# UNRING THE BELL

## TRUDEY MARTIN

# CLAIM YOUR FREE BOOK

You can download a copy of the free Verity Spencer short story, Even Money, if you go to my webpage - there's a form on the front page - just fill in your email and you'll be sent a link to get your copy of the book.

Https://trudeymartin.co.uk

*Can you ever really bury a secret?*

**Unring the bell**

Once something has been done you cannot run away from
it, you can only face the consequences

**theidioms.com**

# FRIDAY

# 1

———

**N**ever do a favour for a friend. That is now my new motto. That was when it all started to unravel. Although, to be fair to Collette it wasn't entirely down to her. And if she'd known what a mess it would lead to, she probably never would have asked me.

Actually, it had all started a few days before that when I'd had a phone call from Detective Sergeant Mike Nash. It was almost a year that I'd known Nash, and our paths had crossed once or twice since he'd interviewed me following the murder of Dr Neasden in Lincoln.

"Nash," I said, picking up the call as I walked through Lincoln city centre. "How are you these days?"

"Good, Verity, all good," Nash replied. He paused, as if choosing his words. "Verity, there's something come up here, and I could do with some help. You came to mind. Have you got a moment to talk?"

"I have," I said. "Can you give me five minutes and I'll go inside somewhere and grab a coffee." It was a dismal grey, damp day. Autumn was setting in, the chill breeze eating at my cheeks. Only a few days before, Lincoln had been ablaze in a sea of sunshine and fire-coloured leaves. Just the last couple of days, though, the weather had turned miserable and all the leaves lay on the pavement forming a slush of grey-brown gloop that everyone trod into all the shops and cafés.

I wondered what Nash might want; it was unlike him to call and ask me for help. It usually happened the other way around. As I trudged to the nearest café I thought about the incident with Dr Neasden; I'd uncovered some serious high-level corruption in Lincoln, left my job lecturing at the local college and had found work as a kind of investigator. In the early days it had all been through word-of-mouth; people had told people about me, who'd told other people, and it had gathered pace over the last year. Fingers crossed, but I had never been without work so far.

I took my coffee and sat down in the corner of the café. Nash picked up almost immediately.

"Verity, thanks for calling back."

"No problem," I said. "How can I help you?"

"How are you fixed for doing some work?"

"Yeah," I said, intrigued. I'd wrapped up a cheating husband case the week before and had enjoyed a few days' rest since then, but I was ready for something new.

"Well, we have a case on file. It's an open case but it's old. Ten years old. We won't close it unless we solve it, but it's unlikely to be honest. We have a prime suspect, but... Well, let me start at the beginning."

"Okay," I said, fishing my notebook out of my bag as I sensed this might not be a two-minute conversation. I wondered why he'd thought of me—I'd never had anything to do with a cold case before. I'd started out with jobs that mainly involved following errant husbands and wives, or reuniting lost relatives, but I'd developed a reputation for dogged determination and had since taken on a couple of missing person cases. My inherent need to dig until I understood what had happened meant that, on the one hand I'd found out where the people were, but on the other, if I worked out the amount I'd got paid versus the hours I'd put in, I'd be on a very low wage indeed. Not that it mattered. I enjoyed the work, and I had my husband's pension to keep the wolves from the door.

"Right," said Nash, taking a deep breath. "Do you remember the child that was murdered in Lincoln ten years ago?"

"Oh yes," I said, wracking my brain. "A little girl. She had an unusual name, didn't she?"

"She did, yes, she certainly did. Her name was Margaret-Elizabeth. Margaret-Elizabeth Ellison."

"That's it. I do remember. She wasn't very old was she? A pretty girl." I remembered the photos in the press and on the television.

"She was eleven when she was murdered, yes. The thing is, the crime scene was completely messed up, but I'll come to that in a bit. There was a prime suspect, still is a prime suspect, his name is Anthony Bridges and he's currently serving time - for unrelated offences. He's been inside a few times in his life, but when Margaret-Elizabeth was murdered, he'd been out for about two years. His previous have involved sex offences, low-level stuff really but he's quite well planned. Oh, and inciting racial hatred."

"Inciting racial hatred? That's pretty strong stuff."

"He was quite a prominent businessman, owned a couple of businesses. And quite political. He ran to be a councillor once or twice, although he didn't ever get elected. He was a member of a far-right political group, Pure Britain. They made a lot of noise about Muslims in the city. And gay people. But that was separate from the other stuff. Flashing, mostly. He'd follow people, young women and adolescent girls, then when he knew their routine he'd wait for them and expose himself."

"Nice…"

"Exactly, well this fitted his modus operandi. Someone had been spotted following Margaret-Elizabeth home. Sometimes after school, sometimes after her gymnastics club. He'd also been spotted watching her over the garden hedge."

"So what happened? Why was he not charged?"

Nash gave a sigh. "Well, there were errors made, Verity, if I'm truthful. Errors by the family, but also by the police."

"By the family? What do you mean?"

"Okay, so you may be able to remember some of the details? The parents went out to their book club as they did every Thursday evening, leaving Margaret-Elizabeth at home with the babysitter. The babysitter had made sure Margaret-Elizabeth was in bed and then watched TV all evening. She'd been up to check a couple of times and there was nothing untoward. It was a hot summer night, and lots of windows and the patio doors were open, but the babysitter didn't spot anything unusual."

"Okay," I said, scribbling frantically in my notebook. "Who was the babysitter?"

"A neighbour. A lady called Phyllis Knight. She was seventy-three, but very sprightly, ran a few local clubs for kids. She'd been a successful sportswoman, a tennis player. Apparently played once at Wimbledon in the fifties and got through to the second round. It finished her, though, the business with Margaret-Elizabeth. People can be cruel, and there were a lot saying she was too old to be babysitting and must have missed something. She gave up the clubs and became quite reclusive. Her physical and mental health went downhill and she died a year or two ago."

"Oh, I think I remember reading something in the local press. But, when she last checked on Margaret-Elizabeth everything was okay?"

"That's what she said. She could remember she'd gone up just after the ten o'clock news, so she was fairly precise on the time. She went to the bathroom and checked in on her way back downstairs. She noticed that the little doll that Margaret-Elizabeth slept with had fallen out of her bed, so she went right into the room and tucked it under her arm."

"Okay, so nothing out of the ordinary there."

"Indeed, nothing unusual. Nothing at all. Anyway, parents came home just before eleven, said goodbye to Mrs Knight, pottered around for a couple of minutes and then Mum went upstairs and that was when they noticed that Margaret-Elizabeth wasn't in her bed."

"I remember reading about this at the time." It was coming back to me, now. "Everyone was going round making sure all their doors and windows were locked the entire time."

"That's right. Paranoia set in in Lincoln for a while."

"So, what happened then? You said the police had messed up a bit?"

"Ah, but you're getting ahead. What happened was that the parents thought the child had wandered off. Apparently she'd been known to sleepwalk sometimes, and so they set off on a search for her. They called their relatives in a bit of a panic when they couldn't find her in the garden and every man and his dog turned up to look for her."

"Is that a bad thing?"

"Well, not so much the looking, but what they did next. One of the uncles found Margaret-Elizabeth's body in the woodland just beyond their house. He saw a man, who he later identified in a line up as Anthony Bridges, crouched down over something. When Bridges saw the uncle approaching, he scarpered. The uncle, a guy named Jonathan Scraggs, ran over and found Margaret-Elizabeth lying there on the ground. He then picked her up and ran with her back to the house, where half of the relatives took turns trying to revive her. The other half ran into the woods after Bridges to try and apprehend him."

"But he got away?"

"He did, indeed. Although the uncle had a good description. The problem was that there'd been so much interference with the crime scene it was impossible. Bridges' DNA was found on Margaret-Elizabeth's body, it was also found inside the kitchen."

"Wouldn't that be enough to convict him?"

"Well, it might have been. But the DNA of a dozen relatives was on her body too. And because they'd moved her body, the forensic people said the fact that his DNA was in the kitchen wouldn't hold up as evidence."

"Really?" I said, surprised, thinking of how easily DNA helped to solve TV murder cases.

Nash appeared to read my thoughts because he then said, "You can't just go into a crime scene wearing your overcoat, like they do on the tele, picking things up with your bare hands. If you touch something, you can transfer the DNA of someone else to another surface. Everyone had touched something. There was DNA on her body that didn't match Bridges or any of the relatives."

"So someone else had been there?"

"Well that's what we thought initially, but forensics eventually decided it was probably DNA that had become

8

so mixed that it was actually from several different people and so never would match up to anyone."

"Wow, I didn't realise that could happen."

"And the area of woodland where Margaret-Elizabeth's body was found had been trampled through too. The relatives hadn't been thinking straight. Well, they'd just found the little girl murdered, so it's understandable. You can imagine they weren't thinking about crime scene preservation. But in their haste to chase Bridges they trampled through the place where she'd been found."

"Disturbing clues there?"

"Exactly," Nash said. "The MO, as I mentioned, matched Bridges. He'd been convicted before after watching children and young adults and then exposing himself to them. His last offence had shown a step up; he'd been convicted after stopping a young lady in a local park and groping her. She was fifteen. He was actually on a licence and he shouldn't have been anywhere near a child. He was on the sex offenders' register."

"Had Margaret-Elizabeth been sexually assaulted?"

"There was evidence of that, yes. But no bodily fluids were found on or in her body, so nothing conclusive there."

"You said the police had messed up too?"

"Yes, well. The fact that Margaret-Elizabeth had possibly been sexually assaulted should never have been in the public domain. We were keeping that piece of information to ourselves." He paused and took in a deep breath, audible down the phone. "The thing was, the team that was working on it were getting nowhere. It's not every day you're dealing with the murder of a child and they all became very emotionally involved. With Bridges' DNA being all over, with the uncle picking him out of a line-up, it matching his MO and all, they were so frustrated that the crown prosecution service said there wasn't enough to take it to court. That was mostly because of the issues with the DNA. A defence barrister would have ripped them apart."

"I can imagine."

"One of the guys, he hadn't been a detective very long, started to suffer. He desperately wanted Bridges brought to justice, as we all did, but without new evidence it was looking unlikely. I think he seriously contemplated taking matters into his own hands, but then Bridges was arrested anyway for another crime. Foster went to the press and gave them information about the investigation. Jesus..." Nash took another huge intake of breath. "He almost scuppered the trial for the case Bridges was arrested for."

"What happened?"

"He lost his job, his pension, everything. There was a flurry of activity in the press. Some vigilantes almost torched Bridges' house. But then things settled down, people forgot about it and we were no further forward."

"Blimey, Mike. That's a terrible situation. So the parents still don't have justice?"

"No, and that's where you might come in."

"I'm not sure what I can do to help, but carry on."

"Friends of the parents, from their church, saw that other, more prominent, cases have been given extra money and resources by the government. They crowdfunded to get money to pay for more manpower for the investigation. I mean, it's an open case, it will be until it's solved, but we can't operate like that. As a force we allocate resources depending on need not on whether some victims' families can pay us more than others. We just couldn't do it. Anyway, they raised over £20,000 and want to spend it trying. To be honest, Verity, to be completely honest, I think it's so late after the event now that it's unlikely to ever be solved. It's not as if we have much that might help if technology advances, either, since the evidence was pretty much screwed up. Unless Bridges has an epiphany and owns up, I think it'll go down as forever unsolved."

"But they need to try, I guess."

"The family want to try, indeed. I believe that if they spend the money they raised and still come up with nothing, then they'll feel like they gave it their all. It might help them to move on."

"But, Mike, if an entire team of police haven't been able to come up with anything, what do you think I'm going to be able to do?"

"Well I know you, Verity, you'll work hard for the money. I said this to the Ellisons, once you've got the bit between your teeth you'll make sure their money is well spent."

## 2
---

"So basically," I said to Sam Charlton when I met him for dinner later that evening, "Nash wants me to work through twenty thousand pounds of someone else's money to make them feel better."

"I guess it may as well be you as anyone else," Charlton said, as down-to-earth as ever.

I looked across at him, the shaved dark skin on his head reflecting the lights from the ceiling above. We were in a restaurant in Nottingham; he'd been there for a conference, and had stayed on so that we could meet up. It had been a few weeks since we'd seen each other, and I'd been looking forward to seeing him more than I'd admitted to anyone. More than I'd dared admit to myself, actually. I didn't know how I'd have managed this past year without Sam's insight; his experience as a detective inspector in the Met had been an invaluable source of support as I'd tumbled into my new line of work.

"I just don't know where to start, Sam. What on earth do they expect me to find that an entire team of police didn't uncover? Especially given the cock up with the evidence."

"I imagine they don't really think you'll come up with much else. But they want to know that they've tried the best they can."

"That's pretty much what Nash said."

"And you won't have to pay for your own lunch or dinner for a while. It doesn't sound like a bad gig, just snoofling around, re-digging dirt that's already well dug. And twenty grand'll keep you going for a while. Sounds like a cushy number to me. Easy money. Not much work and your clients feel better." He leaned his head back and laughed a deep, gravelly laugh.

"Hey, maybe that should be the strapline on my new business cards?"

"Yup." He moved his hand through the air. "'I'll charge you a fortune, not do much work, but you'll feel great'. Huh?"

"You really should consider a switch into PR, you know." I looked across the table at him, and he smiled back at me.

I was grateful he'd been so understanding about the episode a couple of months ago when we'd become really close. Too close for my comfort as a single person not quite adjusted to widowhood. Sam and I had worked around it, our friendship had continued, although it was an uneasy truce. We hadn't quite got our balance back yet.

"How did Mrs Murphy take it when you showed her the pictures of her husband last week?" Sam asked between dinner and dessert.

"Oh, God, she was livid. I thought she was going to kill him. I was worried I'd have a murder on my conscience. I actually offered to stay with her until he came home from work, and I had my hand on the emergency dial button on the phone in my pocket in case I had to call the police. Or an ambulance. Or a hearse."

"That bad, eh?"

"I thought the hardest part would be that he was having an affair with someone the same age as their son. And the same sex." I took a sip of wine. "But actually she was most annoyed because the pictures were taken in one of 'their' places in Anglesey." I made the inverted commas sign with my fingers. "I had photos of him and his toy boy kissing on the balcony of a posh hotel that overlooks the Menai Strait. The hotel he'd always promised to take her to, but said they could never afford. Apparently they stayed in the Premier Inn in Bangor, even on their silver wedding anniversary." I paused. "That's what tipped her over."

Later in the evening, the conversation swung back to Margaret-Elizabeth.

"I think the best thing I can do," I suggested, "is to try to get to know Bridges, find out what he was like, who he was at the time, so I can piece together a picture of him. I can't think where else to start."

"Has Nash given you any information?" he asked.

"Not really, no paperwork or anything. He's given me the contact details of the journalist that Devon Foster went to with the information, and a few other names that might be helpful. I think there's a lot online. Nash said the paper had printed just about everything Foster had given them, which was quite a lot, so there's not much that isn't in the public domain. So I guess Google might help as well."

"I seem to recall lots of people had opinions at the time. Twitter was full of 'how could they leave their daughter with an old woman', and other such stuff."

I drank the last mouthful of cold coffee and thought

about that. Everybody seemed to think they had a right to judge everyone else. I moved the empty coffee cup to one side. "I guess one thing that worries me…" I started.

Sam laid a hand on top of mine. "Yeah?"

"What if I do find something. What if there's proof that Bridges did it? What if there is something, but they still can't convict him? How will the parents feel then? That would be worse, wouldn't it?"

"See how you get on, Verity. They've given you the money, they have to take a chance it won't turn out the way they want."

We paid up and left the restaurant. I pulled my scarf in around my neck and hunched my shoulders as we walked into a biting wind towards the taxi rank. It was late and I'd missed the last train. It would be expensive getting a cab all the way home, but I wasn't in the mood for trains anyway. Besides, I really didn't want to be walking to and from stations in this weather.

Sam put his arm around my shoulders and pulled me close to his body and we leaned into the wind, our bodies keeping one another from getting too cold. The smell of aftershave, washing powder and warm, male body reminded me of how nice it had been to be close to someone, provoking a wave of confusion to swirl around my brain once more. As we reached the taxi rank, I turned to face him. He spread his coat around me, enveloping me in its sanctuary from the stiff, cold breeze, and as I looked up at him he smiled.

"Don't be a stranger," he said.

I kissed him lightly on the lips. "I won't," I said before turning to get into the waiting taxi.

A young man brushed past us, forcing his way between

us. As he barged his way through, he pushed me to one side and I fell into the door of the taxi. He turned towards me, curling his lips into a snarl. "Dirty fucking monkey lover," he shouted and scuttled off.

"What did you say?" I shouted after him, turning and running to catch up with him. "What did you say? Oi! Come back here!"

"Fuck off, go kiss your nigger," the young man shouted and carried on walking away.

Once again I hurried after him. "Come back here! You can't get away with saying things like that. It's evil."

He turned round and flicked a V-sign at me, then darted down an alleyway and out of sight.

Sam was scurrying after me. "Verity," he called. "Leave it."

I swung round and stomped back towards him. "Leave it! Did you hear what he just said?" I gesticulated into the night. "Did you hear what he just called you?" I turned to continue my pursuit of the young man, but Sam caught hold of my wrist and turned me back towards him.

He looked me in the eye, his lips tight, his eyes glistening, pain radiating from his face. I shook my head. I closed my eyes to try to stop the tears, but still one formed and meandered down my face. "Leave it?" I whispered. I touched him on the cheek.

He looked down at his shoes and sighed. He turned his head and gazed off after the young man, long disappeared into the darkness of the night. "It's not worth it," he said eventually. "It's just not worth it."

I climbed into the car without saying another word, unsure what to say, ashamed that anyone could hurl insults at another human because of such a trivial difference. As the taxi pulled off Sam waved his arm then turned away, hunching his shoulders as he walked; maybe against the wind or maybe against the comments of the young man, I wasn't sure.

# SATURDAY

# 3

The following day, the weather was horrendous. I turned the heating up high and lounged around in my comfy pyjamas. I spent some time phoning people, emailing and texting, organising a round of appointments over the next few days. Then I made myself a milky coffee and sat on the sofa with my laptop.

I began by Googling Margaret-Elizabeth Ellison. There were dozens of articles, so I started with the one that came out top, which was from one of the tabloids, and had been written after the CPS had decided not to prosecute Bridges, but before Devon Foster had leaked the details to the Lincoln City Herald.

### No justice for Margaret-Elizabeth's parents
*In a move condemned by the local police, and by Margaret-Elizabeth's parents, the Crown Prosecution Service has announced that Anthony Bridges, 52, will not be charged with the girl's murder. At a press conference yesterday, Matthew Ellison, Margaret-Elizabeth's father, read out a prepared statement. 'I'm devastated by this*

*news. All I want is justice for my beautiful girl. Now I would ask that people leave us alone to grieve. My wife and I have suffered enough. But, rest assured, we will not give up the fight for justice.'*

*Assistant Chief Constable, Michael Moreland, stated 'Lincolnshire Police are disappointed with the news from the CPS. We are not currently looking for anyone else in connection with this horrific crime. We will, however, revisit all the evidence and redouble our efforts to bring her killer to justice.'*

The article went on to describe a timeline of events that had happened on the night of Margaret-Elizabeth's death. It was all sensationalist stuff, with a map of the Ellison's house, the house where they'd been to their book club, and the wood where Margaret-Elizabeth had been found.

*7pm Margaret-Elizabeth's parents leave their daughter at home in the care of their neighbour*
*7.15pm They arrive at their weekly book club, this week held at the home of their good friends Jeffrey and Mary Walker*
*10.30pm In the Ellison's house, the babysitter checks on Margaret-Elizabeth, everything is normal*
*10.45pm Over at the Walker's, the friends wrap up their book club and say their goodbyes*
*10.55pm The Ellisons arrive home and say goodbye to the babysitter*
*11pm Mrs Ellison discovers that Margaret-Elizabeth is not in her bed and the frantic search begins*

It didn't really contain much that I didn't already know,

so I went back to the search page and scrolled through a few more articles.

I paused for some lunch and a coffee, staring out into the back garden as I ate a toasted sandwich. The sky was grey, the rain still falling fast, battering the plants into the ground. There was little else to do so I resumed my position on the sofa and continued searching the Internet.

I started skipping the actual news articles and going directly to the comments section. That made choice reading. Among the majority expressing sympathy for the parents there were some other nuggets. Poor grammar aside, the mental leaps and somersaults people made were astounding.

*JohnnyToogood: Bloody parents should be charged. Who leaves their baby with an old woman when u go out n have a good time? What's more important than the safety of ur child? Glass of wine with friends? Old biddy wun't of heard if someone come in and snatched the child. She probably senile and can't even remember what happened. Ha ha!*

*SimonSue: @JohnnyToogood I completely agree. The police should have a law on the age of babysitters. You can't leave a child with someone under 16 so why can you leave your child with someone too old to chase an intruder? I always believed she saw Bridges take the child and never confessed.*

*PeterR: @SimonSue Totally agree. That old dear knows way more than shes letting on. You can see it in her eyes. My sister is a psychologist and she says its always in peoples eyes. Shes bloody heartless that woman, hiding what she knows from those poor parents.*

*SimonSue: @PeterR Poor parents? There as guilty as the*

*babysitter in my opinion. Why would anyone leave there child in the care of someone incapable of protecting them?*
**JuliaLeach: @JohnnyToogood** *Can you all stop blaming the parents and the babysitter? It wasn't any of them who snatched the little girl, and you're making out that they are as guilty? Focus on the person who actually took the child. Surely every parent has gone out and left their child with a babysitter before! Are we not supposed to enjoy ourselves once we become parents?*
**SimonSue: @JulieLeach** *The fact remains if those selfish parents hadn't gone out there child would still be alive. Is that worth galvanting around? I'm a parent and I can honestly say that my kids have never left my sight since the day they were born. That old woman is lying. I know she knows more than she is letting on. I don't care what anybody says.*

And so it went on. I contemplated the words on my laptop for a while, struggling with the mentality of people prepared to spend their time writing comments about things and circumstances that they knew nothing about.

I looked at my watch then stared at it, convinced it was lying to me. However, a glance out of the window into the darkness beyond corroborated what it was saying. My limbs had been immobile for hours, so I stood up, stretched and moved around a little. I walked over to the window and looked out into the early night; it was still now, the rain having given up, but a shiver ran through me and I turned the heating up. My tummy was growling so I walked through to the kitchen and threw a quick cheese sandwich together. I ate it standing up, leaning against the counter whilst I perused tomorrow's weather forecast for a bit of light entertainment.

Resuming my position at the laptop, only this time with wine rather than coffee, I moved on to look at newspaper reports that had been written following the leak. I searched for Steven Fairbrother, the journalist who'd broken the story. He hadn't held back with the emotion.

### *Evidence of sexual assault dismissed as suspected child sex murderer evades court*

*Alleged child murderer Anthony Bridges, 52, will not be prosecuted for the murder of local little girl, Margaret-Elizabeth Ellison despite evidence that the child had been sexually assaulted before her death. Outraged local police officers were so incensed by the decision of the Crown Prosecution Service that they handed evidence exclusively to this newspaper in the hope that the truth would reach the public. Bridges, who has previous convictions for sexual assault of a minor, was arrested in connection with her murder, but never formally charged.*

*Margaret-Elizabeth was viciously murdered in the shocking events that occurred while her parents were out at their book club. The information the police handed to us reveals that there was evidence of a sexual attack before Margaret-Elizabeth was brutally strangled and left for dead in the woods behind her home. Bridges is currently on remand on a charge of inciting racial hatred for a second time. He was seen at the scene and identified in a line up by Margaret-Elizabeth's favourite uncle, Jonathan Scraggs. Bridges' DNA was found both in the house and on Margaret-Elizabeth's body, yet the CPS, in a staggering move that rocked the local force, decided that there was not enough evidence for a conviction. The heartbroken uncle told us that he could not understand the move. "Perhaps Bridges has friends in high places," he claimed*

*when we asked him about the police information, "because*
*I can't see any other reason why he isn't being charged."*
*Scraggs added, "If it was up to me, I'd be bringing back*
*the death penalty for people like him."*
*Anthony Bridges is a business owner and member of polit-*
*ical group Pure Britain who campaign for a white only*
*British Isles…*

Campaign for a white-only British Isles. My heart gave a
flip, and a fury worked its way through my body once
again, like a raging fire. I thought of Charlton, not wanting
to pursue the young man who'd hurled abuse at him yesterday. 'It's not worth it', Charlton had said. *Not worth it*; I
wasn't sure if I was crosser with the young man for his
blatant racism, or Charlton for not fighting it. Perhaps he'd
grown weary of it over the years. I stood up and shook out
my limbs, shaking the anger from my body. I gave up at
that point, not wanting to read about Bridges' political affiliations. It was late, I'd barely moved all day, and my eyes
ached from looking at the screen for so many hours in
one go.

I snapped the laptop shut and went upstairs to bed.

# SUNDAY

# 4

---

I t was late on Sunday when I woke up. The luxury of lie-ins had eluded me for some time after John had died. Lately, though, I was finding that more often I was sleeping soundly, dreaming deeply and waking up later. I shuffled down to the kitchen where I made some coffee and poured myself a bowl of cereal. I took out my notebook and spent some time trying to organise my scribblings from the previous day's Internet searching. I had two appointments arranged for later in the day. Firstly, I was due to go and meet Margaret-Elizabeth's parents, and following that I had a coffee date with my friend Collette to get to. I started compiling a list of questions I needed to ask the Ellisons, but it became increasingly long. I started again, prioritising those questions that I thought were the most important as I tried to gather my thoughts. Where did you start with a couple who'd come home from a normal evening out to find their life completely ripped apart?

As lunchtime approached, I was still in my pyjamas. After grabbing a quick bite to eat, I ran upstairs to shower and get changed, then I headed outside for the first time in over twenty-four hours and jumped into the car. Margaret-Elizabeth's parents lived to the south of the city, just near Hartsholme Park. I put the postcode into my satnav and dutifully followed the instructions. The house was on a treelined cul-de-sac; the large brick-built detached houses set back from the road with their immaculately kept front gardens on display. I drove slowly down the road, trying to locate the place I needed before spotting the Ellisons' house near the end of the road on the left. Two cars were parked in the driveway, one in front of the double garage and the other by the front door. I parked next to the one by the garage, walked up to the front door then rang the bell.

Mrs Ellison greeted me and led me into the front room. She indicated a chair by the bay window so I sat on that. The room was homely, although devoid of clutter; the furniture positioned to maximise its size. A few modern prints decorated the walls. There were no ornaments, save for a collection of photos on a bookshelf against the far wall. A vase of beautifully arranged cut flowers adorned the windowsill and a book about modern art was displayed on the coffee table. Apart from that there was very little that would gather dust.

"I'm sorry, Matthew isn't here right now," she said as she sat on the sofa opposite me and tucked her legs to one side. "He's just on a call in the office, he'll be done soon." She played with the pearl on her necklace, pulling it from side to side along the gold chain.

"Don't worry, Mrs Ellison," I said and smiled.

"Nicole, please," she said, touching her immaculate hair and pushing an imaginary stray strand back in place. She reached out, stretching her hand as if she were patting my knee although she was too far away to actually touch me. "We're so grateful for you taking this on. I can't tell you."

I nodded. "Nicole," I said after a while, "what is it that you're hoping to achieve by engaging me?"

She looked down and examined her painted fingernails. "I just want closure," she said, looking up at me. "I want to be able to move on, to put the past behind me. You can't begin to imagine…" and she tailed off.

I couldn't; she was right.

"I'm so sorry," I said. "It must be so hard for you." I paused. "My worry is that I won't find anything that the police missed."

At that point, Mr Ellison came into the room, turning off a mobile phone as he entered and putting it into his jacket pocket. He was dressed in jeans and a well-tailored blue blazer with an open-necked maroon shirt that all served to flatter his sturdy frame. He smoothed his hair to one side as he walked across the room and then held out his hand to greet me. I stood up and walked the couple of paces towards him.

"Matthew Ellison," he said. "Welcome, Verity, we're really pleased that you could come." He sat down next to his wife and lay a hand on her knee.

I sat back down. "Tell me a little about Margaret-Elizabeth," I said. "I'm sure she's the best place to start."

"She was a beautiful little girl," he said. "Happy, vivacious. Always laughing."

His wife looked up. "She was just the loveliest child," she agreed. "Such a sunny nature. We were really blessed. She would burst in after school, all full of chat; wanting to tell me everything that had happened all in one go." She wrung her hands, and Mr Ellison took them into his, holding them until they were still.

"It's hard," he said. "For us, we keep expecting her to walk through the door. She'll always be an eleven year old to us. And that's really hard when our friends' children are growing up, turning into adults, going to university. Margaret-Elizabeth's stuck at eleven, we never got to experience those things." He glanced round at the collection of photos.

"Do you mind?" I said, following his gaze.

He said nothing but gestured with his hand, pointing to the pictures as if to say, help yourself. I stood up and walked across the room. There were six in total, carefully arranged in a semi-circle on top of the bookshelf. The Ellisons observed me from across the room as I stood in front of the bookshelf perusing the photos. I picked them up, one by one, careful to put them back exactly as they had been. Mr Ellison left his wife on the sofa and came over to stand beside me. The photos did indeed show a vivacious and bouncy young girl. Margaret-Elizabeth was beautiful. She stared out of the photos like a child model posing in a commercial, playing with the camera. She was a small and dainty child. Her coquettish smile was captivating, her blonde hair cascading over her shoulders and down her back. In one photo she was holding a puppy, waving its paw at the camera. I picked it up and examined it.

"That was her seventh birthday. She'd begged us since she could talk to have a dog and eventually we caved in. She told us she was old enough to walk it and feed it, and that was the bargain. Although, obviously we didn't let her walk him alone. She called him Alvin after that dreadful TV show."

I shrugged. I had no idea about children's television.

"He was devastated when she—" He paused, struggling

after all this time for the right words. "When she…wasn't around anymore. He pined; he went and lay on her bed and wouldn't get off it. He died only about two years after."

I put the photo down and picked up the one next to it. Margaret-Elizabeth looked about two in that one. She was sitting on the lap of a very elderly gentleman.

"That was my Grandad," Mr Ellison explained. "He lived until he was a hundred and one. He must have been in his early nineties at that point. Look," he said, picking up the last photo, "this is four generations. My grandad, me, and my dad holding Margaret-Elizabeth when she had just been born."

I took hold of the frame. "What a beautiful photo," I said. The man holding Margaret-Elizabeth looked painfully thin; his face gaunt, with the skin stretched tight across his cheeks. He looked older than his father.

"My Dad had cancer at the time, but he held on until Margaret-Elizabeth was born. He died a couple of weeks after that photo was taken, but he was determined to meet her."

I put the photo back on the bookshelf and went to sit down. Mr Ellison moved all the frames until they were exactly as they had been and then came to rejoin us.

"What are you hoping for, Mr Ellison, with my involvement?"

"Our friends in the church raised the money for us. We don't go every week, you know, but they wanted to do what they could to help out." He paused. "They've been so supportive. We started going a bit more regularly after… you know? For some comfort."

"And you? What is it that you want from this?"

"We wanted someone who could just dedicate some

time to reviewing all the information, all the evidence. We want to know that every inch of Anthony Bridges' life has been turned over, and if there are any cracks that they'll be found."

"I'll certainly dedicate my time to it. I don't easily give up once I get my teeth into something."

"Good." He nodded. "Good."

"I just don't want you to raise your hopes too much. It may be that I find something but it's not admissible. Or maybe I just come to the same conclusion that the CPS did, that the evidence isn't strong enough to get anywhere with."

Mrs Ellison turned to her husband, and he gave her a reassuring nod. "I think," she said in a small voice, "that we just want to know that we've done everything we can." She paused and picked at her nails. "Even if we can't prove it in a court of law, if he's put under scrutiny...well, it might mean that another family doesn't have to go through what we have."

I nodded. "As I said, you don't have to worry about that, I'll not stop until I'm sure there are no more stones to look under."

"You'll find plenty of stones with that man," Mr Ellison said, raising his eyebrows.

"What do you know about Anthony Bridges?" I asked.

Mrs Ellison visibly flinched at the mention of his name, and her husband quickly laid a hand on her arm as if to calm her. She looked up at me, but let her husband do the talking.

"He's an evil man. I don't just mean because of what he did to Margaret-Elizabeth, but he's so full of hate. Hate for everyone. He built up his businesses, I think through sheer ruthlessness, and used the money to propagate hate. He's in with some very merciless people."

"Are you talking about the political party he belonged to?"

"Well, that. And also, he does business with some of these people. They form allies with other groups. They're very influential. Those people are thugs, but Bridges has money and he's a master at manipulation. He may be in prison at the moment, but he's friends with some very prominent and dangerous people on the outside. Watch your step, Verity, be very careful. Keep looking over your shoulder."

A shiver ran down my spine. "I'll be careful," I said. "Although I won't be easily intimidated."

Mr Ellison nodded but didn't say anything.

"Can I ask you about the night Margaret-Elizabeth died?"

They both looked up. Mrs Ellison's brow furrowed and her husband held onto her hand. He sighed; he looked resigned, as if he really didn't want to relive it all again.

"I'm sorry," I said. "I know it must be painful for you, but it would just help to try to piece together a timeline. You went to your book club?"

Mrs Ellison nodded. "We went every Thursday," she said. She turned to her husband as if she was begging him to take over the story.

He tipped his head. "We went over to the Walkers. We took it in turns to host and it was their turn. We had a pleasant evening, and left about quarter to eleven. It took us about ten minutes to drive home. When we got home everything seemed normal. We spoke to Phyllis for a couple of minutes and she told us she'd checked on Margaret-Elizabeth about fifteen minutes before we got home. She left and we pottered about in the kitchen, putting the kettle on. We closed up the windows and patio doors ready for going to bed, then Nicole went upstairs to check on Margaret-Elizabeth..."

Mrs Ellison caught a sob in her throat. "My beautiful baby," she said. "My beautiful baby."

Mr Ellison continued. "She wasn't in her bed. She wasn't anywhere in the house. She'd sleepwalked a few times before so we assumed she'd found her way out of the house. The patio doors had been open. I ran into the garden, calling her, and Nicole called round some relatives." He swept his hand in the direction of the back garden. "We live just next to the park and we thought they could help to find her. Most of Nicole's family live nearby and they were all here within a few minutes." He paused and looked down. He had kept his composure well, but he rubbed his hands together and then clenched his fists as if he was trying to remain focused on the story. "Nicole's brother came running in, carrying her."

Nicole was breathing heavily, little sobs escaping from her mouth. She leaned into Mr Ellison, who wrapped his arm around her shoulder, gently patting her.

"He put Margaret-Elizabeth's body down on the floor"—Mr Ellison pointed to a spot on the living room carpet, just inside the door—"and we tried to revive her. My baby, lifeless. We tried so hard to revive her. Nicole's sister rang for the ambulance, and they gave us instructions down the phone, but by the time they arrived she was dead. The paramedics kept trying, all the way to the hospital. It was clear that she was dead, but they didn't give up."

Mrs Ellison heaved a great sob and pulled a hanky out of her pocket to cover her mouth. "I'm sorry," she said. "I'm really sorry."

"Don't be sorry," I said.

A little while later, after Nicole had regained her composure, I asked if I could have a look at the spot where Margaret-Elizabeth had been found. Mrs Ellison backed out of walking down there with us, opting instead to make a cafetiere for when we got back.

Mr Ellison and I walked down the hallway and into the dining area, where he grabbed an ancient-looking parka coat with a deep tear down the left front. He offered me a female version, but I shook my head. A large kitchen dining area spanned the width of the back of the house. Large bi-fold doors gave way onto the garden, which swept slightly downhill towards the edge of Hartsholme Park. The rain had stopped, but there was still a biting wind eating into my face and neck as Mr Ellison led me across the manicured lawn. I wrapped my arms around myself, wishing I'd accepted the coat, as we walked past well-kept borders, a busy greenhouse and a cute wooden summer house, to the end of the garden. A fence ran along the end of the garden between the Ellison's property and the Park, but there was a small gate that led directly through. Trees obscured most of the fence, spilling over into the Ellison's garden.

"We've had this all done a few years ago," he explained. "When Margaret-Elizabeth was alive the fence was in poor repair. It barely made a proper border. I'd been meaning to get it fixed for ages..." He tailed off, the consequences of his inaction didn't need to be said out loud.

We made our way through the gate into a thick woodland. Pushing branches and tall weeds to one side, we walked through the trees for a few metres. A little stream babbled past a few feet ahead, but then I spotted a rough wooden cross at the base of one of the trees, in a small clearing covered in fallen leaves. I pointed at the cross, and Mr Ellison nodded.

"Right there," he said, indicating the area around the cross.

We stood in silence. I imagined the body of a small child lying there, under a canopy of leafy branches, in the moonlight of a mid-summer evening ten years ago.

# 5

After I left the Ellisons', I located a parking spot in the city centre, paid an extortionate amount for a parking ticket and went to locate Collette.

Soon after all the business with the notebook, a year or so ago, our favourite coffee shop had closed and we now favoured Café Santos. In the summer it was lovely to sit on the outside terrace, but at this time of year we huddled inside in the cosy interior. I left the car park, pulling my hood up and wrapped my scarf around my neck. I stuffed my hands into my pockets, since I'd forgotten to bring any gloves out with me, and scurried across town as quickly as I could.

Collette was there, sitting in the far corner reading a newspaper while she waited for me. She looked up as I approached and then leaped to her feet to embrace me.

"Hey," she said, "how are you?"

"Good, thanks, and you?" I took off all the trappings of a cold, rainy, autumn day. "It's like the middle of winter," I said, rubbing my hands together, before going off to order my coffee.

Once we were sitting down with our coffees in front of us, we caught up on the progress of her children, the new businesses that were due to open in Lincoln, and general small talk.

"It's Emily's birthday in a few weeks," she said. "I can't believe how badly organised that was, giving birth in the middle of winter. At least when it's Charlotte's birthday they can all run around the garden."

"Can't you take them to one of those indoor places, with all the slides and ball pools and stuff?"

Collette recoiled in her seat and opened her mouth wide. "Verity Spencer, how dare you."

"What," I said, laughing.

"I am not the kind of parent who outsources their children's birthday memories. I am going to organise everything myself."

"More fool you, then," I said, suspecting a lot of Collette's desire to give her children precision-planned parties was more to do with the judgement of the other parents than a need for her children to have perfect childhood memories. But I didn't voice that opinion out loud.

"How did you get on with the Ellisons?" she asked after a while.

"Yeah, it was okay. I just hope that they're realistic about what I can achieve, I don't want to give them false hope."

"I'm sure they're grateful that you've agreed to look into it for them."

"They seemed to be. It's hard isn't it? It's clear the pain of losing a child never goes away."

Collette was silent for a minute. Her eldest, Charlotte, was almost the same age as Margaret-Elizabeth had been when she'd died. She shuddered. "They were out, weren't they, when Margaret-Elizabeth was murdered. I bet that added to the awfulness of it. 'Maybe if we'd been at home?' That kind of thing."

A little later, after drinking down the last of her coffee, she asked, "How did it go with Sam the other night? Your dinner in Nottingham. Was it okay?"

"Yes." I nodded. "It was. It was really nice to see him."

Collette leaned over and touched my arm. She was one of the few people who understood how I'd struggled when Sam and I had got close. Collette had been a friend throughout my marriage to John and she knew how hard his death had been for me. I think she understood the guilt that had torn me apart after I'd slept with Sam.

"You know," she said, "sometimes things don't always happen exactly when they should. Life's a bitch like that. It's like some people spend years trying to find Mr Right and then just when they give up and decide a spinster's life is for them, up pops Mr Perfect. Sometimes, Mr Right comes along too soon. But, Vee, life's too short, you should know that. Sometimes you have to go with what it's throwing at you."

I looked down. She was right. I'd anguished over John; I missed him so much and it was almost as if I'd been unfaithful to him when I'd become involved with another man. It did seem too soon. I wasn't sure I was ready to move on, and I had told Sam as much, but Collette was right. Sometimes these opportunities presented themselves at inopportune moments, and maybe I needed to just take a chance. I glanced up at her and smiled. I cradled my coffee cup in my hand. "I like him," I said, staring into my coffee. "I really like him. A lot. I just don't know how to tell him."

"Well," she said, grinning at me like a Cheshire cat. "If you really like him, a lot, then I guess you need to figure out a way to let him know."

The conversation moved on. Collette seemed somehow nervous. She kept sitting on her hands and opening her mouth as if she was about to say something, but then we'd move on and whatever it was went unsaid. Eventually, she leapt up and said, "Fancy another coffee? There's something I want to ask you." Before I had any chance to enquire further, or even offer a reply, she'd approached the counter and ordered two more coffees.

"Go on..." I said when she sat back down.

She bit her lip and looked away.

"Collette, what is it?" I asked, getting concerned now.

She looked down, pursing her lips. She opened her mouth, but just then the waitress approached with our coffees and Collette fell silent once again. She leaned back in her chair and covered her mouth with her hands. As the waitress went back to the counter to serve a waiting customer, Collette took a deep breath in then blurted out, "I think Marcus is having an affair." The words tumbled out of her mouth in a torrent, crashing into one another as they fell to the ground in front of her, now spoken.

"Marcus?" I asked in disbelief, as if she might be mistaking her husband for someone else.

She nodded and stared at the floor.

"Collette, what makes you think that?" I was stunned. Marcus was the last person I'd have thought would be unfaithful. He adored Collette and their children.

"He's been going out recently. He won't tell me where he's going. He says he's going to work sometimes but I've called the office and he isn't there."

"Have you spoken to him about it?" I leaned across and took her hand. What she was saying sounded awfully similar to some of the other cases I'd dealt with recently. They rarely had a happy ending.

She shook her head. "I daren't," she whispered. "I'm scared he'll say yes. What would I do?" A tear ran down her cheek and she brushed it away with the back of her hand. She looked up and stared into my eyes. "Vee, will you follow him for me?"

I sat back. "I can't, Collette. I can't do that. I know him too well."

She pulled her hand away from mine. "You know me better." She spat the words out, throwing her hands in the air. "I'd pay you, just like everyone else. I'm not asking you to do it for nothing."

"It's not about the money, you know that. You know it wouldn't be right if I followed him. What if he saw me?"

"Oh, it's all about you, isn't it?" Tears started pouring down her cheeks.

I leaned across and put my arms around her.

She rested her head against my shoulder and sobbed. "I don't know what to do, Vee," she said, the words punctuated by deep breaths as she tried to slow her crying down.

I moved back a little and took her chin in my hand. "Hey," I said, lifting her head and looking into her eyes. "We'll get to the bottom of this, but I can't follow him."

Her lip trembled and she looked into my eyes. "Please, Vee. Please. I need to know."

I sighed and sat back. "What will you do if you're right?"

She slumped in her chair, her shoulders drooping. She grabbed a napkin off the table and wiped her eyes and cheeks. "I don't know," she said, her words barely audible. "But if I've got some evidence at least he won't be able to deny it." She looked across at me, grabbing both of my hands with hers and opening her eyes wide. "Please..."

I shook my head and sighed. "I'd have to hire a car, because he'd recognise mine."

"Thank you, Vee," Collette said, leaning back. "I'll pay for a hire car."

"What am I doing?" I said out loud, wondering how I was going to fit in stalking Marcus with finding out more about Anthony Bridges.

# 6

---

By the time I got home, dusk was approaching. The nights were really drawing in and the weather becoming wintery, although the forecast was promising a mini Indian summer for the end of the week. I looked forward to that as I shivered and reached into my wardrobe for a jumper.

I spent the evening scouring the Internet for any more information on Anthony Bridges. I found little that I didn't already know about the murder of Margaret-Elizabeth but I did come across some interesting information about his political group Pure Britain. Pure Britain was quite clearly still politically active. Although they were a small, Lincolnshire based group, they appeared to have high ambitions, setting out their stall on the homepage of their website.

*Our aims, hopes, and goals...a return to an all-white Britain*
*Pure Britain is a political activist group, fighting for the ever diminishing rights of the true British citizen. We will*

*fight the elite as they continue to mislead the public,*
*pumping out propaganda and stifling free speech. We will*
*fight them as they allow our country to be overrun by reli-*
*gious fanatics who rape our children. We will fight them*
*as they allow our country to be overrun by non-whites*
*wanting to impose their abusive culture on us. We will*
*fight as they allow these fanatics to kill our citizens and*
*terrorise the country. We will fight as they jail us for*
*speaking the truth. They're scared and they know. We will*
*come for them. We will win the fight for an all-white*
*Britain.*

*Our vision is for a Christian country, a country that*
*adheres to our traditional values. We need to cease the*
*immoral practice of same-sex couples living together,*
*marrying and having children. This debauched activity*
*should be purged from our shores.*

*Pure Britain protests against the current regime who do*
*not want you to know the truth. We peacefully target*
*prominent figures, including MPs and activists on the*
*left, on social media, television, in the press, and in person.*
*We support mass deportations and zero acceptance of*
*refugees and asylum seekers. Join our new revolution*
*now...*

And so it went on, through every page I clicked. I gave a great sigh. The irony that these people were citing propaganda as something they were fighting against seemed to get lost in the rhetoric.

The website was filled with pictures of rallies and marches. Mostly attended by white middle-aged pot-bellied men, but there were a few women too, their fists raised above their heads. Many were holding banners that said, 'No more mosques' or wearing T-shirts that declared

'Whites will overcome', 'If you're not white you're not British' and other such slogans. On the foot of each page was a link to a YouTube channel, so I clicked on that and watched a few minutes of hate-filled outrage before I'd had enough.

I searched through for reports of Anthony Bridges in connection with Pure Britain and it appeared that his latest imprisonment had stirred his followers into action. There had been some considerable outrage. It was seen as an affront to free speech and, apparently, membership of Pure Britain had grown three-fold in the aftermath of his sentence. Bridges had been arrested outside the home of a local Imam, shouting into a microphone about child abuse, rape, sharia law and terrorism. I found an article in the local press.

### *Far-right activist arrested after inciting racial hatred*

*Anthony Bridges, 52, a founder member of Lincolnshire far-right group Pure Britain, was arrested today outside the home of Dr Mohammed Zafar, Imam of the local mosque. Bridges had been repeatedly warned by police to cease harassing Dr Zafar. Following a hate-filled speech earlier in the week, the homes of two local Muslims were badly damaged after rags drenched in petrol were posted through their letter boxes and set alight. Nobody was hurt in either attack, but one family managed to escape only minutes before the house became engulfed in flames.*

The article was accompanied by a photo of Bridges being taken away by three police officers, his mouth twisted, his face contorted, as he continued to shout as he was dragged off. He was surrounded by angry supporters shaking their fists at the police. At the end of the article one of them was quoted:

*"This is an affront to freedom of speech. The authorities don't want the public to know what is going on in the Muslim community, it should be them that are being arrested, not us."*

# MONDAY

# 7

The following morning I had an appointment with Steven Fairbrother, the journalist who had received all the leaked information from the police. Fairbrother worked for the Lincoln City Herald and they had an office in the city centre. I also needed to pick up the hire car; Collette had told me that Marcus was allegedly working late today but she didn't believe him. I'd decided to go and see Fairbrother first, then pick up the car. That would save me having to find a parking space in the city, which wasn't always easy.

I wrapped myself in a winter coat, wound a scarf tightly round my neck, and pulled some sheepskin gloves on. The promised Indian summer seemed a long way off. A slate-grey sky threatened rain, the colours blending in with the lead roof of the cathedral as I headed into town. Steep Hill was shiny with the remains of a heavy rainfall, making the descent a little hazardous in places, but I reached the bottom unscathed.

I announced myself at the Herald reception desk and took a seat. The waiting area had wide padded box-type seats that looked comfortable but weren't. You couldn't lean back, and they were just slightly too high to comfortably rest your feet on the floor. Several doors led off in various directions so I had no idea where Fairbrother would appear from. I didn't have to wait long. I heard my name and turned to my right to see a face poking around a half-open door.

"Steven Fairbrother?" I asked.

He nodded and held out his hand. "Great to meet you," he said as I approached, and I took his hand and shook it.

I followed him through the door and he bounced up a flight of stairs as I struggled to keep up. We walked through a small but busy room, full of people, their desks piled high with papers and files. Fairbrother offered no explanation about who they were or what they were doing. He paused by a desk, scooped up a thick pink cardboard file and pointed to a vacant room a little further on.

A glass wall looked out over the people in the room beyond, their heads buried in paperwork or glued to their computers. The odour of the previous meeting's attendees hung in the air, and with no window was unlikely to dissipate soon.

"Sorry about the facilities," Fairbrother said and, giving no pause for me to answer, asked, "Can I get you a drink?"

I told him I was fine, so he closed the door.

"Please," he said indicating the chairs.

I sat down at the far end of the table and he took a seat diagonally opposite me. He put the file on the table, its contents almost spilling onto the table.

"Thanks for seeing me."

"Not a problem," he replied. "If we can get any closure for the Ellisons it'll be time well spent."

"Mr Fairbrother—"

"Stephen, please."

"Stephen, can I start by asking you why you think Devon Foster took his information to the press?"

He rested his hand on the file in front of him, as if he were guarding its secrets for a little while longer. "He was a destroyed man when he came to see me." He glanced out at the people busy working in the office beyond. "It was about a week or so after they'd had the decision from the CPS and he'd been wrestling with his conscience since then." He sighed and looked across at me. "It was Devon who went and told the Ellisons, you know."

"That can't have been easy."

"No." He shook his head. "They blamed themselves for moving her body, for the DNA getting mixed. But what do you do when your daughter's just been murdered?" He shrugged and furrowed his brow.

"Did the Ellisons know that he was going to leak the information?"

"I don't think so, no." He paused. "Foster was destroyed by the whole thing, he wasn't thinking straight. He became quite close to the Ellisons during the investigation; well you would. He was part of the family liaison team. But by the time he gave me the information he was broken."

"But you took the information from him anyway?"

"I'm a journalist," he said holding his hands palm up as if that provided plenty of explanation. "And, if I'm honest I did have other motives. I mean, Bridges was never high on anyone's top ten most likeable people, and he had powerful friends, people with not just influence but money. And muscle too. He played the media for his own ends. At the time, he was organising marches and protests about Muslims in the city. The city had taken in some refugees, I forget from where, and Bridges organised protests about them being given housing that should have gone to local people. He had papers, and not just local ones, the more gutter-leaning national press, lining up to interview a heap of local families who'd been waiting for houses for a hundred years or something. Whipping people up into a frenzy over nothing. The refugees were housed by a charity in private housing, but of course that didn't fit the story."

"So, you saw it as an opportunity to get back at him?"

"Like I say, he knew people. There'd been stories that he'd managed to keep out of the press. But this"—he stabbed his finger at the file—"this, he couldn't control." Finally, Fairbrother opened the file. Papers and photos spilled out in a jumble and he tucked them back into a rough semblance of order. He fumbled through the papers until he found a photo. He pushed it across the table towards me. "They obviously couldn't photograph her at the crime scene, so this is from the morgue, just before the post-mortem."

With some reluctance I forced myself to look down at the photo of eleven-year-old Margaret-Elizabeth. She looked younger than eleven, her beautiful features were still, her long wavy hair flowing over her shoulders. Her neck was dark with bruising but apart from that she looked as if she were sleeping.

"What was she strangled with?" I asked, looking at the bruising.

"Her dressing gown cord. She wasn't wearing her dressing gown, but it had recently been washed so it was hanging in the utility room, drying. So either Margaret-Elizabeth had walked out into the garden carrying just the cord of her dressing gown. Unlikely." He tipped his head from side to side. "Or someone had been into the house."

"Bridges' DNA was found in the house, wasn't it?"

"In the kitchen, yes."

"On the dressing gown cord?"

"The cord was never found."

I pushed the photo back to him. He slid it in amongst the papers and closed the file. He pushed the file over to me and said, "Here, you can take this. This is what Foster gave me. Sorry it's a bit of a mess, but it's been ten years. Peruse it at your leisure."

"Do you think the CPS were wrong not to prosecute?"

"Well, I'm not really in a position to say. Bridges is an unpleasant character, who hates everyone that isn't a straight white man who shares his political affiliations. He treats women with contempt and he's got previous for sexual assault." He tilted his hands, balancing, weighing things up. "But when you look at the file, objectively, you'd have a job proving it beyond reasonable doubt. A defence lawyer would rip the DNA evidence apart and what are you left with? He was there, he was definitely there. He was seen bending over Margaret-Elizabeth's body. But again, any decent lawyer would claim that was circumstantial." He shrugged. "So, I guess I can see where they were coming from."

"He'd been seen following her, or hanging around hadn't he?"

"That was his MO. Yes, Margaret-Elizabeth had mentioned that someone had followed her home one day from school. And then she saw the same man in the woods beyond the house watching her over the fence. He'd done it before, he had a history."

"Flashing, wasn't it?"

"It had been. Although he'd apparently groped some-one. Not sure where that went, I don't think he was put away for it. So, by printing that"—he pointed at the file—"I felt I was doing my bit, you know, to balance things up a bit."

"You say he had connections. Didn't he try to get an injunction? Or stop you printing the stories?"

"We had some good lawyers looking over what we were saying. We were always very careful not to directly accuse. But, you can infer, you know, within the law."

I pulled the file towards me and opened it up. "What will be the most use?" I flicked through a couple of the pages.

"There's all the police interviews, that's probably a good place to start. It kind of builds up a picture of what happened that night from various different points of view."

"I think I might see if I can go and see Bridges," I said, more to myself than anything, as I closed the file.

"Now that'll be a pleasure, I'm sure."

"Well, thanks for seeing me." I stood up, clutching the unruly file under my arm.

Steven Fairbrother showed me down the stairs and back to the reception area, where he ran over and held the door open for me. The sun was making an admirable attempt to break through the thick layer of clouds and I wondered if it might, perhaps, start to warm up later.

## 8

I left the Herald offices and walked through town towards the car hire place. The street was quiet, a little dappled sunlight dancing on the pavement. Looking up into the sky, I could see that the clouds were clearing, and it was noticeably warmer so I reached into my handbag and pulled out a fabric shopping bag. I placed my scarf, gloves and the untidy file inside it and continued walking, deciding to go through the city centre, although it wasn't necessary. I needed a few bits and pieces and it wasn't far out of my way.

Lost in thought, I almost missed the crossing and I glanced around to check the road was clear. A movement in the corner of my eye made me linger a little, and I turned my head to see what it had been, but there was nothing there. A shiver worked its way down my back, but I shook my head. There was nothing there. I carried on walking, crossing the road and dipping through a little alleyway to get into the centre. Footsteps approached, the sounds getting closer. Halfway down the alley I turned round, peering over my shoulder. Just the merest fraction of a movement indicated that someone had dipped behind the entrance as I had turned round. My heart picked up a beat, and I quickened my pace. I left the alley and headed for the nearest shop, which happened to be a baker's, and stood inside the door peering out into the street. It wasn't busy and a few tired shoppers walked past, but nobody that aroused any suspicion. I left the shop without buying anything and headed over to Marks and Spencer, looking around me as I went. I couldn't shake the sensation that I was being followed, but every time I looked round there was no one there. No one obvious anyway.

I made a mental note of the people around me; the sixty-something woman in the red coat; the young mum with a buggy; the man in a suit with a newspaper tucked under his arm. I tried to memorise the dozen or so people I could see and continued with my shopping, placing the items in my basket with increasing speed and heading for the check-out. I peered over my shoulder every few seconds, but the only person I saw more than once was the young mum with the buggy and she was lowest on my list of potential suspects.

I paid for my things and made my way back through the store, doubling back a couple of times to see if I could catch anyone out. Apart from fluttering movements out of the corner of my eye every now and again there was nothing and I decided I was being paranoid. All the same I was relieved that I would be driving home in the hire car, so no one would be able to follow me and find out where I lived.

At a pace so fast I was practically running, I made my way to pick up the car and wallowed in the sanctuary of the reception. For once, I wasn't hit with frustration at the long-winded process of filling in all the relevant documentation, signing here, there and everywhere. At least it felt secure there. Still, eventually I had to leave. I walked out the back of the reception and into the car park to locate my car. There was definitely nobody else in the car park and as I looked at myself in the rear-view mirror, I shook my head and scolded myself for my paranoia.

# 9

A little later on, the hire car parked on the road outside, I sat at my dining table, papers spread out covering every inch of it. I'd made some attempt to sort out and categorise the contents of the file, although I kept changing my mind about how I should organise them, so the piles had been arranged and rearranged several times already.

Basically I had a pile of family statements; a pile of statements from people who weren't family, like the members of the Ellisons' book club; a couple of statements from 'others' such as associates of Bridges, and various assorted individuals. Then I had a pile of stuff such as Bridges' interview under caution, financial details, his Internet browsing history, messages he'd sent, his criminal history and so on. There were details of his political affiliations and contributions, as well as information on his activities as a protester. There were specialist reports such as the post-mortem. There were print offs from the private Facebook group that the book club had used to communicate, various email trails, text messages, photos, receipts and bank statements. I held the still from a CCTV camera in my hand and perused my piles. It really didn't fit into any of my, admittedly rather arbitrary, categories. The photo showed a grainy image of the city centre, a man that I took to be Bridges walking down a deserted street. The time in the corner of the image showed just past midnight and I assumed that this was him walking home, although I could find no accompanying explanation. I placed the photo on the table and gave up with my categorising.

I sat down and decided to make a start on the statements, taking notes of any interesting information as I went. The police had interviewed a host of people, so I began with the ones who had been involved that night from the parents' perspective. The members of the book club had all been seen, and they all had pretty much said the same thing; that they'd finished up just after ten-thirty and the Ellisons had left soon after. What more could they say?

The book club was made up of seven people; three couples and a divorcee. They all had children of various ages and they took it in turns to host the club once every four weeks. I wrote their names down in my notebook, wondering whether it would shed any fresh light on anything for me if I went to see them. I had £20,000 to work my way through, so I didn't see that it would do any harm.


*Matthew and Nicole Ellison*
*Margaret-Elizabeth      11*


*Dan and Theresa Johnson*
*Jake                          13*
*Grace                          5*

*Jeffrey and Mary Walker*

| | |
|---|---|
| *Isabella* | 12 |
| *Jasmine* | 11 |
| *Sebastian* | 9 |

*Angela Thompson*

| | |
|---|---|
| *Hannah* | 11 |
| *Callum* | 2 |

The interviews with the Ellisons covered much the same ground as when I'd seen them yesterday. The police had obviously asked them about the whereabouts of the dressing gown cord, because both statements had a sentence about it, but there was little there that I didn't already know. They had no idea about the cord, each saying separately that the dressing gown had been hanging in the utility room after being washed. Both said they hadn't noticed the cord had gone until later.

The statements contained the names of all the relatives who had turned up at the house and I started a new page in my notebook and wrote them down.

> *Jonathan and Christina Scraggs (Nicole's brother and his wife)*
> *Karl and Judith Ryan (Nicole's sister and her husband)*
> *David, Marion and Diane Todd (Nicole's cousin, his wife and their adult daughter)*

I knew that it had been Jonathan who'd found Margaret-Elizabeth's body, but the statements informed me that Karl, David and Diane had gone with Jonathan to look for her. I looked through Jonathan's statement. It had been taken by DC Devon Foster.

...so we went into the garden to see if we could find out where she had gone. It was dark but I saw a movement. I shouted out and someone stood up and looked directly at me. I thought he was going to say something but then he ran off. I could see that it was a man. I got a clear look at him. When he stood up, his face was clear in the moon-light. I'm confident I would recognise him again if I saw him. I ran over to where he'd been and that's when I saw Margaret-Elizabeth. She was lying on the ground, face down. Her hair all spread out. Her arms were up above her head and her legs out behind her. She was wearing her nightie. I shouted out to the others, that's Karl and David who'd come out with me to the garden. Then I turned her over. I picked her up and ran with her back to the house. I was shouting for the others to chase after the man I'd seen. I pointed in the direction he'd run and they went off to try and find him. I ran back with Margaret-Elizabeth to the house.

Nicole was in the front room with Judith. I'm not sure where everyone was. I think Chrissy, and maybe Matthew, had gone out the front, down the street in case she'd wandered off that way. And, Marion, was maybe in the kitchen. Everything was confused. I wasn't really paying attention to where everyone was, I just wanted to get help. I shouted for them to call an ambulance. Judith called for the ambulance and she was giving instruction to me to try to help Margaret-Elizabeth but I couldn't do it. Marion came in and she took over. Nicole was bending over Margaret-Elizabeth and stroking her and then the others came in from the garden and Diane led her away. Marion became upset. Judith was on the phone to the ambulance people and they said we must keep trying till the ambulance arrived. So David took over. Then the

63

*ambulance arrived and they put Margaret-Elizabeth in the*
*ambulance. Nicole went in the ambulance and Judith went*
*with her. Matthew came into the room just as they were*
*putting Margaret-Elizabeth in the ambulance. He asked*
*David to take him, to follow the ambulance. The rest of us*
*went back through the woods to see if we could find the*
*man, but there was no sign. Then we got the message that*
*Margaret-Elizabeth was dead and we just sat there…*

The interviews with the other family members all said pretty much the same thing. There had clearly been utter confusion, with some placing various family members in different places at different times. There were a couple of versions of who had tried to revive Margaret-Elizabeth but nothing surprising given the circumstances.

In his interview, Anthony Bridges had answered almost every question with 'no comment'. He did admit to being there, in the woods. He did admit that he had seen Margaret-Elizabeth walking home from school, although he denied that he'd been following her. When he was asked what he'd been doing in the woods at half-past ten at night he said, "None of your fucking business. But I wasn't there to kill a fucking child." The interviewer had asked Bridges directly if he had killed Margaret-Elizabeth. He denied that he had. He also denied being in the house, or entering the garden.

I shuffled the papers around a little, scanning the contents for anything important. There was a long printout of people spoken to but who hadn't given statements, presumably because they'd had nothing useful to say. I took out my notebook and turned to another page. I wrote down a list of people who'd given statements about Bridges. It would be useful to talk to them and get a good feel for who he was and what he'd been doing at the time.

| | |
|---|---|
| *Colin O'Gorman* | *Business Partner* |
| *James Poole* | *Fellow founder of Pure Britain* |
| *Zoe Hepworth* | *Ex-girlfriend* |

I looked at my watch. I needed to get into position to follow Marcus. I momentarily considered the idea of staying at home and wondered if Collette would find out if I didn't actually follow him. Following a friend wasn't something that I was happy doing, but I'd been unable to resist her doe eyes. And she'd clearly been distressed at the idea that he was having an affair, understandably so. I was convinced that he'd be working late, or that there must be some other logical explanation, but I had promised her. I guessed that once I'd proved her wrong I could hand the hire car back and get on with looking into Margaret-Elizabeth's murder.

Before I left the house, I took photos on my phone of as much of the information as I could. If I was going to be sitting in a car waiting for Marcus to appear I may as well have something to keep me interested. I started with what I assumed to be the most important things, then moved on through until I had everything I thought would be useful. I left anything I thought could wait, or that wouldn't make very interesting reading, like the financial records and then gathered it all together, walked through to the dining room and placed the file in my set of lockable drawers.

## 10

**M**arcus worked at Lincoln University in a role I never quite understood, but had something to do with student numbers, recruitment, or generally making sure that people wanted to attend. He usually left work around half-past five. From what Collette had told me over the years he seemed to keep more or less to that routine, wanting to get home to see the girls in plenty of time for bed. There were a couple of staff car parks so I drove round until I spotted his car and then parked several spaces down so that I could see him approaching. I made sure that I had my camera to hand so that I could record exactly what was happening and when. The car park was gloomily lit, and the light would be fading soon, but one of my first purchases after I'd had a couple of pay cheques had been a new camera and I was fairly confident it would take some nice clear pictures.

I stared out into the early evening light and hoped that I was far enough away from Marcus' car to be well-hidden. I was just contemplating turning on the heater when he appeared around the corner of the nearest building. My hands were freezing so I rubbed them together in an attempt to warm them up, before grabbing my camera and firing off a round of shots of Marcus walking to his car so that the time was recorded. Not wanting to draw too much attention to myself, I waited until he was in the car before turning on the engine.

We pulled out of the car park, skirted round the city centre and headed out of the city on Canwick Road. He clearly wasn't heading home. I followed him along the same road until we hit Branston. I hung back a little as there were only a few cars on the road and I didn't want him to realise he was being followed. He slowed down to drive through the attractive village. Stone houses lined the main street, their small front gardens brimming over with shrubs and flowers. We were about to reach the village limits when he indicated to turn left. I followed, but hung back even more. There was nothing in-between him and me, and thanks to the gloominess of approaching night and his bright tail lights I could see where he was going from a reasonable distance.

Marcus meandered down a couple of roads before eventually entering a modern-looking estate. A combination of yellow and red bricks, semis and detached houses added some variety but for the most part the buildings were fairly uniform. Each house had a little lawn and a drive. Some owners had planted shrubs along the edge of the lawn or a tree in the garden but it was a fairly characterless area. I imagined it provided affordable housing to people who worked in Lincoln or one of the bigger towns, as the connections would be reasonably good.

I slowed down as Marcus turned into a cul-de-sac and parked up on the drive of a small red brick semi-detached house. I drove past the end of the road, turned round in somebody's drive, then crawled back so that I could see what he was doing. He got out of his car and approached the house, a motion-sensitive light coming on as he neared the front door. I took out my camera and snapped him ringing the doorbell and taking a step back to wait. At least he didn't have a key.

From my vantage point up the road I could see the front door clearly, and although I was quite a way up the street my digital camera zoomed right in on the front door. Seconds later a smiling, and very attractive, blonde lady opened the door and indicated for him to go in. With that, Marcus disappeared inside and the front door closed.

I examined the pictures and a trickle of worry started worming its way through my body. Maybe Collette had been right. They clearly knew each other well. In fact, now that I looked at the pictures I could see the blonde woman leaning into Marcus and pecking him on what looked to be the cheek, although from the angle it wasn't clear. It could have been his lips. My heart sank, as much for me having to break the news, as for Collette having to deal with it.

I put the camera down on the passenger seat and moved the car so that I was still down the cul-de-sac but positioned between the end of the road and the house. Marcus wouldn't be able to leave without me seeing, even if I didn't spend every second looking at the door. If nothing else his headlights would alert me to him leaving.

I settled in and reached for my phone so that I could study the pictures I'd taken of all the information in the Margaret-Elizabeth file. I read through the statements of Bridges' associates who described him as an upstanding, albeit ruthless, businessman with patriotic political views. There were email trails and texts—in some he'd been organising protest marches, in others he was discussing figures about the number of foreign nationals who were living in the city. Bridges owned a business providing vending machines; renting spaces in an office, a shopping centre, a station or similar and then going round filling them up and collecting the money. It seemed the trend at the time had been that, more often, people were wanting to pay for their purchases with bank cards. Some of the information seemed to hint at a disagreement between Bridges and his fellow directors, with Bridges in favour of the move to modernity. Although based in Lincoln, the business had machines all over the country and employed dozens of staff to fill the machines, service them, change them, buy the stock and so on.

He clearly used his money for political gain and several of the associates made allusions to him being friendly with people in Westminster as well as bribing local councillors to make decisions in his favour. What those decisions had been was not clear, but the image of a man used to blustering his way through life using power, money and threats to get what he wanted came through loud and clear.

I switched tack and started looking at something less likely to cause my blood to boil. I read through a few of the messages on the Facebook group that the book club had used to keep in touch about their activities. For the most part this seemed to be a whole trail of what books they were reading, not unsurprisingly. Although it wasn't just the adults; they all discussed what books their children were reading too.

The sounds of voices in the distance drew my consciousness back to the task in hand and I looked up to see that Marcus was about to leave. I grabbed my camera and started clicking pictures. The same blonde woman was at the door and although I couldn't hear what they were saying I could see that they were bidding each other a friendly farewell. A smile, a raised hand, a quick wave. I kept photographing until Marcus was in his car.

He'd been in there about an hour and a half. Long enough for a secret shag, I thought, but not really long enough for a bit of romance as well. Maybe that's all it was, emotionless sex. Perhaps the blonde lady was a working girl, turning tricks from her home. It didn't appear that way though. They'd seemed really friendly. I tossed the camera onto the passenger seat and followed Marcus back to the city. I wanted to make sure that he went home and I didn't miss him going anywhere else. From a hundred yards down the road, I spied on my best friend's house and watched her husband go home to her and their children as if he'd been in the office working late. What was he up to?

I drove home, puzzling it through in my mind until I pulled up on the road, in a parking space conveniently available right in front of my house. I snatched up my camera, locked the car, and headed down the drive, and then all thoughts of Marcus disappeared from my head in an instant.

## 11

The front door was open. Only slightly, but it was definitely open. My blood froze in my veins, and my breathing quickened as I struggled with the sudden need for oxygen. An elevated level of adrenaline coursed through my body, causing my pulse to gallop away like a stampeding horse. The house was in darkness, an eerie quiet highlighting the beating of my heart, which I was sure was so loud that it would alert anyone to my presence.

Without even thinking about what I was doing, I pushed open the door, and slid inside on tiptoes, holding my breath while I rested the camera and my handbag on the hall table, just inside the door. I stood still, trying not to make a sound, straining my ears for a clue as to whether there was anyone inside. It felt like hours but it must have only been seconds. As I let out a breath, silently, between pursed lips, a faint rustling emanated from the dining room. Attempting to stay as quiet as possible, I pulled my dad's old walking stick little by little from the umbrella stand, grateful that I had never been able to bring myself to give it away. I crept towards the door. Placing each step carefully on the carpet, I inched my way forward, pulling the walking stick above my head as I edged down the hallway.

I hadn't quite made it when the dining room door swung open, and a tall male figure emerged, clad in black from head to foot, a balaclava obscuring his face and a black bag slung over his shoulders. I was only a few feet from the door and I swung the walking stick in an arc towards him. He glanced to his left just as I started my swing and he bolted towards the kitchen. The walking stick landed with a crash on the door jamb causing shudders of pain to reverberate up my arms.

"Hey!" I shouted out and hurtled after the figure, shaking my arms to try to release the aching still pulsing through them. "Hey! Come back!"

He took no notice and continued running. He crashed through the kitchen door, pulling it shut behind him. I tore through the door, holding the walking stick aloft with my right arm as I did so. He was fumbling with the back door, trying to work the lock, and I slammed the walking stick down onto his back. He buckled with the pain, letting go of the door handle and he fell to the floor. He rolled over onto his back and as I attempted to bring the walking stick down on him one more time, he lashed out with his arms and grabbed my right ankle. With one swift movement he yanked my leg towards him and I flew through the air, hitting the kitchen floor with a thump that vibrated through my entire body. Pain ripped up my back as I landed, yelling out and the walking stick tumbled from my hands.

He seized the opportunity and leapt to his feet, but I kicked up at him with the sole of my foot and caught him square in the chest, sending him smashing into the counter, pieces of crockery falling around him. It barely stopped him at all. He pushed himself forward, heaving me up by my coat lapels and pulling me to a standing position. Then he shoved me with both hands on my chest. I flew back into the fridge causing a box of wine glasses to tumble from the top and shatter on the floor. I staggered as I tried to keep myself from falling, but before I could stand squarely on both feet, he kicked at my leg, pushing it from underneath me. I fell onto my side, smashing my outstretched arm into the broken glass. Whilst I was on the floor he fumbled once more with the back door, this time with success. As I scrabbled back onto my feet I was able to scoop up the walking stick just as he yanked open the door. I swung the stick wildly, trying to land it on him as he ran through the door and out into the back garden.

I chased after him but he was quick, running down the garden and leaping over the wall at the bottom. I sprinted to the end of the garden, watching him as he disappeared, engulfed in the blackness of the night. It was useless; I stopped, resting my hands on my knees, struggling for breath and gazing into the emptiness of the gardens beyond. I stayed where I was for several minutes, leaning on my knees and staring out into the darkness. I didn't know what I was hoping for. Maybe that I'd catch sight of him and be able to give chase once more.

I sighed and stood up. There was no hope of finding where he'd gone. With shoulders bent in resignation, I sloped back up to the house to try to understand what had just happened.

The kitchen had sustained some damage. Bits of crockery and glass covered the floor and there was a dent in the fridge where I'd crashed into it. I ignored the mess and went through to the dining room. I put on the light and surveyed the scene in front of me. Drawers in the bookcase had been emptied, papers spilling onto the floor in front of it. A few books had tumbled onto the floor and the spider plant that sat on top was laying splayed across the papers, a mixture of compost and leaves like confetti across the carpet.

Then my eyes were drawn to the corner of the room. To my set of locked drawers. The drawers had all been pulled out, the wood splintered where they'd been prised from their housing against their will. I ran over and pulled through the jumble of papers, but I already knew what was missing. There was no pink file. Someone had stolen the information about Margaret-Elizabeth's murder that the journalist had given me that morning.

## 12

------

A little while later I stood in the kitchen and faced a reluctant young police officer who'd been dispatched to the house. The timbre of her voice and her arched eyebrows hinted at disbelief; her pinched mouth suggested she'd much rather be in the police station drinking a cup of tea. Her uniform strained across her ample chest and I found myself wondering if she'd put on some weight since joining the force.

"Mrs Spencer?" she said.

"I'm sorry." I shook my head. "Sorry, I'm a little shaken, that's all. What were you saying?"

"Hmmm," she replied and folded her arms. She'd already given me a long lecture explaining in some detail why I'd been reckless to enter the house if, as she put it, I suspected there was someone inside. I may have been wrong, but her tone appeared to be casting doubt on my version of events. "I asked whether you locked the door on your way out?"

"Um, yes, of course. Why?"

"Well, there's no sign of forced entry. So, I wonder if you could have forgotten?"

I could clearly remember locking the door, because I'd got the wrong car keys and had to unlock it to go back in and pick up the ones for the hire car. Unless...maybe I hadn't locked it when I went out the second time? I was sure that I had.

"And there's nothing else missing apart from a file of papers?"

"Not that I can see, no."

"I see," she said, unfolding her arms and scribbling in her pocketbook.

"Are you going to check for fingerprints?"

"You said the man was wearing gloves," she replied, peering up at me without moving her head.

"I just thought he might have taken them off whilst he was searching, that's all." It sounded stupid even before the words had left my mouth, but her attitude was making me nervous.

"Well..." Her gaze returned to her notebook. "We have to prioritise the use of resources such as that, and as I'm sure you can appreciate, there are burglaries with rather more valuable items stolen. I'm sure you understand." She snapped the book shut and replaced it in her top pocket.

"So what happens now?"

"I'll file the report," she said moving towards the door. "If you need a number for insurance purposes, give us a ring." She pointed to the door lock on her way out. "And don't forget to lock the door next time," she said, shutting the door before I had a chance to reply.

I stomped back into the kitchen and cleared up the broken crockery and glass. Then I went and surveyed the damage in the dining room. It wasn't so bad, apart from the poor plant. I'd need to buy a new set of drawers but the rest was easily put back together again. I looked at my watch—it was heading towards ten o'clock, but I thought I ought to call the Ellisons and let them know that Margaret-Elizabeth's file had been stolen.

Mr Ellison picked up on the second ring.

"How are you getting on?" he asked after I'd explained who it was and apologised for the late hour.

"Well, I thought you ought to know that someone broke into my house this evening."

"Are you okay?"

"I'm fine, thanks. I was out at the time." I thought I'd keep quiet on my 'reckless' pursuit of the intruder. "It's just that...well, I went to see Steven Fairbrother this morning. The journalist who printed the leaked information?"

"Yes, I see."

"Well, I put the file in a locked drawer when I went out, but that's what the burglar stole. Just that, there's nothing else. Obviously someone was wanting that file." I thought about the sensation I'd had of being followed earlier. Someone clearly knew that I'd been into the Herald offices.

"I did ask to see the file," he said at length. "After the articles had been printed. Steven Fairbrother asked me if I wanted it, but what good would it have done me? I can't imagine why anyone would want to steal it."

"I don't know either. But there's obviously something in there that somebody doesn't want to be found."

"I don't know what on earth there could be. Most of the content of the interviews was printed in the papers." He paused. "Are you sure you're okay? Are you sure you want to keep going with this? I'd understand completely if you wanted to give up."

"Oh, absolutely. Don't worry about that. I'm not going

to let anyone put me off. In fact, it's made me more determined to make sure I leave no stone unturned. I promise,
I'll do my best for you, Matthew."

"Well, do be careful, please."

"I will. I'm going to see Devon Foster tomorrow, to see
what he has to say."

"A lovely, lovely man. Such a shame, this hit him so
hard. Well, clearly it hit us all, but Nicole and I had each
other to lean on when we needed it. Devon was so dedi-
cated and so badly wanted to get a resolution for us." He
sighed. That resolution was still being elusive.

"Yes, it'll be interesting to get his perspective. Then, I'm
going to see if I can arrange to meet up with Anthony
Bridges."

"He's not a big fan of women, apparently."

"Well, with prison guards hanging around I'm hoping
I'll be safe."

"Yes, that will be interesting. He did get quite cosy with
a female journalist once, so you never know he might open
up if you can get his sympathy soon enough. He hardly
answered any of the questions in his police interview so,
who knows, maybe he'll tell you something that he hasn't
mentioned before."

"I'll do my best. I thought about having a chat with your
relatives, the ones who were in the house that night."

"Well," he mused. "I'm not sure they'd be able to tell
you much, nothing that they haven't already said, but I'm
sure they'll be willing to help out if they can."

"You never know, with the passage of time there might
be something that clicks. And Jonathan Scraggs did see
Bridges, so it might be worth a shot. I also wondered about
the book club members. Just for a bit of background."

"I doubt it's worth bothering them. They were all at the

Walkers' and didn't see anything at all. I can't think that they'll be able to add anything that'll help."

"Okay, well I'll let you get off. Give my regards to Nicole and I'll keep in touch with progress."

"Stay safe, Verity. Be careful."

"I will. Goodnight."

# TUESDAY

# 13

The following morning I sent a text to Charlton to see if he was around for a chat, and we arranged to talk later in the morning, before I went to see Devon Foster. Then I tried Nash and was surprised when he picked up the call. His phone almost always went to voicemail.

"Verity, hi," he said. "How are you?"

I filled him in on the details of the night before.

"Why would someone want to steal the file?" he asked, his voice filled with surprise.

"I have no idea. And what are they going to do with the information?"

"Well, thankfully, that's all in the public domain now. So why they would need to steal it, I don't know. They could read most of the statements online if they wanted to. The Herald archive still has the majority of it."

"I guess there might be something in the file that they don't want me to see."

"Well, it's a possibility," he agreed. "But I can't think what."

I laughed. "I suppose if we knew it wouldn't be a secret."

"That's true, yes, that's very true."

"Actually, I'd taken photos of most of the stuff anyway, so unless it was some receipt or invoice or bank statement or something like that they were trying to retrieve, I still have the information on my phone." I paused. "I wonder if someone was trying to frighten me?"

He cackled. "I bet that didn't work, Verity. That won't have worked at all!"

"Well, no. I promised Mr Ellison I'd do all I could."

"I told him you were determined."

"Nash?" I ventured, after a short pause. "I was wondering if I could go and visit Anthony Bridges in prison?"

"Hmmm…" he pondered. "I can see what I can arrange. He'd have to agree to see you, though. There's a chance, there's a fair chance that he might not."

"If you could ask, or find out for me?"

"I will, Verity, I certainly will. I'm not sure he'll say anything even if he does agree to see you. He's not said anything to anyone else yet."

"I know," I said. "But I'd like to try. You never know, and I won't have lost anything, except a bit of time." And a bit more of the Ellison's £20,000 I thought.

"I'll do what I can," he said.

There was an hour or so before I'd arranged to call Charlton, so I scrolled through all the information on my phone, sending several of the pictures to my laptop so that I could see them better. I took out my notebook and next to the names of the relatives and the book club members I noted down their contact details. Then I rang round to see if I could arrange to go and visit them.

Out of the book club members, Jeffrey Walker's phone gave an unobtainable signal, so I assumed he'd not only changed his mobile, but also his number, in the last ten years. Both Mary Walker's and Angela Thompson's phones did ring, but there was no answer and they went to voice-mail so I left a message on each saying who I was, what the Ellisons had asked me to do, and asked them to call me back. Lastly, I tried Theresa Johnson. The phone rang for ages and I was just about to disconnect when someone answered.

"Well," she said, after I'd done my introductions. "I'm really not sure what we'd be able to tell you. We weren't anywhere near the house, as you probably know."

"I appreciate that, Mrs Johnson," I said. "But it would be really useful for me to just build up a picture of what was happening generally around that time, so that I can get an idea of Margaret-Elizabeth's life and what was going on for her back then."

"Okay," she said. "Well, late afternoon is probably good for me."

I was about to call Jonathan Scraggs, but then something in the pictures on my laptop caught my eye. I'd not noticed the day before as I'd skimmed over the statements from Bridges' political affiliates, but alongside the statements from his allies there was one from the chairperson of a group called Action and Assistance Lincoln, an organisation that offered support to a range of vulnerable people, including refugees. They had clearly been involved in plenty of counter-protests against Pure Britain during the time that Bridges had been leading marches and rallies. The chairman was a man called Paul Hardy and I imagined he'd been interviewed because he had a history of clashes with Bridges and had openly challenged him, calling him a liar and a racist. The antagonism came through in his statement. It went on:

> ...*that was when I started to get the threats. Bridges himself came up to me after the rally in October and said if I didn't back down he'd see to it that I never walked again. He was deadly serious. Then in the spring of the following year, one of his bodyguards started pushing me, shoving me as the march moved forward. He was trying to push me over and would have succeeded except that there were way more of us, and other people saw what was happening and huddled around me. He told me again that if I didn't back off I'd live to regret it. I remember he said, 'You'll live to regret, or put it another way, you'll regret to live.' Which I took to mean life would be so bad I'd wish I'd died....*

The fact that Bridges had needed bodyguards at his marches said something. I Googled Action and Assistance Lincoln. It was still in existence and it was still working to help refugees and other vulnerable families. It seemed that they did a lot of work in conjunction with the local mosque, including helping them out with the delivery of food parcels. Bridges wouldn't like that. The chairperson was no longer Paul Hardy though. I searched for him, and before very long I found out that he was now the landlord of The Steam Hammer pub, just towards the foot of Steep Hill in Lincoln. I knew the pub well; I must have seen him in there, although I couldn't remember.

The Steam Hammer pub had a website full of arty pictures of artisan beers, unusual gins, cocktails, mixers and wines. The male bar staff all sported beards and wore waist-coats and tinted glasses. I located the 'contact us' page and sent a quick message, for the attention of Paul Hardy, asking if I could go and have a chat with him with a brief explanation of what it was regarding.

It was time to talk to Charlton, so I grabbed my laptop, put it down on the coffee table and video called him. As his smiling face appeared I waved at him. "Hi," I said. "How are you?"

"Good, thanks. How's things with you?"

"All good here thanks. Well, apart from a break-in last night."

Sam's face crinkled up in concern.

"Oh, I'm fine," I added hastily. I filled him in on the details as well as the police officer's assertion that I'd been 'reckless' to enter the house.

"Well, she has a point, Verity. He could have been armed, or something. He could have grabbed a knife while you were in the kitchen and stabbed you. All sorts of things could have happened."

I hadn't really thought about kitchen knives. "Well, luckily I'm still here to tell the tale," I said, wishing I'd kept quiet. "Anyway, my search of Bridges as a character is continuing and he seems like a really pleasant chap." I rolled my eyes. "Have you heard of Pure Britain?"

"Is that one of those far-right movements? They're generally pretty badly organised and full of in-fighting."

"I don't know about that, but their website is full of vitriol. Anyone who isn't white and straight they want banished from our shores forever."

"I wonder where they think they'll send us all," he said, pulling his mouth to one side and gazing at his ceiling. "If we get a choice, maybe I could go to Barbados." He laughed.

"I'll come with you if that lot are in charge. I just don't get the hatred against anyone who's different to them."

"People are frightened by anything different, that's the thing. It's easy to believe that someone who's from a different race or religion is to blame for all your problems. There are people in power who love groups like this. It takes the heat off them."

"The website says they're anti-establishment."

"Yeah, that's why people buy into the rhetoric. They think these groups represent them; that they're against the elite. They think they're on their side, but they're not. I mean, your everyday working man in the street might just be convinced that foreigners are out to steal his job but the organisers know. They help the establishment."

"Apparently Bridges had friends in Westminster."

"I bet he does. Groups like this are useful to the powers that be. When your average man has a pay cut, or loses his job, or his house, the government don't want to be blamed or people wouldn't vote for them anymore. Much better to blame the poor guy that just came from Romania, or Afghanistan or somewhere, than a government policy."

"Well, hopefully I'll get to ask him about all that. I've asked Nash if he can organise for me to go and see him, if he gets back to me." I looked at my watch as if I'd been counting the minutes since asking him.

"Patience, my dear. You need patience," Charlton said, throwing his head back and laughing.

"I don't have time for that," I retorted.

We chatted a little about the change in the weather, Netflix choices and the possibility of me buying a new laptop, before I realised it was almost time for me to go.

"Listen, Sam, I have to go but I'm going to see Devon

Foster, the policeman who leaked the information to the press. Everyone tells me he's a bit reclusive, broken even. Any advice?"

"Go easy on him, Verity."

## 14

Devon Foster lived in a flat towards the end of Monks Road so I set off in plenty of time to arrive ahead of our planned meeting time. A golden hue bathed Steep Hill, the colour of the low afternoon sun enhancing the stone of the shops on either side. The temperature was about fifteen degrees higher than it had been a day or two ago. The vagaries of the English climate never ceased to amaze me, but it was confusing the hell out of the general public. No one knew what to wear. Some were wearing the coats and scarves they'd become used to needing for the last couple of weeks, others had sought out their shorts and sandals. I had plumped for a half-way house, with jeans and a light jacket and it was refreshing to walk along without the cold biting into any exposed flesh. I held my head up to the autumn sun to feel the warmth of it on my face.

The flats where Foster lived were arranged in two and three storey blocks, and I checked the address, confused by the numbering. It was a good job I'd left early because by the time I'd figured out which was Foster's flat I only had a couple of minutes spare. He lived in a ground floor flat and I rang the bell and waited, standing back a little and surveying the neighbours' bikes and washing. After some time, shuffling noises began to work their way through the door and a shadow fell over the glass panel. Foster opened the door an inch, a charcoal black eye peering through the gap.

"Verity Spencer," I said, and he opened the door to let me in.

A potent mix of smells hit my nose; old tobacco, stale body odour, urine and mouldy food. I followed him in, blinking back tears as the stench stung into my eyes.

We walked down a hallway cluttered on all sides with newspapers, books, empty takeaway containers, half-drunk cider bottles and full ashtrays. He led me into a front room, equally cluttered, and indicated a sofa. I pushed a pile of newspapers and magazines to one side and balanced myself on the few inches of free space I'd created. Foster sat down in a chair by the window. He perched on the edge of the chair, his legs spread out. He leaned forward and rested his elbows on his knees. Remote controls lined the arm of the chair, and a little table to his left held glasses that were variously full with some kind of golden liquid. I hoped it was cider.

Foster stared across at me, his jet black eyes showing no emotion. With dark sagging skin and aged, deep creases furrowing his forehead, he looked three decades older than the thirty-something years he'd lived.

"Thank you for seeing me, Devon," I said.

He nodded slowly, but said nothing. He held up a packet of cigarettes, pointing them towards himself, and he arched his eyebrows. I gave a short nod. He shook one out and lit it up, before taking in a deep draw, then breathing out a fog of smoke.

Normally I'd have asked him to tell me a little bit about Margaret-Elizabeth or her family or ask for some background, but I got the impression that Foster wasn't going to want me to hang around for any longer than absolutely necessary, so I dived straight in.

"Tell me about why you went to the press?"

He coughed, pulling his hand up to his mouth. "I wanted people to know. To know what she'd been through." His voice was scratchy, gravelly with the wear of constant smoking.

"You mean the sexual assault?"

He nodded again and swallowed.

"Did you think it would help?"

He looked at his hands, turning the cigarette between his fingers, and then looked up. "No. Not really. I just didn't want it to be buried. I didn't want her to be yesterday's news."

"It must have been tough, after all the work you put in, that the CPS decided not to prosecute."

"Yeah." He spread out his hand, the one that wasn't holding the cigarette, and turned it over, examining his palm and picking at the skin. "It happens, you know. And I could sense what their decision was going to be; all the evidence was circumstantial and would have been thoroughly raked over by a defence team." He sighed. "It doesn't ever make it easy though."

"Even with the DNA evidence?"

"DNA is only good if you have everything else stacked up. Even if you can place two guys in a room together, try proving one killed the other without any other evidence. The defence team would have all kinds of reasons stacked up to explain why they were there." He coughed, a phlegmy cough from deep within his lungs.

"You didn't look for anyone else after the decision?"

"No, there was no one else to look for. We had no other leads at all."

"I read somewhere about there being DNA that didn't match anyone?"

He nodded and flicked the ash of his cigarette in the vague direction of the ashtray. Most of it missed, drifting down onto the worn carpet like a light snowstorm. "Forensics said it was most probably a mash up of other people's DNA. I guess if another suspect came along they'd be able to check if it matched." He paused, lingered over a last drag then stubbed his cigarette out in an overflowing ashtray.

"How did the Ellisons feel about you going to the press?"

"They wanted everyone to know what a monster Bridges was." Foster looked up, and for the first time he became quite animated; his eyes opening wide and his hands gesticulating. "That poor girl had been sexually assaulted and they wanted that out there." He pointed through the window to indicate the world in general. "If they couldn't get Bridges locked up for it, the next best thing would be to let everyone know what he'd done." He picked up his packet of cigarettes, took another one out and lit it up. The fug of smoke filled the already thick air in the room.

"Did you tell them you were going to leak the information?"

"No. But I knew they'd be supportive. Can you imagine what it's like having your daughter murdered and not getting justice for it?" His voice cracked as he spoke.

"No," I said, "I can't even begin to imagine." My mind

flicked to Collette's children, my Goddaughters, and a chill ran down my spine.

"What was Bridges like? Did you interview him?"

"No. I was on the family liaison team, we took statements from all the family and friends. But I did meet him. And he was well known anyway for his political activities. He'd been arrested lots of times." He looked off to one side. "Odious man." He wiped his mouth with the back of his hand and gazed down at the floor.

"Politically?"

"Well that, yes, but he'd been caught several times flashing at teenagers and young girls. He'd follow them, get used to their routine and wait for them." He shook his head as if he couldn't quite believe that someone would do that.

"Did you talk to any of them after Margaret-Elizabeth's murder? I couldn't see any statements in the papers Steven Fairbrother gave me."

"We did, yes. I didn't pass those on. I didn't want their identities to get into the media."

"What did they say? About Bridges."

"That they'd noticed someone following them, most said a couple of times. Or watching them from a distance. Then one day he'd be waiting, on their route home, and expose himself to them. He'd have an erection and as they walked towards him he'd start touching himself." Foster started coughing again.

I waited until he'd recovered. "The last time, before Margaret-Elizabeth, he assaulted that young lady didn't he?"

"Yes," Foster said quietly, moving his foot on the carpet as if he were stubbing out one of his cigarettes.

"What happened there?"

"She was on her way home from some club; an after-school club. I can't remember, guides or something. She'd noticed at least twice that someone was behind her, but she'd put it down to someone else's routine matching hers. Then he was waiting one day, by the edge of the park. In plain sight, but there was no one else around. He opened his jacket to reveal his erection, just as she got level with him. As she turned to look at him he reached out and grabbed her breasts, pulling her towards him. She almost fell into him and he tried to grab her down below"—he indicated his crotch area—"but she ran away."

"Did he chase after her?"

"No, she said he just laughed as she ran off."

"And Margaret-Elizabeth was followed wasn't she?"

"Yes," he whispered, "yes she was. She told her parents that she thought a strange man had followed her a couple of times."

"Do you have the contact details for the girl who he assaulted?"

Foster shook his head. "No. I can remember her name though. Jade Griffiths. She was fifteen at the time. Just coming up to doing her GCSEs." He rubbed his face and continued staring at the filthy carpet.

We chatted a little about Jade Griffiths, but it soon became obvious that Foster had grown tired and weary. He rubbed his eyes and then stared without expression at the carpet. I wasn't going to get anything more from him so I stood up and said my goodbyes, leaving him resting his elbows on his knees in a fog of thick smoke.


As I left Devon Foster's house, I gulped in the fresh air. The smell of cigarettes and stale urine clung to me as I walked along. I scurried up the hill, barely lifting my gaze from the pavement, and jumped into the shower the minute I got home.

The water did nothing to get rid of the smell, it seemed to have penetrated my skin, but at least I felt cleaner. I put my clothes in the washing machine on as hot a wash as I thought they'd stand and then checked my emails. I'd had a reply from Paul Hardy saying that he would be at The Steam Hammer pub tomorrow about one o'clock if I was around, so I zipped off a quick reply saying that suited me fine. I could go and see him before my appointment with the Johnsons at five.

Then I got ready to follow Marcus again. I hadn't heard anything from Collette so I wasn't sure what he would be doing when he left work, perhaps he'd go straight home. But I was keen to get to the bottom of things, not just to allow me to concentrate on Margaret-Elizabeth but for Collette's peace of mind too. So, as I had no plans for the evening, I thought I'd go and wait for him and see what happened.

## 15

Marcus scuttled across the car park fifteen minutes early, piles of papers under his arm, so I was relieved that I'd arrived in plenty of time. Several cars all pulled out of spaces at the same time and we queued to get through the barrier. I pulled up with two cars between me and Marcus, and several behind me. Luckily, the traffic lights just down the road were at red so I could see which direction Marcus was heading. I followed him on the familiar route, out of town and towards Branston. I kept a safe distance, knowing this time where he'd be turning off and I parked just down the road while he pulled up outside the semi-detached house. A grey car pulling past me and parking just along the road barely registered in my conscience as I prepared myself to gather more evidence for Collette.

Marcus left his car on the road and walked over to the house, although the angle he was standing at meant that I couldn't get a clear shot of who was opening the door. This time, Marcus wasn't in the house very long before he re-emerged. The light was fading but I could see he was accompanied by the same blonde lady who I'd seen before. The pair of them came out of the front door, accompanied by what looked like a teenage boy, and they climbed into Marcus' car; the lady in the front, the teenager in the back. I snapped off a few quick pictures and then slung the camera onto the passenger seat, waited a little while and then pulled off after them.

As I paused at the junction, the grey car drew away from the curb and waited behind me. Coincidence, I thought, and pulled out behind Marcus. As we re-joined the main road, the grey car slotted in behind me. After a while, Marcus indicated that he was going to turn right and I followed suit, keeping one eye on my rear-view mirror. A niggling worry was snaking its way from the pit of my stomach, winding its way across my chest and tightening around my neck. Something told me that this was not right. My breaths came quickly, fighting the constriction in my throat. The car behind turned right as well, although it was now a couple of spaces behind me. I carried on, following Marcus along the road for a couple of miles, peering every few seconds into my mirror. The headlights of the grey car behind shot out into the road as it overtook one of the cars between us. Horns blared as it shot back into the traffic, narrowly missing a head-on collision with oncoming traffic.

At the next junction, I let Marcus continue and I turned right; if I really was being followed then I didn't want Marcus getting involved. The grey car turned right as well.

I drove carefully through the first village I came to. My hands were clammy with sweat, and they slipped on the steering wheel. One at a time I wiped them against my jeans and gripped the wheel hard, my nails cutting into the palms of my hands. I turned left without indicating, putting my foot down, then quickly left again. The car behind sped up, keeping up with me. I peered into the darkness as I left the village and I twisted through a few country roads, turning back on myself every now and then but I couldn't shake the grey car. It flew along behind me and I increased my speed even more, pushing the hire car to its limits. I wound through the country lanes, throwing the car around the corners, pulling away from my tail. As I accelerated out of a particularly sharp corner I sighed with relief as no headlights appeared in the mirrors. And then, out of nowhere, it bore down on me, hurtling up behind and smashing into the boot. The car lurched forward, my head reeling with the force, and I put my foot down, trying to pull away. I pushed the accelerator hard, bouncing in the driver's seat as I attempted to escape. My chest thumped hard into the seatbelt as the car took another hit from behind and the seatbelt locked down, digging into my shoulder. I glanced in my rear-view mirror for any clues as to who was in the car behind. The combination of darkness and bright headlights meant that I could see very little. I couldn't tell what sort of car it was and beyond a shadowy figure there was nothing to give any indication as to who was driving it. I made a mental note to take more notice of what was happening around me when I was staking out in future. If I'd paid more attention earlier, I might have seen who'd been at the wheel.

The driver did their best to pull alongside me on the tiny country road but with deep ditches on either side there was nowhere for them to go. I thumped the car into reverse and slammed into its front bumper before pulling off with all the speed I could muster, stiffening my neck in an attempt to prevent another jolt to my head. Tyres screeched against the tarmac as I sped off down the road. I must have thrown the driver a little because I managed to get a small distance ahead. I pushed the accelerator as hard as I could, almost lifting myself out of the seat in an effort to get the car to go faster.

Ignoring the speed limit, I headed towards a junction looming ahead. I pulled up at the crossroad, my heart thundering in my chest, and I waited momentarily, bracing myself in case the car tried to hit me again. As it sped up the road towards me I steadied myself, and took a deep breath. I indicated right, although I had no intention of going that way. I was trying anything that might cause a slight delay to my pursuer. Headlights were approaching along the main road and I revved up the car, put it into first gear and waited, waited, waited until the headlights were almost upon me and then I slammed my foot onto the accelerator and pulled out across the road in front of it.

Screeching brakes and the loud blare of a horn combined into a cacophony behind me. My heart seemed to simultaneously stop and pound all at the same time as if it was unsure whether to explode or give in. I threw the poor hire car through the gears, stamping each time on the accelerator and shouting, "Come on, come on!" as I urged it to go faster. It seemed like minutes before I dared to glance in my rear-view mirror, although I hadn't gone far down the road. My pursuer had been held up by the, still stationary, car in the road and was pulling around it, weaving through the oncoming traffic. I pounded the accelerator, turning into a sharp left-hand bend as fast as I dared, slipping sideways across the narrow road, and giving silent thanks that I wasn't driving Frank, my Fiat 500. I hurtled around the next bend, spotting the headlights in the distance some way behind me but getting closer. Then I turned sharply off the road towards a small village, the speedometer measuring eighty as I approached the thirty miles an hour sign.

I screeched round a bend and, before the car behind could see where I was going, I took a sharp left into a modern housing estate. I turned and twisted around corners, into roads and out again, randomly weaving round and round until I was certain that I had lost them. Then almost without thinking, I pulled onto the drive of someone's house and cut the lights. I sat there in the silence, breathing as shallowly as I could, although I wasn't sure why. Perhaps I thought my heavy breaths would alert the driver to my presence; that he would be able to hear me from his car and track me down.

I waited, sitting there for over half an hour, before I dared to move, the violent shaking refusing to stop. I wouldn't allow myself to dwell on what the consequences of my driving could have been. PC Fletcher would no doubt have adjectives other than 'reckless' she would use to describe it. The shaking from fear had been rapidly replaced by shaking from the thought of what might have been had there been a dog walker, or cyclist, out on the dark lanes. After some time, I peered at my hands, holding them out in front of me until I was convinced I could hold them steady.

Eventually, I pulled off the drive, the house still in darkness, and inched out of the quiet street back into the maze of the estate. After a few wrong turns and having to reverse out of several cul-de-sacs I found my way onto one of the country roads I'd not long been speeding down. I had no idea where I was but I had no intention of stopping to find out. The flood-lit cathedral shone in the distance, high on its hill above the city, like a beacon guiding me home, and I used that to navigate back towards the city centre. I drove like someone on their first ever lesson, staying well below the speed limit. Every time a car caught up with me I indicated to pull over and let it overtake me. I drove home via a circuitous route, checking obsessively that nothing was following me and even after I pulled up on the street outside my house I waited for twenty minutes, making doubly sure there was nothing there before I climbed out of the car. I decided not to even look at the damage. I said a silent thank you that I'd taken out the comprehensive insurance and rushed inside.

# 16

I deployed all the locks and chains on both the front and back doors, and rested the walking stick against the front door, just in case I needed it. Then I went into the kitchen and removed the carving knives from the drawer and, after wrapping them in several tea towels, I hid them under the chest of drawers in my bedroom. You could never be too sure.

Back in the kitchen I reached into one of the cupboards where, way in the back, there was a bottle of whiskey. I didn't really like whiskey; it had been given to me a few months ago and I'd been going to give it away, but now felt like a good time to reacquaint my tastebuds. I cracked open the bottle, poured a healthy measure into a glass and took a large mouthful, swirling the liquid around my mouth before swallowing it down.

I wasn't sure what to make of the evening's events. Why had someone been following me, and what were they doing crashing into my car in the middle of nowhere. If they'd been trying to send me a message I was confused as to what it was. My musings were interrupted by a buzzing on my wrist. It was an incoming phone call from Robert, spinning me back into the everyday world.

"Robert, hi!" I said, more brightly than I felt. "How are you guys?" I poured a little more whiskey into my glass then took it through to the living room, making myself comfortable on the sofa to chat.

"We're good, thanks," he replied, and we caught up on some small talk and gossip for a couple of minutes.

Thinking about everyday stuff rather than the extraordinary, and not a little surreal, events of the last couple of days was a welcome interruption. It was good to have the distraction of normality, and my body relaxed a little as I spoke to him. Whether that was his calming influence or the whiskey I wasn't quite sure, but it was a welcome change.

"I was just ringing about the gala dinner," he carried on.

I was looking forward to that, and hoped it hadn't been cancelled or anything. "Oh, how's Keith? Is it all going smoothly?"

"Well, you know how stressed he gets about these things. People cancel, change their plans, suddenly want another table, you know how it is."

"He loves it though. He's a born organiser. I'd have him on my committee if I were organising a gala."

Robert scoffed. "You're welcome to him. He's a nightmare in the final run up. I don't know how I put up with him."

The gala was being held in the Doubletree Hotel, near the Brayford Pool in Lincoln a week on Saturday. After the dinner there was going to be awards and recognitions for people in Keith's field, the entertainment industry. Then an evening of dancing and merriment making. He'd want it to be perfect.

"So, is there a problem?" I asked.

"Hm. It's just that one of Keith's colleagues can't make it now so we have a spare seat. So we wondered if you'd like to invite Sam Charlton."

Robert and Keith had yet to meet Charlton, and I smiled to myself, not entirely sure that this hadn't been engineered by Keith to try to ensure they could eventually meet him.

"I can ask him," I said, instantly excited about the prospect but at the same time a little nervous that he might have something else already organised. And, I had to admit, the thought of Sam in a dinner jacket and bow tie sent an unknown sensation tingling down my spine and around into my stomach.

"Great, well let me know," Robert said, "because I think Keith had someone else in mind if Sam can't make it."

"I will," I replied. "It'll be nice if you can meet him."

"Keith's beginning to suspect he's a figment of your imagination."

"Ha! My mind is nowhere near that imaginative, sadly. I'd be able to keep myself amused for hours if it was."

As soon as I'd finished the call with Robert, I gave Charlton a ring, and he seemed quite enthusiastic about the prospect of a gala dinner.

"I wasn't sure you'd be able to make it at short notice," I said.

"Well, perhaps I don't have many friends," he suggested, laughing.

"Ha! Like that movie," I offered, admittedly a little vaguely.

"Give me more of a clue," Charlton said.

"You know, the one with the guy who drove the taxi, that wasn't Al Pacino."

"You mean Taxi Driver? Now to be known as The Guy Who Drove the Taxi instead."

"Oh, yes, that's the one. Who was it? I always get them muddled up."

"I think you'll find it was Robert De Niro. Although I haven't got that desperate that I've started plotting to kill people. Well, not so far…"

"Give it time."

"Is it a posh do?" Charlton asked.

"It is, yes. An opportunity to dress up. I haven't decided what to wear yet," I said. "I do have a couple of long dresses, but it might be a good excuse to buy something new."

"Well, there you have the benefit of being male," he laughed. "We have little else to think about but whether to wear a black bow tie or a white one."

"That's a little sexist," I retorted. "Perhaps you'd really like to wear an evening gown?"

"It's not for everyone," he said. "Although it would be nice if people could, if they'd like. I think I have the figure for it."

"Well, you have a few days to decide."

Charlton mused for a while about which hotel to stay in and I suggested that the Doubletree, where the gala was being held, might be a good one. I remembered his suggestion from a few months ago that I stayed at his flat when I went down to London, and where that decision had led us. I looked around me at the house I'd shared with John and thought about my discussion with Collette about timing. But I kept quiet and let Charlton make a reservation online while we talked.

The conversation moved on to Margaret-Elizabeth and I filled Charlton in on what I'd been doing so far. I failed to mention the hidden kitchen knives, not least because I thought I was being a little paranoid and had maybe taken his warning the other night a little too literally. Someone had definitely followed me, but that didn't mean they wanted to kill me. Or maybe they did? They'd certainly been quite aggressive. But I didn't want to throw it into the conversation with Charlton. Not right now.

"I'm just taking the approach that the more I can find out about what was happening at the time, the better."

"Well, you have a lot of money to spend on it."

"Exactly. Well, tomorrow I'm going to see the guy who organised protests against Bridges' protests. Anti-anti-Muslim protests."

"That'll be interesting. Might give you a little insight into what made Bridges tick."

"Yes, I'm hoping so. It sounds as if Bridges had been threatening this guy." I told him what I'd read in the statement.

"It could be useful, yes," he said. "It'll give you another perspective on what this Bridges' character is like."

A little later, I asked Charlton about whether it was true what Devon Foster had said in relation to the DNA evidence.

"Yeah, he's right," Charlton stated. "DNA on its own won't convict someone. If you say there's a one in a million chance this DNA belongs to your suspect, think about it. There are over sixty million inhabitants in the UK alone, so that means it could feasibly have been at least fifty nine other people, and that's before you start counting any visitors to the country."

"Hmm, I see what you mean."

"The DNA is just one part of a picture that you have to build up."

"Okay," I said.

"So, if you find a claw hammer that matches marks on a broken-down door and it has your suspect's fingerprints all over it, well you might be getting closer. Or maybe a piece of hair, skin or clothes that snagged on a broken window or fence or something. If someone's found with a blood-soaked ornament, or covered in bodily fluids not entirely of their own making you might have something. Then you can start to build up your evidence, piece all those little bits together so that the coincidences pile up until they don't seem coincidental anymore. But DNA on its own…well the defence would rip holes in that, I'm afraid."

"Oh well," I sighed. "I'd better just keep trying to do what I can then."

After I'd put the phone down I fished out all my notes and started to write down some questions for the people I was going to meet tomorrow. The whiskey was going down nicely so I stuck with that and poured myself another glass. I was sitting cross-legged on the sofa, my notes spread out around me when my phone rang–and then all thoughts of questions disappeared from my head.

"Jake Johnson has been found dead, Verity," Nash said, a sombre tone to his voice. "I thought I ought to let you know."

## 17

Jake Johnson, the son of the Johnsons who I'd been planning on going to see the following day, had been found hanging from a tree in the woods. In Hartsholme Park. Not that far from where Margaret-Elizabeth was found.

"Oh my God, Nash. What happened? Was it suicide?"

"Well, it's too early, Verity, too early to be sure, but it looks that way."

"Was there a note?" I asked.

"We haven't found one yet. But then a surprising number of people don't write anything."

"Who found him?"

"Someone was out walking in the park, earlier this evening. He'd told his parents he was going out to meet a friend for a drink, but he never arrived."

"I was going to talk to his parents tomorrow."

"I'd leave off with that if I were you," Nash suggested. "They'll be in no fit state to talk to anybody."

"I can imagine. How old was he?"

"Twenty-two."

"Jesus. Was there any indication that he was going to do something like that?"

"Well, as you'd expect the parents are distraught, but there's nothing so far to suggest that anyone had any idea that he was thinking of ending his life. His parents described him as excited that he had a job interview next week, for what they said was a dream job."

"Do you think its connected in any way to Margaret-Elizabeth's murder?"

"What makes you ask that, Verity?"

"Well it all seems a bit coincidental don't you think."

"It could be that something has triggered in him. Maybe it's a result of renewed interest in Margaret-Elizabeth, who knows? Hopefully we'll get to the bottom of it. The sad fact is, with suicide, the people left behind often never know what caused it."

I sighed. It seemed such a waste of another life. "Has anyone told the Ellisons yet?"

"We will do. The parents asked that we told their close friends and the Ellisons were on the list. They'll know later today."

"Oh, Nash?"

"Yes."

"I was followed today. I was out in the car and someone was following me." It seemed sensible to tell him, although I decided to be a little economical with the fact that I had actually been following someone else at the time. "They crashed into the back of the car whilst I was driving. I managed to shake them off…" Not least because I was driving considerably faster than the recommended speed limit, but I didn't mention that. "But they were definitely following me. I couldn't see who it was, or what kind of car because of the dark and their headlights shining in my eyes."

"Are you sure you're okay to keep going with this?" he asked.

"Yes, of course."

"I can arrange for patrols to drop by? Keep an eye on you?"

"I'll be fine, Mike. Honestly, don't worry."

"Well, be careful, Verity. Be very careful."

After I ended the call, I sat there staring at my phone and the notes spread around me. I wondered what thoughts might have been circling round a young man's head as he walked through the woods carrying a length of rope with the intent of ending his life. Would he be thinking about what he was doing? *'This is the last time I'll walk through this wood; this is the last step I'll ever take; this is the last sight I'll ever see before my eyes don't see anything ever again.'* Would he have been thinking about his parents frantically ringing friends to find out where he was as he put the noose around his neck? Maybe he'd been walking through the woods towards his death as I was being chased around the country roads, assessing the trees for a good one to hang from; branches not too difficult to climb but not too close to the ground.

I shuddered and shook my head, trying to shake the thoughts loose but they wouldn't leave. I walked around the house, checking that all the doors and windows were shut, locked and bolted. The more I thought about it, the more sinister it seemed. Someone had tried to run me off the road just as Jake Johnson was trying to end his life.

But if whoever had been chasing me thought they would put me off, they'd have to think again. I had no idea who, but someone was trying to prevent me finding something out. There was obviously a crucial fact of some sort hidden in among all the papers, or maybe in the interviews; or perhaps it was a memory they were worried about, a memory in somebody's head, something they might let slip. I was determined to do my best for the Ellisons, determined not to give up. I clenched my jaw as my resolve to get to the bottom of things gradually overcame my nervousness.

Once I was absolutely sure that no one could get into the house without causing some kind of commotion I returned to the sofa, and my notes. I made a list of people that I would call round tomorrow and try to arrange to see. After that, a wave of exhaustion rolled over me and I packed everything away and went into the bedroom. I knelt down and pulled out the knives, deciding it was safer if they were closer to me so I hid them under the bed, just in case.

# WEDNESDAY

# 18

Morning arrived and I had managed to survive the night without the need to stab anyone. After showering and changing I took the knives and put them back in the drawer in the kitchen. Then I worked through my list, making calls to various of Margaret-Elizabeth's family members, associates and other assorted contacts that I had come across in the paperwork. Many of the numbers were no longer in use; I guessed people changed their numbers quite a lot. Some went to voicemail, where I left messages asking people to ring me back. Only a couple were answered.

James Poole, the co-founder of Pure Britain refused point blank to talk to me.

"I said what I had to say to the police at the time," he said, stressing on the word police as if to emphasise that I wasn't official. "I have no idea why the parents have dragged in some amateur to rake over old ground."

"They just want justice, Mr Poole," I ventured.

"Well they need to look in a different direction then. The police didn't prosecute Tony for a reason. Because there was no evidence. When will they grasp that? There was no evidence. End of."

"I guess it might help me to put what happened in some kind of context."

"I have absolutely no intention of talking to anyone. You or anyone else." And he ended the call without another word.

After a couple more unobtainable signals, I managed to get hold of Judith Ryan, Nicole Ellison's sister, who had called the ambulance on the night of Margaret-Elizabeth's death.

"My sister mentioned that you might call," she said. "I'm really not sure that there's much I'll be able to tell you, but you're welcome to come round tomorrow afternoon if it's convenient."

I said that tomorrow afternoon would be great and I wrote down her address and postcode.

I decided to drive over to the Ellison's house to see if they were in. It seemed that it would be a nice gesture, given that one of their best friends had just lost their child. It might have raised some issues for them. I grabbed the keys to Frank, the little car that Robert had helped me buy a few months ago, and headed out. The warm autumn sun sent dappled shadows dancing across the pavement, with just a few cotton wool clouds intermittently passing across its face. A light denim jacket was enough to keep the chill off. Before driving off, I examined the damage to the hire car. There was a large dent in the driver's side at the back. The whole door was pushed in, extending towards the boot area. Walking round the back, I spotted that the rear bumper was cracked, with one end hanging down and the rear light smashed into pieces. I'd have to come up with a good story when I handed it back.

. . .

I parked on the Ellisons' drive where I had the other day, in front of the double garage, although the car that had been parked there the last time was gone. Mrs Ellison answered the door, a tea towel clutched in one hand, and led me through to the kitchen.

"I've just made some coffee," she said, indicating that I should take a seat at the kitchen table. "I'm sorry Matthew isn't here, he's got a day of meetings at the office."

"That's no problem, I just thought I'd come and see you after hearing about Jake Johnson yesterday."

Mrs Ellison placed her hands on the back of one of the kitchen chairs, sighing as she did so, the set of her mouth emphasising the lines that ran down towards her jaw. "He always was a weak boy," she said.

"How do you mean?" I said, a little surprised at her apparent lack of sympathy.

"I'm sorry, that doesn't sound very nice. I am very upset for the Johnsons, it's just that I'm not really that surprised." She paused, her hand hovering over the plunger of the cafetiere. "He was always snivelling as a child. Always complaining that the other children were bullying him but he never stood up for himself. He'd just stand there crying for no reason."

"He sounds like quite a sensitive soul."

"Hmm," she said, pressing the plunger down with some force. She reached into a cupboard and brought out some china mugs, dividing the coffee between the two. She glanced around the kitchen, her eyebrows knitted together. "I don't think I have any milk," she said without making a move towards the fridge.

"Black is fine, don't worry."

She stared into a vacant space somewhere in the middle distance. "I wonder how Grace is feeling at the moment."

"His sister?"

She nodded, her eyes glazed as if they weren't actually seeing anything. "She must be devastated. She has her own issues, you know, problems at school. This isn't going to help her is it?" She pulled out a chair and plonked herself down on it.

"I suppose if you're in the frame of mind to end your life, you might not be thinking very straight. I imagine other people's feelings might not be your top priority."

She snapped her eyes shut. When she opened them she was looking directly at me. "Yes, well. Like I said, a bit weak. Those poor parents. Believe me, I know that losing a child is hard, so hard. You never recover. But thinking that they chose to go, chose to leave you…" She looked into her coffee cup and bit on her bottom lip. "I can't imagine how that must be. Thinking that your own child has made the choice that it's better they're not here with you." She was wringing her hands together, her knuckles whitening with the effort. "What a terrible thing to do," she added.

I gave a brief smile, then changed the subject. "Your sister has agreed to see me tomorrow. Judith."

Nicole looked up and studied my face. "She's been a rock. An absolute rock. She called the ambulance that night. She was giving out instructions, trying to keep…trying…"

I reached out and patted her hand.

"She was gone. I think we knew she was gone, but nobody gave up trying. Even the ambulance people kept trying. All the way to the hospital. It was only when we got there that they stopped. They said there was no point. I remember begging them to keep trying, begging them to give it one more chance. But it was hopeless. I just wanted to turn back time. I wanted to come home again, to have my time again. To do it all differently. To find her in her bed, kiss her on her head, stroke her soft hair and leave her there sleeping."

After a while I said, "I'm trying to arrange to see Anthony Bridges in prison. I want to look him in the eye. I want to see what he has to say." I wanted to find out what it was that someone was trying to prevent me knowing, and I thought he was my best bet. My mind flitted to the battered hire car, but it didn't seem the time to talk about the woes of being followed, so I kept quiet.

She stared down at her hands but didn't say anything. At length she said, "Do you think there's anything new to find out? Do you think he'll tell you anything different?"

"I don't know, Nicole," I said. "But I can try. I want to get to the bottom of this if I possibly can. And I want justice for Margaret-Elizabeth. If there's anything at all that I can do to understand what happened that night, rest assured I will do everything I can to find it."

Nicole gazed into her empty coffee cup. A tear worked its way down her cheek and fell onto the table. I stood up, patted her on the shoulder and made my way to the door.

"I'll let myself out," I said, looking back at her.

She sat, motionless and silent for what felt like an eternity, tears forming a small puddle on the table in front of her. Eventually she gave a short nod and I turned, leaving her there with her thoughts and memories.

## 19

After getting home I had lunch whilst I stood at the kitchen counter and then I set off to see Paul Hardy at The Steam Hammer pub. The rosy autumn sun cast a glow over the city, bouncing off the few remaining rust-coloured leaves as they danced and shone in the light breeze. I hoped the weather would last; people were smiling so much more than last week when everyone had been huddling under brollies and scuttling along to get out of the wind at the first opportunity.

Paul Hardy was cleaning glasses behind the bar when I arrived. He turned round as I walked in and stroked a little plait that grew from his chin. He came through the bar door and into the pub, indicating that we should go and sit in a quiet corner. He wore moccasins without socks and a thick cotton top with a hood.

"Would you like a drink?" he asked, rubbing his hand over his close-cropped hair.

A large coffee machine stood on the shelf behind the bar so I asked the barman for a coffee. Hardy led me to the table and we sat down. The Steam Hammer was a pub that John and I had visited often. They had a large selection of beers, which John was determined to work his way through. He didn't make it to the end of their list, which was chalked up on the wall on a massive blackboard in amongst a display of branded beer glasses from around the world. Soon after getting comfortable, we were interrupted by the barman coming over with a coffee for me and a glass of water for Paul.

"Now then," he said. "You want me to tell you about Anthony Bridges?"

I nodded.

"Well," he said, stroking his little plait. "Where to start, where to start."

"Perhaps tell me a little about the rallies and marches he organised. And the counter protests," I suggested.

"He was forever organising protests." He nodded. "He really didn't like Muslims. Still doesn't, I'm guessing."

"Did many people attend?"

"More as time went on. He was very clever. Very good at tapping into people's fears. He had a great rhetoric. He could whip people up. He loved it, revelled in it. He especially liked it when he got arrested because it garnered support. People became almost like disciples, and when he got arrested they saw that as proof that he was right. Proof that the authorities were trying to silence him. He pitched himself as a friend of the working classes, a friend of the oppressed, the silent majority who had no one to speak for them."

"He gave speeches at his rallies?"

"He did speeches all the time. Sometimes he'd just pitch up in the city centre and start talking."

I nodded, a memory coming back to me. "I remember now. I remember seeing him a couple of times. I didn't realise that's who it was. I can't remember him though. I think I maybe just walked past without stopping to look at him."

"Probably best," he said. "He'd pray on people's troubles. Unemployment, crime, lack of money and housing. He'd get them on side agreeing that yes, they were poorer than they used to be, that yes, there was less housing than there used to be. They all knew someone who couldn't find anywhere to live. They'd all lost jobs or knew people who had. They all knew someone who'd been mugged, or burgled. Then he'd start blaming immigrants, saying that it was their fault people were missing out on jobs and housing; their fault that crime was rising. That the immigrants were lazy and feckless and came here for easy money and free accommodation."

"Stealing jobs whilst lazing about claiming benefits and mugging people?"

"They drank it all in. It made sense to them. And it fed into their fears. It could only get worse, he'd tell them. The country was going to hell in a handcart and the government were complicit; letting us get overrun by the very people causing the problems. The only way to stop it was to stop these people coming here. To refuse entry. To rid ourselves of the people already here."

"He threatened you once or twice, didn't he?"

"Many times. Him and his henchmen. They were worried that we'd publicise their secrets."

"Secrets?"

"Mostly that he knew there was no truth in a lot of what he was saying. He's a clever man. He knows the statistics, but he knew the best way to get any political support was to play to people's fears. But there was virtually no point saying it anyway. If we ever tried to provide counter statistics, which we did, his followers just took it as proof that we were scared. Scared of 'the truth'. They'd accuse us of lying and it entrenched their belief that Bridges was an honest man up against the establishment."

"They needed someone on their side, perhaps?"

"That's exactly it. But he wasn't really one of them. He was a wealthy man. Still is. And the louder he shouted, the more he protested, the more money they donated to the cause. The poor, paying money to a wealthy man to protect them from people who posed no threat to them."

"So you kept trying?"

"Well, we gathered quite a lot of support along the way. Like him, we were mainly preaching to the converted, but there were people willing to support us to help the people he was vilifying. He used to accuse us of treason. There were occasions when factions broke out within Pure Britain; those who wanted to take up their pitchforks, round up the Muslims and hound them out of the city against those who favoured a more political approach. A lot of these types of organisations spilt up, but he was more intelligent than most. He kept it together, pulled everyone along. He could be quite charismatic if you were into that kind of thing."

I nodded.

He carried on, "But it was after he was arrested that we really discovered how devious he was at manipulating people."

"How do you mean?" I asked.

"What's the best way of convincing people that Muslims are stealing your homes and your jobs?"

I shrugged, pulling my mouth down. I had no idea.

"By making sure that there are Muslims living and working in your city."

"I don't understand," I said, frowning in puzzlement.

"Bridges owned a company. Well, I say he owned it, it wasn't actually in his name but the profits found their way into his accounts by a circuitous route. It was a company assisting refugees, especially from Muslim countries, to get housing and jobs. For a reasonable fee, they helped families to move into housing in the city. Housing owned by a charity funded by donations from one source, which could also be linked back to him and his family. The people who worked in the charity were oblivious, they were genuinely there to support the families."

"So, you're saying that Bridges actively encouraged Muslims to live and work in the city, and then accused them of taking jobs and houses from the locals?"

"That's exactly what he was doing. His anti-Muslim rhetoric wouldn't have worked so well if he couldn't point to more than a couple of families. The more of them he encouraged to live here, the better for him politically."

"And he made money whilst doing this?"

"Quite a considerable amount, yes."

We both sat in silence for a moment. I thought about the mentality needed to try to create a problem for political gain by helping vulnerable people, only to point at the people you'd helped and accuse them of creating the problem in the first place.

After a little while, I said, "What do you know about his other activities? The flashing, you know."

"Not a lot really. I know he had a reputation for being a womaniser."

"I heard he didn't like women much."

"I don't think he did. I don't think he saw them as equals, rather as something to be played with and tossed aside. He seemed to relish in the power; that women found him attractive."

"I don't think he'd do it for me," I said, remembering the pictures I'd seen.

"It wasn't his looks, it was the power he commanded that attracted them. To have hundreds of people hanging on your every word. He had a bit of a name for letting his hands wander whenever he got the chance. I don't think people complained, I don't think there was much concrete proof, you know? Just rumours."

"But it fits with someone who might feel they have the right to watch children whenever they want. And expose themselves."

"He certainly had a sense of entitlement. That he could do what he wanted. And get away with it. I think the police sometimes turned a blind eye to his rallies and speeches because they knew arresting him was counter-productive. Every time he was arrested, more people joined Pure Britain, more people donated to the cause, and he became wealthier."

"Is Pure Britain still active?" I asked.

"God, yes. And they've expanded their repertoire to include, well basically anyone who isn't British, white, straight and called Smith probably. And these days they don't need so many rallies to pick up the cash. PayPal, Twitter and Facebook made that all much easier. Anyone can set up a donation page and people can pay instantly, at the click of a button."

"I looked at their website. It's not an easy read."

"It's better since the authorities came down a bit harder on hate speech."

"Really? It still seemed quite hateful to me."

"They're careful what they say. The website words will be carefully chosen to make sure they're not actively seen to be encouraging violence. They save that for their social media sites."

"So who's in charge, with Bridges in prison?"

"He is. He has people doing the donkey work for him, but I'm sure it's still him who's pulling the strings."

"Do they still organise events?"

"They use Facebook, and other platforms, you know? They can say hateful things there by using code words."

"Code words? What do you mean?"

"Well, if they say 'nigger' or 'paki' outright—" He reached over and touched my arm, pulling his mouth into a grimace. "I'm sorry, I hate using those words even when I'm not actually saying them myself, if you see what I mean."

"I do," I said, nodding. "Go on."

"Where was I? Yes, they can't use those terms, or language that incites people, because the pages will be closed down. The authorities do understand some of the code words; they often say 'boogaloo' for example, as a code for the fight they see themselves on. The words change often, but if you look at their social media pages you'll see how they differ to normal groups with the repetition of certain words, numbers or particular emojis and other codes or memes." He glanced across at me, the confusion obviously writ large across my face, because he followed up with, " Hang on, I'll show you what I mean." He stood up, went behind the bar then came back clutching his phone.

He opened up his phone and scrolled through a few pages. "Hmmm…let's see. Oh yes, here's a thread, look. People are talking about a 'discussion club' that means they're having a meeting. "Look," he said pointing to a comment.

My eyes followed his finger, and I read:

*Discussion club. Too much cultural enrichment. 88*

The replies were:

*Lincoln's blues, (((you know who))) 14/88*

*Yes, give him a nose check and a free helicopter ride. Lincoln's too blueish.*

*Our guy George be there on skype. Lincoln should be red not blue 88.*

I looked up at him blankly.

"Basically they're talking about Jews in Lincoln, implying that the Jews are in control in Lincoln. Lots of those words refer to Jewish people – blues, the triple brackets and so on. The free helicopter ride means killing people off – you know, it comes from Pinochet and others who used to throw their opponents out of planes and helicopters."

I ruckled my nose in disgust.

"And the numbers refer to extreme right-wing phrases, or in the case of the eighty-eight HH, or Heil Hitler, H being the eighth letter of the alphabet. But you see how the words repeat, and this is what they do when they're planning something. This 'discussion club' could well be to organise something against the Jews."

I sat back and thought about that for a minute. After a moment, I said, "I think there's something about the events surrounding Margaret-Elizabeth's death that someone is desperate that I don't find out. I don't have any idea what it is, but I've been followed," I said. An understatement. "And burgled. Someone stole the file of stuff I had about the murder."

"He's a wealthy and powerful man. He has a lot of supporters out here. A lot still in the city. I'd tread carefully."

My phone lit up, vibrating against the table. The name

'Mike Nash' popped up and I indicated that I would need to take the call. Paul nodded and moved away. He pointed at my coffee cup and raised his eyebrows but I shook my head.

"Mike, hi," I said as I connected with Nash. "How are you?"

"Good, Verity, very good. How about you?"

"Yep, all good here too. How can I help?"

"Well, to start with," he said, "I have an appointment for you to visit Bridges at the prison. It's on Friday at three in the afternoon. Is that ok?"

"That's fantastic. Thanks, Mike, I really appreciate your help. Do I need to get there early or anything?"

He talked me through the process, where to park and what to say when I arrived. He heaved a sigh down the phone, then paused. "There's something else, Verity, something else I thought you'd want to know." His voice was tinged with a note of puzzlement, the tones rising as he spoke. "I thought you'd like to know…" He paused. "There are signs, there are a few signs, that Jake Johnson may not have committed suicide."

I sat back in my chair, open mouthed. At length I said, "If he didn't commit suicide, then…?"

"They need to do more tests, but initial reports suggest that there was some kind of a struggle."

"Are you suggesting that somebody murdered him?"

"I'm afraid it's looking that way, yes."

## 20

I needed to clear my head. I needed to think. When I left The Steam Hammer I wandered through the city, lost in thought, paying no attention to my surroundings at all. If Jake Johnson had been murdered that put a whole new perspective on things. Why would someone murder him? There had to be some connection, surely, to Margaret-Elizabeth's death, but what? Was it that he'd been involved? That seemed impossible; he'd been at home being looked after by his own babysitter at the time. Even at age twelve, or thirteen, if he'd had the inclination, he wouldn't have had the time. He'd not have been able to sneak out, go round to the Ellisons', take Margaret-Elizabeth from her bed, murder her and get back home before his parents got back. And all without anyone noticing.

So what could it be? Maybe there was no connection. Maybe it was purely coincidental. Perhaps he'd just been in the wrong place at the wrong time. I sighed. I didn't believe that; there had to be a link. Was it something to do with my investigation? Perhaps he would have helped me. If that was the case then I'd never know now. I looked around me.

I'd walked all the way to the south end of the city. I was almost at Collette's house so I carried on in that direction. When I arrived I gave a knock on the front door, but walked in without waiting for an answer.

"Hello?" I called out.

"Vee," a voice drifted down from upstairs. "Down in a sec, we've just got back from school. How are you? Have you got any news?" She appeared at the top of the stairs, and ran down towards me.

"News about…?" I stopped myself. It hadn't occurred to me that she'd think I was there to tell her whether or not Marcus was having an affair. I'd been so absorbed in my own thoughts I hadn't given space to what she might think when I turned up unannounced at her house. "Well, nothing much. I thought I'd pop by and just let you know how things were going," I lied.

"And?" she said expectantly, giving me a hug and pulling me into the front room. She closed the door behind us. "I don't want the girls to hear," she said, nodding towards upstairs.

"Well, I haven't really found much out," I said.

"But you followed him?"

We both sat down, me on the sofa and her on a chair. "Well, yes, but…"

"Where did he go?" she asked, leaning forward.

"It's too early, Collette. I don't know what's going on yet."

She shoved herself backwards into the chair and folded her arms. "You're being vague. You're lying to me, I can tell. I know you, Vee, you're no good at lying."

I didn't used to be. I was getting quite good at it these days. "I lost him," I said, half truthfully. "I followed him but I lost him."

"You lost him? What kind of investigator are you?" she said, throwing her hands into the air.

I didn't mention the extenuating circumstances. "I did follow him the other day, to a house, but I don't know what he was doing. I didn't see anyone else," I said, mixing truth with fiction.

"Where was the house?"

"I'm not telling you. I don't want you going there when I have no evidence yet of anything."

"So you thought you'd come and tell me that you don't really know what's happening?"

I shuffled in my seat. "I just wanted to keep you informed, you know. That's what I do with people. Let them know how things are going."

"But you haven't got anything to tell me?"

"Well, no. Not really."

Collette slouched further down in the chair. "He is having an affair. I knew it." She looked crestfallen, sitting there slumped in the chair, her mouth turned down and her chin squashing into her neck. She closed her eyes and ran her hands across her face.

"Oh, Collette, we don't know that. I really, honestly, don't know yet."

"Honestly?"

I nodded, not willing to say an outright lie to my best friend. I had every reason to suspect that Marcus was having an affair, but I wasn't completely sure and I didn't want her to confront him without solid evidence.

She sat up a little in the chair. Whatever she was thinking, she was interrupted by Emily breezing in through the door. She ran over and gave me a hug, then twirled on one foot around the room.

"Aunty Vee, Aunty Vee, I've started going to ballet

131

classes. Look at what I've learned." And she twisted and turned, dancing and whirling her way across the floor. "I can do third position, look!" She placed the heel of her right foot against the middle of her left foot, and held her right arm out to the side.

"Wow!" I exclaimed and clapped. "Can I have front row seats when you're the prima ballerina?"

"Yes," she said, laughing, and she pirouetted out of the living room.

When we were alone Collette appeared to have relaxed a little. "So, have you had a talk with Charlton yet?" she asked.

"No. Not really."

"What do you mean 'not really'?"

"Well, he has agreed to come to the gala ball with me. You know, the one Keith's involved with."

She became quite animated, sitting up and smiling, her eyes open wide. "Well, that's good then. But you haven't actually told him that you like him. How did you put it? That you really like him. A lot."

"Not yet. Maybe at the gala. That might be a good time." I paused, gazing into the space between us. "I do keep imagining him in his dinner suit, with a bow tie. Like a member of the Rat Pack. Sammy Davies Junior, maybe, only better looking." I couldn't stop the smile from spreading across my face.

Collette laughed. "Well at least that's some good news," she said. "And do you think you'll get your head around the timing not being perfect?"

I bit my lip. "I hope so. I hope so…"

She came over to the sofa, sat down beside me and hugged me so tightly that I struggled to breathe. After a little while she sat back but kept her arm around my shoulders. "I know it sounds like a cliché, but John would want you to be happy. What would you want, if it had been the other way round?"

"I'd want him to mourn me forever and be desperately sad, walking around in his sackcloth and ashes. Who could possibly ever compare to me?" I looked at her and laughed. "No, I know. I'd want him to be happy. And I'd know that if he found someone else, they wouldn't replace me. They'd just be different. A different relationship. I know that, logically. It's just my heart doesn't always keep up with my head."

Both girls burst through the door shouting for attention. "When's it teatime?"

"Look at my drawing!"

"Mummy, Mummy, is Verity staying the night?"

I said I'd leave her to it, and that I would let her know when I had something more concrete, although I didn't mention about what in front of the children. I called for a taxi as I couldn't be bothered to walk all the way back home. We said our goodbyes and I ran out to the waiting cab. The sun was sinking fast to the west of the city, the light casting long shadows across the road in front of us.

I sat in the taxi mulling over what Collette had said about Sam and timing, rehearsing what I might say to him. I'd told him I wasn't ready to move on, wasn't ready for a relationship, and in many ways that was still true. But Collette was right, things didn't always happen in a perfect order and I guessed I had to just make the most of what life threw in my direction.

## 21

I sat on the sofa thinking about what Paul Hardy had said in relation to Facebook groups and the use of codewords. The thread he'd shown me hadn't meant much to me, so I thought I'd compare it to another Facebook thread, to see if I could spot how it differed from a normal conversation. I had the pages from the Ellisons' book club so I fired up my laptop and scrolled through my photos until I got to the ones showing all the Facebook messages. I scanned through all their chats about what books they were reading and, if I was honest, differences didn't leap off the page to me.

Paul had spoken about repetition, but there was lots of repetition here too. I reviewed a few of the threads again. Of course there was repetition, people were discussing the same subject. I struggled to see where Paul had been coming from. Surely any subject would have repetition? If you were talking about making jam, the words jam, fruit and sugar would surely repeat themselves dozens of time. For the book club, clearly books featured heavily. Each week the participants spoke about what they were reading, what they were enjoying about it and what they were looking forward to discussing. There was also a fair amount of chat about what their children were reading.

'Grace is so looking forward to the Very Hungry Caterpillar'

'Isabella is loving Little Women. Last time she had fun with The Witches, but I think Little Women might be more her style'

'Remember Margaret-Elizabeth loved Little Women a few of weeks ago? She didn't want to try The Witches either, but seemed to get stuck in once she started.'

'Jasmine is going to read Little Women again, she loved it so much.'

And so it went on. The children all reading similar books but at different times. I sat there, staring at my screen, completely bemused and unable, still, to fully grasp what Paul Hardy had been saying. I thought I'd add it to my list of questions for Anthony Bridges. If he'd answer any of them, that was. He might throw some light on the use of codes and how the users of certain social media groups understood them, because at the moment I was struggling to comprehend it.

The shrill ring of my landline sliced through my thoughts. I jolted upright. My landline hardly ever rang, and when it did it was almost always an unsolicited call, some robot suggesting I might have had an accident that wasn't my fault, or similar. I answered it, preparing myself for the inevitable. But there was nothing.

"Hello?" I said into the silence. The phone crackled a little, and I held it away from my ear to check it was still connected. "Hello?"

A click followed by a dial tone told me that, whoever it had been, had hung up. I walked back over to the sofa, but the impetus to look into Facebook groups and threads had deserted me, so I started gathering my things together and thinking about what I would have for dinner. Since living alone, my eating habits had become much more haphazard than previously. I ate when I was hungry, rather than at set mealtimes, and not always as healthily as I should, although striding up and down Steep Hill kept me fit enough.

As I went through to the kitchen to peruse the contents of the cupboards, my wrist vibrated and my mobile began to ring. I glanced down; it was a mobile number I didn't recognise. I paused in the hallway to answer it.

"Hello?"

A crackly female voice spoke in a hoarse whisper, "Hello, is that Verity Spencer?"

"It is, yes, speaking," I replied.

Silence.

"Can I help?"

There was more crackling and the whispering voice said something that I couldn't quite hear.

"I'm sorry, can you repeat that?" I asked. "The line is really unclear."

"It's Jade," the voice croaked down the phone.

"I'm sorry?" I replied, eyeing up a granary loaf I'd bought earlier, thinking I'd have a slice of that to keep me going.

"Jade." The voice almost disappeared. There was a cough, a deep breath, and then she rasped, "Jade Griffiths."

It took me a moment to recall where I'd heard the name before. Jade Griffiths had been the young lady that Bridges had assaulted on her way home from school. "Oh, Jade, hi," I said, trying to hide my surprise. "Thanks for calling. How can I help?" I wondered how she'd got my phone number but the line was so crackly I wasn't going to ask anything that wasn't strictly necessary. I tucked the phone under my ear, reached for the loaf and pulled a bread knife and chopping board out of the drawer.

"Can I talk to you?"

"Of course, although the phone connection is really bad. Do you want to try calling back?"

"Can you come out here?"

I sighed and looked at my watch. It was just after six and my tummy was rumbling. "It's probably best if I come tomorrow now," I ventured.

Another cough drifted down the phoneline and a whisper too quiet to hear. Then Jade said, "Can you come out here now? I really need to talk to you."

I glanced longingly at the granary loaf and threw the knife and chopping board back in the drawer.

"Okay," I said. "Give me the address and I'll come over. But I can't stay long, I need to be back home within an hour as I have an appointment." I tapped the top of a nearby bottle of wine, then pushed it to the back of the counter, silently promising to come home and open it as soon as possible.

In her hoarse whisper, she gave me the address. It took several attempts, but eventually I got it down right, scribbling it on a piece of paper and stuffing it into my pocket. The house was in an area to the north of the city, not too far away, so I told her I'd be there in about ten minutes. I put the loaf back in its paper wrapper, thinking I could last out for an hour. I grabbed my coat, my handbag, my notebook and my car keys and left the house, throwing the phone in my handbag as I went.

I found Jade's house quite easily, and parked on the street outside. The houses looked as if they were old local authority, but each had been individualised over time with cladding, new windows or a new coat of paint. Some children played out on the street although the sun had just disappeared over the horizon; young teenagers kicking a ball to each other. As I pulled up they moved a little further along the road. I locked the car and peered down front paths to make sure I had the right house; half of the street-lights were not working and it was hard to make them out. Jade's was an end of terrace with a little patch of grass and some well-cared for tubs lining the path outside the front door.

The living room light beamed out across the small front garden, as did the hallway light, through the decorated glass panel in the front door. A television flickered in the corner of the front room, broadcasting some soap or other. I knocked on the door and waited. There was no answer, so I knocked again. I walked over to the window and peered in. The programme continued, a couple arguing on screen, the story beaming out to an empty room. A half-drunk cup of tea on a little coffee table by the sofa indicated that this might not have been the case for very long. I tried the front door again. Nothing.

I moved away and peered along the side of the house, down a tiny pathway blocked by a couple of wheelie bins. A little window towards the back of the house glowed with a light and I decided to try the back door. As I headed towards the wheelie bins, the light in the side window went out and I was plunged into darkness. At least that meant someone was there. I waited a moment until my eyes adjusted to the change in the light. I edged along the side of the house and rounded a corner into the back garden. My foot caught on something and I threw my arms out to try to stop my fall, but I tumbled onto the concrete path. Pain bored through my shoulder as I bounced off the step by the back door and rolled into the garden.

A light flashed on above me and the silhouette of a shadowy figure loomed overhead. "Jade?" I said in a small, quiet voice, watching as the figure's arms rose, lifting something high above its head. Then it brought its arms crashing down towards my face, and the world went black.

## 22

A searing pain jabbed into my head and I opened one eye, unsure of where I was, what time of day it was, or what I was doing. The darkness was enveloping and I had no idea where I was. Was I at home? I reached out with my left hand, which came into contact with something hard, something concrete-like. Not in bed, then. Was it the morning? I opened my other eye and glanced around me. The half-moon in a dark night sky cast a faint glow across my surroundings. I could make out grass and a fence. What on earth was I doing in the garden, lying on the grass? But as I scanned around and my eyes took in the unfamiliar sights I realised that I was not at home. This was not my garden.

I lifted a hand up to my head. The thumping to the side of my skull was so severe it was distorting my vision and I blinked a few times in an attempt to clear my eyes. I tried to sit up and an intense wave of nausea caused me to groan out loud. I rested back against the ground and then lifted my head up again, this time at a pace that didn't make me feel as if I'd been spinning for hours on a carousel.

When I moved, a light from above me sent out a dull beam of light, and I looked up towards it; it was a motion sensor light to one side of the back door. I was sitting outside somebody's house but I had no idea whose or what I was doing there. I blinked in the light and took in the outline of a small garden, the features becoming clearer as my eyes adjusted. And then I saw it; somebody was lying on the grass just a few feet away from me.

I struggled to my feet, and staggered a little as I made my way over to see who it was. My handbag was still slung across my body and it swung as I stood up, banging into my hip. I peered through the semi-dark and studied the dim shape in front of me. A young lady wearing jeans and a leather jacket lay face down on the ground, her left arm high above her head and her right arm bent up under her chest. One of her trainers laid on the grass in front of her, the other still on her foot. I bent down to ask her if she was okay, but the words got caught in my throat. Her eyes stared out ahead of her, her mouth open as if in mid-shout. Her forehead had caved in to one side, a deep gash above her left eyebrow. I looked at her, fear crawling across my skin like hundreds of spiders.

I threw myself onto the lawn, falling to my knees and vomiting into the grass; my whole body contracting as my stomach rid itself of what little there was inside. Despite being sick, waves of nausea still surged through me from the top of my head to the tips of my toes. I leaned close to the grass, gagging as each contraction swept through me, the nausea refusing to go away even though there was nothing left to bring up. As I wiped my mouth on the back of my sleeve, I leaned back on my heels and gasped for air. What the fuck had happened? Memories were creeping back into my mind; a phone call, Jade's house, the darkness at the back of the house. I looked back down at the young lady. I'd never seen her before. I had no idea who she was. Blood pumped in my ears, loud drum-like beats, as I circled round her. I reached down for her left wrist, flopped on the ground above her head and I tried to find a pulse. I knew it was useless; her unblinking eyes continued to stare into the darkness. Her skin was cold to the touch and I had an over-whelming urge to wrap her up and try to keep her warm. Thoughts of Margaret-Elizabeth's family destroying evidence flooded into my brain and I left her exactly as she was.

The light above the kitchen door went out, so I waved my arm around trying to catch the sensor. After a few seconds it sprang back to life with a click and I yanked my phone out of my bag and dialled 999. I fought to keep the phone steady as my hands shook with a violence I hadn't experienced before. Little more than a whisper came out as I attempted to describe the scene in front of me. I had to rummage in my pocket for the scrap of paper I'd scribbled the address down on. I was told to stay where I was, that the police and an ambulance would be there as soon as possible, not to touch anything, not to go anywhere.

I sat back on my heels, a million thoughts racing through my mind, all fighting to be the one I'd grasp hold of. Thoughts careered through my brain like cars on a race-track, hurtling round and round, except they weren't following a path, they were all crashing into one another, smashing around my aching head, and I growled out loud in an effort to slow them down. I steadied myself against the grass, the shaking in my limbs causing great shudders to run up and down my body, my knees juddering against the ground. All I wanted to do was get up and run away.

Instead I just sat there, holding my arms tight across my chest, rocking backwards and forwards and looking at the body before me. I could understand Margaret-Elizabeth's family desperately trying to revive her. I didn't know this young woman but every fibre of my body wanted to touch her, to warm her up, to comfort her, to move a stray hair that had caught in the corner of her mouth. I fought to steady my breathing, to slow my body down, to calm my galloping brain.

"What happened?" I whispered to her. "What happened here?"

I waited in the silence and studied the garden around me. There was no obvious murder weapon lying around, carelessly discarded on the lawn by someone in a haste to get away. A bucket of weeds stood in amongst the plants, some gardening gloves flung over the side and a pair of secateurs balanced on top of the gloves. A job that would be forever half finished. A pair of boots leaned against the wall by the back door, never to be worn again. The back door had a cat flap in the bottom, and an image of a cat waiting in vain to be fed drifted through my brain. I gazed back down at the young woman sprawled out on the lawn and wondered if she'd seen the beginning of the TV soap; threads of stories that she'd never know the ending to. I asked her what the cat was called, but I got no answer.

I stayed there with her, motionless, until distant sirens began drifting through the air. I sat there on my heels, staring into the night as the sirens grew louder and blue lights flashed through the darkness. I didn't move as the footsteps approached down the side of the house and what seemed to be dozens of police officers appeared in the garden, sparking the light back into action. I didn't move until someone came up to me and took me by the elbow, guiding me to my feet and away around the side of the house. I looked back as I was led away, the garden lit now by lights, the silence destroyed by voices shouting, talking, radios crackling, protective clothing being donned.

## 23

A young female officer patted me down and asked me again what had happened. We were at the front of the house, standing on the path by the road. A small crowd of local residents had gathered to see what all the commotion was about, the distant murmuring growing louder as more people came, Chinese whispers clearly circulating from one to another.

"I have no recollection," I said, not for the first time. "I remember coming here. There was a light on in the front room, a television playing in the corner but no one in there." I pointed to the house, the front room now pitch black, no light, no television. "So I went down the side to see if anyone would answer the back door, and that's the last thing I remember until I woke up." I glanced at my watch, it was just after seven, slightly more than an hour since I'd left home.

"The light was definitely on in the front room?"

"Yes, I remember thinking it looked as if someone had just left the room. The television was on, it was some soap. I don't know which one."

"And you received a phone call?"

"Yes, Jade called me and asked if I'd come round and see her. She seemed very keen that I came this evening."

"And you woke up and she was lying there on the grass?"

I nodded. "I didn't even realise she was there until a few minutes after I'd come round." I touched the wound on my head. "I think I need someone to look at this," I said. "I was unconscious for a while, I don't know how long."

The police officer went off to confer with a colleague. Together, they made their way back towards me.

"We need to take you to the station," the male officer said. "To give us a witness statement. We'll make sure the doctor sees you when you get to the station, just in case."

I nodded. "Yes, fine," I said. One of the buttons on his polo shirt was broken. The top half had cracked off, although the button was still fastened. Funny the things you notice.

The police officer was indicating that I should get in the car, and he held the back door open for me. Necks craned and heads bobbed as the gathering crowd tried to get a glimpse of what was happening. Several of them took out their phones and started taking photos and I kept my head low, like a fugitive, in an attempt to stay anonymous.

I sat in silence as we made our way to the police station and, once we'd cleared the excited onlookers, I stared out into the night. People were walking up and down the streets, coming and going as if somebody hadn't just been murdered. In town, people sat in softly lit pubs drinking beer and laughing. They wouldn't know. They wouldn't know that my evening plans had been so drastically derailed. They carried about their business without a care, sharing jokes and anecdotes over their drinks. I thought about Charlton talking about the coincidences, the DNA and other factors piling up until they didn't seem coincidental anymore. I glanced ahead at the two officers in front of me whose job it would be to find the pieces of the puzzle and put them together, like a jigsaw, until they had a murderer's face in front of them.

I shut my eyes and trawled my brain in a desperate search to find a memory, anything that might give me a clue as to why I'd been drawn round to Jade's house. The car pulled to a halt and I opened my eyes to find myself in a fenced-in compound. No chance of running away, the massive green gates were locking automatically behind me. The two officers leapt out of the car, the male one opening the door and holding it until I'd climbed out. I was led into the police station, through a door and directly into the custody suite, where I was asked to have my fingerprints taken. I didn't have to, the officer behind the enormous white desk explained, but it would be a huge help to their enquiries. After that, I was shown into an interview room. The officer told me he'd ask the doctor to come and have a look at my head, and then asked if I'd agree to have the contents of my phone downloaded. I hadn't noticed, but the female officer seemed to have disappeared along the route.

I nodded without saying anything, my brain too numb to come up with actual words.

"It's just that you said you'd received a phone call. It'll help with evidence if we can corroborate the time."

I handed my phone to him, mulling over what would happen if I'd said that no, I wasn't in agreement. I didn't have the energy to argue with him, even if I'd felt the inclination. Most of what I had on my phone would bore the pants off anyone else, so I wasn't particularly bothered.

"Would you like a coffee? Or tea?" the police officer asked.

I coughed, trying to find my voice. "Yes, please. Coffee please. Black will be fine," I said. Mainly because I wanted someone to come back within a reasonable time. I wasn't sure whether coffee would help or hinder the nausea that had taken root in my stomach, but I didn't have to drink it. I just didn't want to be left alone too long.

He shut the door behind him and I was left by myself, sitting staring at the plain walls with no phone to amuse me. Everything in the room was screwed down, including the uncomfortable wooden chairs. I started to look for patterns in the wood grain, anything to distract my brain from mulling over what might have happened earlier in the evening. Fierce clenches tightened my stomach every few seconds, causing acid to rise up my throat. I swallowed hard, hoping that the promised coffee might appear before too long. I perched on the edge of the wooden chair, clutching at the seat with both hands, digging my fingers into the underneath until they ached with the effort.

My bottom was completely numb by the time the door opened and a well-groomed young lady appeared. Her blonde hair bobbed as she kicked the door shut behind her and placed a polystyrene cup full of coffee in front of me.

"Hello," she said, flashing me a friendly smile.

After only a second, a thin middle-aged man in a tweed jacket followed her into the room. He was carrying an old-fashioned doctor's bag, which he rested on the table and opened, before pulling on some latex gloves and removing a blood-pressure pump. I touched the wound on my head—a great lump was appearing around the cut. The doctor leaned my head down and felt around the lump, then pulled my hair to one side. He rummaged in his bag and pulled out an alcohol wipe.

"Just look down can you?" he asked. Before he added, "This might sting a little."

He wiped the wound. His assessment of the amount it might sting fell woefully short of the mark and I breathed in sharply as the alcohol hit my nerve endings.

He peered again at the wound. "It's a superficial cut," he declared. "It's swelling up quite nicely, which will protect it. You were unconscious?"

"Yes," I answered, forcing the words through my dry and scratchy throat. "I don't know for how long though."

After establishing that I wasn't in too much pain, that I could only see one of everything, and that I wasn't suffering from loss of memory he asked if I was experiencing any nausea.

"Yes." I nodded. "But I'm not sure if that's because of the blow to my head, or stumbling over a dead body."

The doctor snorted, a rough laugh. I guessed he came across dead bodies more often than most.

He took my blood pressure and declared it elevated. I could have told him that without the need for measuring. He snapped off his gloves and threw them in his bag.

"If you experience pain, take some ibuprofen or parac-etamol," he said. "And if the nausea persists, if you get any double vision or if you suffer any memory loss go to A and E." He snapped his bag closed and left the room without saying another word.

The police officer closed the door after him and sat down opposite me. My stomach contracted once again, but as I took in her efficient appearance the nausea subsided a little. I tried to steady my hand enough to pick up the cup without spilling the coffee and took a sip of the barely warm, sludge brown liquid, hoping it might calm me a little.

"I'm Detective Constable Jenny Shepherd," she said, holding out her hand. "I'm going to take your statement."

"Okay," I said.

"So." She smiled. "Tell me about the events of tonight."

"There's not much to tell," I said and went through my evening, starting with the strange call from Jade and finishing with waking up unsure of where I was.

"What time did Jade call you?"

"I don't know exactly. It'll be on my phone."

"Approximately."

"I think it was about six. When I left the house, the sun was just about down and when I reached Jade's house it was dark."

"What did she say? Try to remember exactly."

"It was a really bad line. I was struggling to hear her. I think she asked if it was me, and I said yes it was. Um…" I tried to think back. "Then she told me who she was and I remember wondering how she'd got my number, but the line was so bad I didn't bother asking. She said she wanted to talk to me. I was really hungry and so I suggested that I saw her the next day, but she was insistent that I went round so I agreed to go there right then. I lied that I had an appointment in an hour, as I really hadn't wanted to be out long. That was it. She gave me the address, which I scribbled down on a piece of paper and I left."

"Have you ever spoken to her before?"

"No, I've never met her. I'd never heard of her until the other day. You know I'm looking into the murder of Margaret-Elizabeth Ellison?"

"I had heard, yes."

"Well, I went to see Devon Foster. I can't remember

which day it was now, it'll be in my notebook, but he mentioned that Jade had been assaulted by Anthony Bridges. He had no details for her though. That was the first time I'd ever heard her name."

"I see." She pursed her lips. "So did you think it was strange that she called you up?"

"I was surprised, definitely. But I thought maybe Foster had passed on my number. It probably would've been good to get her perspective on what Bridges had been like, too. If he'd given me her number when I saw him I may well have tried calling her."

"What were you doing earlier in the day? Before you got the call?"

"I'd been to see Paul Hardy at The Steam Hammer. He used to lock horns with Bridges, and it was interesting to get his perspective. Then, let's see...I walked over to Collette's. Oh yes, I had a call from Nash. He told me that Jake Johnson's death probably hadn't been a suicide."

She looked up, raising an eyebrow. "Did he now?" she said, making a note.

I hoped I hadn't landed Nash in trouble. "Er, well," I stammered, a little thrown at the thought that I shouldn't have mentioned anything to her. I got back on track with the story of my afternoon before she thought to ask me anymore about what Nash had said. "Then I went for a walk, to clear my head and I ended up at Collette's."

She checked a wadge of notes. "Collette Smith? Your friend?"

"Yes, I stayed there for a while, maybe three quarters of an hour and then got a taxi home."

"What time was that?"

I couldn't remember. "The call to the taxi will be on my phone, but...um...well, the kids had just got back in from school when I arrived, so I guess that would have been some time around four, maybe. So I must have got the taxi just before five."

"And when you got home?"

"I looked at some notes to do with Margaret-Elizabeth then I was just about to make a sandwich when Jade rang." I paused. "Oh, and I had a silent call on my landline. That's what made me realise how hungry I was." I clutched at my stomach, aching now with hunger.

"A silent call?"

"Yes. My landline hardly ever rings. I don't know why I bother with it. There was nothing, then it went dead."

"When you left the house to go to Jade's, what did you do?"

"I put the postcode in the satnav and drove straight there."

"Tell me what you did when you got there."

"I knocked on the front door but there was no response. The light in the front room was on, so I peered in. The television was on. It looked as if someone had just left the room so I went round the side." A memory came back. "There was a light on, down the side, just beyond the wheelie bins but as I got closer to the back of the house it went out and I was left in the dark. I had to feel along the wall. I remember thinking I'd been right about someone leaving the front room. Then I rounded the corner and fell over. I hurt my shoulder on the back doorstep." I rubbed my shoulder to indicate where I'd hurt it. "Then nothing until I woke up."

"Uh-huh," she said, perusing her notes. She pulled her mouth to one side. "Do you know anyone who would want to cause you any harm?"

"Me?"

"Yes, anyone want to hurt you?"

I thought about the last few days. Someone was trying to derail my investigation into Margaret-Elizabeth's murder, that was for sure.

"Well," I started, and I told Detective Constable Shepherd about the events of the last couple of days, including my speeding through the countryside. I reasoned she had bigger fish to fry than worrying about my driving. Then there was a knock at the door.

She stood up. "One moment, please," she said. She scooped up all her notes and opened the door. A uniformed officer loitered on the other side and DC Shepherd stood by the open door talking to him in whispers.

I closed my eyes and breathed out. I looked down at my hands and tried to hold them still, but I couldn't stop them shaking. I took slow and deliberate breaths, heaving in deeply through my nose and puffing out slowly through my mouth. The butterflies still fluttered around my stomach, which was gnawing with hunger. I looked down at the cold coffee and took a large mouthful, trying to moisten my dry lips and tongue.

The hushed conversation just outside the door was mostly too quiet to hear, but a few words drifted into my consciousness and I started to take notice.

"Dead for how long?" DC Shepherd asked.

A few whispered words came back through the open door. "...not sure...several hours by the look...time to get cold...no bleeding from the..." I remembered how cold Jade's wrist had been when I'd tried to take her pulse.

"Maybe moved...?" DC Shepherd was asking but I lost the rest of her question and the other officer had turned away slightly and I could no longer hear any of his responses.

After some time, DC Shepherd returned. "Okay," she

said then paused. "What we're going to do is complete the statement and then you can go home. It's probably best if you don't go away from Lincoln without letting me know, at least for the next week or two."

I nodded, and we spent the next hour or so writing and revisiting my statement until it had everything in it that DC Shepherd thought she'd need. After some time, she stood up and led me out of the room. Relief was threatening to overwhelm me but I held it at bay, not sure that my trauma was anywhere close to over yet.

As we walked through the door I said, "When I tried to find a pulse, I noticed that Jade's skin was really cold. She can't have just been killed, she'd have still been warm if she was killed after I got to the house."

"I'm afraid I can't comment on that."

I stopped and turned to her. "So who rang me up, if Jade was already dead?"

"I'm sorry, I can't..." DC Shepherd carried on walking down the corridor

"I know. It just doesn't make sense. Somebody killed Jade, then rang me up and lured me round there? They hit me over the head. And left me there with her body. Were they trying to kill us both? Is that what you're suggesting, that someone was trying to kill me?"

DC Shepherd just raised her eyebrows, but said nothing. She passed over my possessions, my phone was there in the bag, with the SIM card taped to the back of it. Someone had obviously downloaded all the information. I followed her through the corridors to the front reception area.

"I'm sorry we haven't got anyone available to drive you back to your car," she said. "Will you be okay getting home?"

I nodded, although I didn't want to go back to my car. It could stay where it was for the time being.

The officer behind the reception desk took one look at me and agreed to call me a taxi. I sat in silence in the reception area staring out into the darkness of the night while I waited, blinking back tears. I knew they would come but I wouldn't let them. Not now, not here.

## 24

The taxi driver filled the air with friendly banter all the way home. I said nothing, but at least it occupied my head with words. Words that didn't involve murder. I sat back and closed my eyes and let his constant chatter drift over me, keeping my brain distracted; allowing me to enjoy a little respite from thoughts of a strange phone call, a dead body, a gash to my head...

When I got in I ran up the stairs and ripped off my clothes, then I stood for some time under the shower, trying to rid myself of the memories of the evening. It didn't work. Every time I turned round I saw it again, as if it were a new sight—Jade lying on the grass in front of me, the stray hair caught in her mouth. The cat flap, the half-completed weeding, the unworn boots.

When I walked back downstairs I looked at my watch. It was late, but I was desperate to talk to Charlton about the events of the night. Desperate for some kind words and some sage advice. He'd conducted lots of murder investigations and I knew he'd be able to put a different perspective on things. Maybe put my mind at rest a little. I imagined his deep voice offering encouragement, explanations, soothing the scurrying thoughts that scrabbled around my brain.

I fumbled with the phone, trying to open the little SIM card holder but after a couple of minutes I gave up, throwing the phone down on the sofa in frustration. I was too tired. I reached for my laptop, found Charlton's number and dialled from my landline.

The phone rang for quite a while and I thought it was going to go to voicemail, but then Sam's welcome, deep voice said, "Yes?"

Of course, he wouldn't recognise my landline number.

"It's me," I said, fighting back the tears that appeared the minute I heard his familiar voice.

"Hello, Verity, what is it?" His sluggish words hinted at tiredness.

"Oh, I'm sorry, Sam, were you asleep?"

"No, no," he said, although the rustling of the sheets, and a soft groan, told me he was just sitting up in bed. "Are you okay?"

"Not really," I said. "I've had a really tough evening. But, look, I'm being selfish, it's late, I can call in the morning. I didn't mean to wake you up."

"It's not a problem," he said, and although he stifled it I could tell that he was yawning. "Give me a second. We can talk." I heard him moving at the other end of the phone, the sound of bedclothes being pushed to one side. And then a moment later, "Okay, what's up?"

I looked down at my hands and took in a deep breath, relief at being able to share what had happened that evening threatening to spill out and overwhelm me before I'd even begun. I wasn't sure where to start with the strange story of my night. Memories zipped through my mind, flashbacks that arrived in random sequences cascading through my brain like falling leaves. I took in another breath. *Just start at the beginning, Verity.* But just as I started to form my first sentence another soporific sounding voice drifted down the line. A female voice.

The words drawn out and drowsy. "Sam," the female voice drawled. "Sam, what is it?"

And then I realised that it wasn't sleepiness I was detecting in their voices. "I...I..." I stuttered, thrown into uncertainty. "Have you got someone there with you?" The words spluttered out of my mouth.

"Verity, listen—"

But I cut him off, a fireball of fury rising through my body, overtaking me, the blood coursing through my veins with a speed that was almost palpable. I leapt to my feet. "Oh, don't you worry about me," I snapped.

"Verity, don't be like—"

"You get back to it," I said, swaying from one foot to the other, waving my free hand in the air.

"Let me—"

"Don't even start. I shan't interrupt you for a moment longer," I blurted, unable to keep the bitterness out of my voice. I held the phone away from my ear, no longer wanting to hear his reply and I stabbed at it to end the call. I smashed the phone into the floor, its component pieces scattering across the carpet. Then I stamped on them, every piece, crushing them beneath my slippers, pounding my feet down, over and over. I gritted my teeth and let out a growl, picking up the cushions one by one and flinging them across the room, then hurling them back towards the sofa, kicking the furniture as I stomped backwards and forwards.

Then the tears came. Pouring down my face, my shoulders heaving with the effort to try to rid my body of the unwelcome emotions. I threw myself onto the sofa and grabbed the nearest cushion, hugging it tight into my chest as if it might protect me from the hurt. Defeated, I curled into a tight ball until the crying subsided and I fell into an exhausted sleep.

# THURSDAY

## 25

The morning light streaming through the windows woke me up, still hunched over and clutching the cushion as if my life depended on it. For a brief moment, I wondered what on earth I was doing sleeping on the sofa, but then a flood of memories surged into my brain; a dead body, betrayal, rejection. The mental pain seemed to make the physical pain from the blow to my head even worse. I rubbed my temples, not sure if I was trying to allay the headache or erase the thoughts of Charlton in bed with another woman.

"Urgh," I said to the empty room and lay back down, spreading myself along the sofa and pulling the cushion in close against my chest. I churned over the brief conversation I'd had with Charlton last night, a wave of despair blowing through me like a gust of wind. The smooth, silky woman's voice that had wafted down the phone replayed over and over again. "Sam..." I heard her drawl, and I clutched the cushion tight over my mouth and growled into it until my jaw ached. I'd need to let Robert and Keith know that there'd be a spare seat at the gala dinner after all, but that could wait. I couldn't face verbalising what had happened to anyone else; not right now.

Tears welled up in the corners of my eyes, but I clenched my jaw and stared at the ceiling until they disappeared. I wouldn't give over more tears or emotions to that right now. As a way of distraction from Charlton, I lay back on the sofa and closed my eyes revisiting the events of the previous night. I ran things over and over in my mind, preferring the memory of waking up in a lonely garden with a dead body to that of the sleepy woman's voice drifting down the phone. After a while I moved the cushion to one side and sat up, leaning back against the sofa. I surveyed the broken splinters of phone littering the carpet and shuffled into the utility room to find the vacuum cleaner.

Once the room was looking less like a battlefield, I reached for my laptop and Googled how long it would take a dead body to go cold. Consensus seemed to be that it was around about 1.5 degrees an hour, although the ambient temperature would have an effect. I remembered how cold Jade's body had been, surely more than a couple of degrees colder than normal. She must have been dead for some time. If Jade had been killed after I'd arrived at the house she'd have still been fairly warm to the touch. But that begged the question—who had rung me up last night? If Jade had already been dead at the time, somebody else had made the call to me yesterday, with the intention of luring me out there. Then they'd knocked me unconscious and left me to discover the body. What was that all about?

I was determined not to give up. I'd told the Ellisons that once I got the bit between my teeth I wouldn't let go, and I honestly couldn't think of what else to do but carry on. I could slope about at home feeling sorry for myself, piling on the misery with each passing thought, or I could occupy my brain by digging some more and trying to get to the bottom of what was going on. At least that way I wouldn't have to entertain the thought of Sam Charlton in bed with another woman. I definitely didn't want to allow that to happen.

I got dressed and headed into the kitchen. I fumbled with my phone, eventually getting the SIM card back inside. When it sprang into life it pinged with several texts and voice messages. Nothing from Charlton. There was a text from Collette asking me to call her, and another from Keith asking if Charlton had confirmed about the gala. That voice span through my brain again. "Sam…"

My heart sank; I'd deal with that later. There were some other texts, from my bank and telephone providers telling me that my bills were available online. I listened to the voicemails. The first one was from Colin O'Gorman, Anthony Bridges' business partner. He'd left the message yesterday evening about the time I'd been crouching over the body of Jade Griffiths.

*"You asked if I'd be happy to talk to you about Margaret-Elizabeth Ellison. Yeah, sure, I don't see why not. I doubt I'll be able to tell you anything but if you think there's anything I can help with…well, just drop me a text or call. I'll be around tomorrow if you're free."*

I sent a text suggesting I went to see him later that morning and he replied almost straight away saying that suited him fine and he gave me the address of his office.

The other voicemail was from Mary Walker, one of the book club parents suggesting she could see me later that day. I called her back and we arranged to meet in town at

Café Santos after I'd finished my meeting with Colin O'Gorman. I had a couple of hours to kill before then, so I donned my rubber gloves and busied myself with doing a few chores, thinking I'd settle down to think about what I needed to ask everyone once I'd got the house looking a bit neater.

I scrubbed at the kitchen floor with a fervour I didn't usually feel for cleaning, pushing the brush backwards and forwards, almost taking the veneer off the tiles. My rubber gloves developed a hole and I stood up, ripping them from my hands. I pushed the pedal on the bin and the lid caught on something, refusing to open. "Stupid, stupid bin," I shouted, banging my foot down on the pedal and yanking the lid up with my hands. I took a deep breath; this was supposed to be cathartic. I stood looking at the recalcitrant bin for several seconds and then took in a deep breath, closed my eyes and released the breath slowly. Then I donned a new pair of rubber gloves, picked up the scrubbing brush and cleaned the sparkling floor once again.

After tidying the kitchen to industrial catering standards, I scooped up a bag of rubbish and took it outside to put in the wheelie bin. As I opened the lid and lowered the bag down, something glinted in the sunlight. I hauled the bag back up again and placed it on the ground, peering into the bin to see what was in there. Laying on top of the rubbish was an ornament. A brass ballerina. She was about twelve inches long, standing atop a sturdy wooden base. Holding her arms aloft and pointing her toes, she didn't look dissimilar to Emily when she'd been dancing around yesterday afternoon. I reached into the bin and picked her up, bemused as to where she'd come from. And then I noticed a few hairs sticking to the wooden base. When I examined her more closely, the hairs were mingled with blood and something else that I could only conclude was skin. Or worse.

I flicked my head around as if someone might be watching me over my shoulder and I lay the ballerina back down exactly as I'd found her, breathing a sigh of relief that I'd been wearing rubber gloves when I'd picked her up. I wasn't sure what I expected to see behind me. Someone lurking in the bushes maybe? Or DC Shepherd, ready to pronounce me guilty of murder. The garden span before me and I grabbed hold of the bin to steady myself, glancing around and gulping in air to try to bring my head back down to earth. I leaned into the bin, my head hanging over the edge, and I tried to clear my brain and give a little space to thinking about what this might mean.

I let go of the bin and leaned my back against the wall of the house. I sank to the ground, pulling my knees up against my chest and hugging them close to my body as I fought to make sense of what I'd just found. Was this the weapon that had caused the great fissure in Jade's skull? And if it was, what the fuck was it doing in my bin? I sat there for some time, thinking it all through but none of it made any sense. I ached with the urge to call Charlton and discuss it, but that option had been closed to me. I sat there, leaning against the wall for some time, mulling over what I knew. Fact one; someone knew where I lived. Fact two; someone was determined to hinder my investigation into Margaret-Elizabeth's murder. I had to assume that those were one and the same person. But what on earth were they worried I would discover that no one else had managed to find?

After some time, I went back into the house and, for the second time in less than twenty-four hours, I called the police.

# 26

D C Jenny Shepherd was in a huddle just outside my back door with a couple of uniformed offi-cers and someone else who was covered from head to toe in what looked like a hooded paper onesie. She glanced from time to time in my direction, looking at me with what I was convinced was an air of suspicion. After some considerable time they began to depart, carrying the contents of my rubbish bin with them, the ballerina encased in a labelled plastic bag.

"You're sure you didn't touch it?" DC Shepherd asked me for the umpteenth time.

"I did pick it up, yes," I repeated, "but I was wearing my rubber gloves. But as soon as I realised what was on the base, I put it back down so I was only holding it for a few seconds at the most."

"And where did you hold it when you picked it up?"

"I pulled her up by her arms. She was laying across the top of the bag with her arms pointing towards me. Then I noticed the hairs on the base and I put it straight back where I'd found it."

"Well," said DC Shepherd, pursing her lips and furrowing her brow. "We'll be in touch. I should advise you, once again, that it wouldn't be wise for you to go anywhere out of Lincoln at the moment. I think that's even more important now."

I watched them all leave, wondering what the neighbours would make of there being two police cars outside my house. It was only three days since the break in, when that surly PC had been round. People were probably thinking I had some kind of criminal activity going on. Not that I particularly cared what people thought, but Steeple Lane was a quiet little street and I couldn't remember the last time I'd seen a police car in the road. I went around the house, double checking that everything was secure, inspecting all the windows in case they'd mysteriously unlocked themselves since the last time I'd checked. I locked the back door and threw the bolt across. Then I went into the dining room and grabbed a chair and wedged it under the door handle. I had no idea if that would stop anyone, but it seemed to work in movies, so it surely couldn't hurt.

As I locked up the front door I made a mental note to call a locksmith and have a second lock fitted. I was just about on time for my appointment with Colin O'Gorman, so I upped my pace and headed down Steep Hill and into the city centre. About halfway down the hill my phone rang; it was Collette.

"Morning!" I chirruped down the phone, trying to appear more carefree than I felt.

"Verity, what's happening?" she blurted down the phone, a hint of fear tainting her words. "I've had the police call, asking me what time you were round here yesterday."

169

"What did you tell them?" I asked, probably not allaying her worries as much as she'd hoped.

"I told them the truth. What did you expect?" she demanded.

"No, no, that's good," I said. "It's just that something happened after I left you and I ended up going to the police station so they're just checking my story that's all."

"Your story? You didn't lie to them did you?"

"No, of course not."

"Don't sound so prissy. I remember the saga with that bloody notebook."

"Collette, it's nothing like that. Look, I have an appointment I have to get to. I haven't got time to explain right now." I didn't really want to, more to the point, but that would have been a little rude to say out loud.

"Okay, well call me back later," she said. "Oh and, Vee?"

"Yeah."

"Marcus is going to be late again this evening."

"I'll see what I can do, darling, but I am really busy with this case at the moment."

"Please, Vee. I need to know what's going on. I can't stand it."

"I'll do my best."

There was no response.

"I promise, Collette, I'll follow him if I can."

I pushed all thoughts of Marcus to one side, and stood outside Colin O'Gorman's office feeling utterly unprepared, events having overtaken the time I'd set aside for thinking about questions. I took in a deep breath and closed my eyes for a moment, focusing on the image I'd developed over the last few days, of Margaret-Elizabeth lying dead amongst the trees. What I needed to find out was a little more information about the man who'd been arrested on suspicion of murdering her. I had been building a picture, and the information from Paul Hardy had been useful, but this man had worked as his business partner for years. He'd know him better than most. I pulled my shoulders back, held my head up high and brushed thoughts of the silky soft voice from my mind. I walked through the doors and announced myself at the reception desk.

Colin O'Gorman looked nothing like I'd been expecting. In fact, I wasn't quite sure what I had been expecting until he arrived and I found myself surprised. To start with, he was younger than I'd anticipated. He looked to be in his mid-forties, with a full head of hair and a closely cropped beard. His office was on the third floor and we took the lift, standing in silence as it shuddered and stuttered upwards. I resolved to take the stairs on my way out; getting stuck in an ancient lift was the last thing I needed at the moment.

"Take a seat," he said, indicating some chairs with a swift gesture of his hand. A dark wood desk occupied the far wall, standing next to a window that gave a fantastic view of the cathedral. Close to the desk was another table housing a coffee machine, cups, little coffee capsules and so on. Colin pointed towards the machine and raised his eyebrows but said nothing.

I nodded in response. "Black's good," I answered.

He picked up some capsules. "Brazilian or Ethiopian?"

I shrugged. "Whichever one you have in your hand will be okay," I said.

He studied the capsule. "Ethiopian then," he announced. He made the coffee and came and sat opposite me. "Now then," he said. "How can I help?"

"Well, as you know the Ellisons have asked me to have a look into the murder of their daughter, Margaret-Elizabeth, and, well, as I'm sure you're aware, Anthony Bridges was the main suspect, so I thought you'd be able to tell me a little bit about him. I'm just trying to build up a picture."

"He didn't kill that girl, you know." He wagged his finger at me, before picking up the coffee and putting it down on the desk in front of me.

"You sound very convinced. The police seemed to think that he did."

"The police didn't have another suspect so they'd have liked for it to have been Tony. But he didn't do it. I'm absolutely convinced of that."

"His DNA was found on Margaret-Elizabeth's body," I ventured.

"Yeah, so was half of her family's apparently."

"And he admitted to being there."

He raised his eyebrows. "That doesn't make him a murderer."

"And he'd been convicted of assaulting young women."

"Ditto," he said. "It's a leap from a quick grope of a teenager to murdering a child."

"Do you share his political views?" I asked, changing the subject.

He sat back in his chair and stroked his beard. "Tony has some interesting things to say." He shrugged. "But no, I've never been a member of Pure Britain. We don't mix business with politics. But, like I say, he has an interesting take on things. Makes you think."

"Like hatred of Muslims?"

"We live in a free country. He's entitled to have his opinion, and to speak out about it. But he doesn't, and never did, *hate* Muslims. He just didn't like the way the government seemed to favour them. He didn't want them over-running the country and taking all the jobs so locals can't find employment."

"And what do you think about that?"

He leaned forward, resting his elbows on the table. "What's my opinion got to do with anything?"

"Just curious. You two worked together for quite some time. Set up the company together. I can't imagine working with someone who I didn't share at least some political opinions with."

"Do you own a successful nationwide company?" He leaned back in his chair and folded his arms.

I thought about my investigating. It was pretty much hand to mouth. "No," I said.

"Well, as I said, business and politics don't necessarily go together. Tony's a shrewd businessman. With some interesting opinions."

"I gather his opinions make him quite a bit of money too." I finished up my coffee and pushed my cup across the table.

"What do you mean?"

"Well, it seems that he makes quite a bit out of contributions to Pure Britain."

"A lot of people agree with him. They're prepared to support his campaigning."

"And he makes a lot of money from them."

"The party does."

I shook my head. "So he doesn't spend the money himself?"

"He spends it on promoting the party." He tipped his head to one side. "Are you insinuating Tony uses the contributions for his own ends?"

"Maybe. Maybe the party promotion includes quite a bit in the way of expenses?"

"I'm sure that whatever he spends the money on, it's all above board. Shrewd. As I said. And if people want to contribute to his personal expenses…well, who are we to tell them what to spend their money on." He paused and glanced down. "In any case, I'm unclear how Tony's political affiliations, or his business practices for that matter, have got anything to do with whether he's capable of murder. Which he isn't. He made a few enemies, that's for sure. The left-leaning do-gooders and socialist activists didn't like him. But I don't think he particularly cared about that, if I'm honest." He lifted his hands and shrugged.

"I've heard that he'd been arrested a few times too."

"The police took a dim view of his speeches, but they forget that we're still allowed free speech in this country. For now, anyway. He's allowed to have whatever opinions he wants, even if people disagree with him or find it unpalatable."

"So his views weren't popular?"

"They were very popular. Trouble is he railed against not being allowed to voice opinions that go against the latest politically correct diktat. Tony said what people were thinking. He chimed with them. He said what they thought, but felt unable to say. He gave them a voice."

"He's not allowed to incite people though."

"He didn't incite people." He spread his hands out, palms up. "He's a great speaker, that's all. He could carry people along with him."

"I heard that he was the round-a-bout owner of a business that helped refugees settle in Lincoln. That the company worked in conjunction with a charity offering support. Housing and helping people find jobs."

Colin O'Gorman leaned back in his chair and laughed. He refolded his arms across his chest. "Are you serious?"

"I'm just saying what I've heard. That it gave more weight to his argument. The more Muslims there were in the city, the more he could claim they were taking housing and jobs."

"Honestly. I don't know who you've been talking to, but you need to check your sources. Tony didn't need to manipulate things. He was just speaking his mind." He held up his hands and shook his head.

"A good speaker, as you said. He could encourage people to do things, yes?"

"Yeah. That's what made him a good businessman also. Even people who thought his opinions were a bit unsavoury would get swept along with him. But what people did after listening to him…well, they should take responsibility for their own actions."

"I gather he gave out addresses and names of local Muslim leaders. Then their houses got torched."

"As I say, personal responsibility." He shrugged.

"Do you think he tried to get arrested?"

"Why would anyone do that?"

"More publicity. More outrage. That leads to more people joining the party, more subscriptions, more political sway. You said he was shrewd."

"Shrewd. Yes. But that's not why we're here, is it. Being shrewd doesn't make you a murderer."

"What was he doing in the woods at that time of night?" I asked.

"You'd have to ask him that."

I had my mouth open to tell him that I was going to go and see Bridges tomorrow, and that I would definitely have that question on my list, but something stopped me. I decided it was probably best not to tell anyone who I was going to see or what I was going to do. That way, nobody would be able to try to stop me. Instead, I said, "Why are you so convinced that he didn't do it?"

He nodded. "I know him," he said. "I've known him for years. You might not like the way that he does things. You might not agree with his political views. Or his aspirations for Britain. But one thing I can tell you"—he pointed his finger at me—"is that he isn't capable of murder." He stood up. "Now, if you'll forgive me, I have things I need to be doing."

I looked at my watch and stood up. "Yes, me too. But thanks for your time. I appreciate you agreeing to meet me."

He showed me back to the stairs where I told him I was happy to walk down by myself, and I left the building feeling a little uneasy; unsure what to make of O'Gorman's conviction that Bridges was not guilty. I guessed if you'd worked with someone for such a length of time you wouldn't want to admit that you'd misjudged their character, would you? I'd read about this somewhere, although I couldn't recall what they called it. It was like when religious leaders were proved to be wrong, when they'd predicted the end of the world or something, and it hadn't happened. Instead of becoming disillusioned, their followers became more convinced in their leader. Subconsciously, they didn't want to admit to themselves that they'd made an error of judgement so their brains convinced them that they'd been right. That the world had been given a stay of execution because of some reason or another, and they became even more fervent, even more entrenched in their views. Cognitive dissonance or something. I couldn't quite remember, but it was an interesting theory.

## 27

---

I walked across town towards Café Santos. It was another warm day, although the sun was dipping behind clouds every now and again, leaving the temperature noticeably cooler each time. I scanned around but couldn't see anyone who met Mary Walker's description so I ordered a coffee to arrive when my guest appeared and I found a comfy seat in a corner to wait for her.

I glanced at my watch. Mary Walker must have been running late and I used the time to review my notes whilst I waited. I wasn't really sure what I could glean from her that I didn't already know but it would be interesting to look at things from the point of view of someone who hadn't been involved at all, someone on the periphery. She'd have known the Ellisons well and known Margaret-Elizabeth too, so it would add something to my general background information. And, as Charlton had pointed out, I had twenty grand to work my way through and so far I'd only made a small dent in that, so the extra time would add to my tally. My heart sank as thoughts of Charlton swirled around my head, the disappointment crushing me, and I shook my head to try to loosen their grip. To my relief, a woman had appeared in the doorway, looking around surveying all the tables and I stood up and waved. She was shaking out an umbrella; the weather must have taken a sudden turn for the worse.

She approached me with her hand held out. "Verity?" she asked. She shook out her shoulder-length dark brown hair. Not a peep of a grey hair despite the deep furrows her crow's feet and brow lines made in her face.

I nodded and offered to go and order her a drink. I left her removing various layers of clothing and making herself comfortable. When I returned we exchanged a few pleasantries and she confirmed that it had started raining a few minutes ago and, yes, the temperature had taken a dive as well.

I sat forward in my chair. "Thanks for coming out to meet me," I said. "As you know I'm looking into Margaret-Elizabeth's murder and I'm just trying to get a feel for what was happening at the time."

"Yes, I see. What do you want to know? I'm not sure I'll be any help to you, but I'm happy to talk to you, if you think it'll do any good."

"I'm not sure either," I agreed. "But it'll help build up a picture of what was going on, what was happening in Margaret-Elizabeth's life, you know? The more comprehensive a picture I have, the more likely I'll be able to understand her life as it was just before she died."

"But if a complete stranger killed her, then why will it matter what her life was like?"

"Well, in a sense, Bridges wasn't a complete stranger because he'd been seen following Margaret-Elizabeth home from school once or twice. And, apparently, watching her over the garden fence. So, if it was him who she'd seen following her, then their paths had already crossed a few times before she died."

"I see." She nodded. "Well, what can I tell you?"

The waitress appeared with our drinks and we both leaned back to allow her room to place them on the coffee table. I waited a minute after she'd disappeared and then moved my head towards Mary Walker. She was an attractive woman, with a long horsey face. Not pretty, but I imagined she'd been quite captivating in her youth.

"Tell me a little bit about the Ellisons and how you knew them," I suggested as an opener.

She rested her elbow on her knee and cupped her chin in her hand. "Well, I've known Matthew for years," she said. "Since before he met Nicole. In fact, we dated for a while when we were younger. He was at university and I was working in a dressmaker's shop."

"In Lincoln?" I asked.

"No, Lincoln University would have been very new in those days. It was tiny when it first began."

I nodded. I remembered. It must have been the late nineties that they started the first building on the site, but I didn't think the university had really gathered much pace until the early noughties.

"We lived in Durham at the time," she carried on. "It was pure coincidence that we both ended up in Lincoln. He came because of his job, and I came because of Jeffrey. We bumped into each other in the city centre one day and our friendship kind of reignited. We were both married by then, but we used to get together for dinner and stuff. You know."

"And you had children about the same age?"

"Yes, Jasmine and Margaret-Elizabeth were almost the same age exactly. I think there were only weeks between their birthdays. Isabella's a little older and Sebastian a couple of years younger." She glanced off to one side, watching as an elderly gentleman shuffled through the stiff door, inched towards a table, and sat down. "They all got on very well. Very well." She nodded as if reaffirming to herself.

"How did the children cope when Margaret-Elizabeth died?"

"Well, I didn't tell them the circumstances to start with." She looked down at her hands. "But obviously it all came out. Children at school spread rumours and they'd come home and ask questions. So I had to be honest with them." She paused, pushing her hair behind her ears. "They were devastated, obviously. I don't think Seb has ever got over it. He's always stayed close to home. He even goes to uni here. The girls have flown the nest now, but I can't see Seb leaving anytime soon."

"Tell me a little bit about Margaret-Elizabeth. What was she like?"

I could sense the memories of a child's life passing past her eyes as she gazed into nothingness.

After a moment she said, "She was a beautiful child. I don't just mean physically, although she was a pretty little girl. She was tiny and delicate with that lovely long blonde hair. But she had a kind of radiance about her, you know, like a charisma that attracted people. She was popular with everyone, all ages. Everybody loved Margaret-Elizabeth." She said the last sentence with a hint of bitterness tainting her voice. Like a parent who might be jealous that someone else's daughter was prettier, or more popular, than their own.

I changed tack. "And the book club? When did you all start that?"

She sighed and wrung her hands together. Perhaps it was the memories of Margaret-Elizabeth's death clawing at her. "It was Matthew and Nicole's idea. Well, mostly Matthew's I think. He started it up with the Johnsons, you know Dan and Theresa. Oh, bless them," she said with a visible shiver. "Poor Jakey, that poor boy. And Grace, of course, she's had her own problems. How they're all still managing to put one foot in front of the other, I do not know."

I agreed that it was, indeed, a sad situation. I didn't divulge what Nash had told me about Jake's death probably not being suicide. I thought I'd already got him into enough trouble with what I'd told DC Shepherd.

"So," I prompted, trying to keep her on track, "the Johnsons and the Ellisons started up the book club?"

"Yes, then they asked us if we wanted to join." She pulled her mouth to one side. "And Angela was the last. She joined when Callum was a tiny baby."

"Were there ever any other members?"

"No." She shook her head. "No, we kept it small. I wasn't really sure about Angela joining to be honest, but she seemed to fit in okay."

"And you took it in turns to host?"

"Latterly we did. In the beginning we used to all go round to the Ellisons, but..." She paused and glanced up at me then looked back down at her hands "...but then as the children got older..."

"It was more manageable to have them in their own homes?" I suggested.

"Yes," she said. "Much easier as they got older."

"And the children read books too?"

"The children?"

"Yes, I was reading the messages on the Facebook group

and there were comments about the books the children were reading too."

"Oh, yes, I see what you mean." She nodded. "Yes, we did. They did. They read books too and we all exchanged ideas and things about it. Yes."

"And did the book club carry on after Margaret-Elizabeth's murder?"

Her mouth opened, her eyes did too. "No," she said, shaking her head. "No, we couldn't face carrying on after that. No, the last time we met was the night Margaret-Elizabeth died."

"And was that when the Facebook group closed down too?"

She thought for a moment, then nodded. "Yes, that's right. We wound that up. We closed it down straight after— we couldn't bear to be reminded of it."

We chatted a little more; Mary started talking about what she needed to buy for dinner later and I realised that I wasn't going to learn anything more of any use from the conversation so I said my goodbyes and thanked her for her time.

By the time I left the café the rain had stopped and the sun had come back out, so I decided to walk home and get the keys so that I could go and reclaim my car from outside Jade Griffith's house.

## 28

M y car was exactly where I'd left it. I wasn't sure why that pulled me up, but it did. Perhaps it was the memory of parking yesterday evening, the thoughts that had been circling in my mind at the time; thoughts of an immediate future very different to the one I'd ended up living through. In that alternative universe I'd gone home and eaten granary bread and drunk red wine. It was only a few hours ago, but it felt like a lifetime. How things had changed since then.

Curious to take a look at the scene of last night's events, I didn't just pick up the car and drive off. I wanted to see the garden in daylight. I walked down the narrow path along the side of the house and checked to make sure there were no police officers still lingering. At the corner a deep split in the pavement showed where I must have tripped over. I'd have been unable to see it in the dark. Police tape stretched across from the corner of the wall to the fence that ran along the back of the garden. I peeped over my shoulder and ducked under the tape. The lawn was flattened in places; by the weight of Jade's body and by the number of people who'd been trampling around. An eerie quietness sent goosebumps racing up my arms and neck, and I imagined Jade's body laid out, one arm above her head. I hoped someone had moved the hair from her mouth. The bucket of weeds and the secateurs were standing where they'd been last night. Obviously of no interest to the police. I peered in through the kitchen window. It was a neat little room with a few appliances out on the counter. Fridge magnets held notes against the door; lists and reminders, phone numbers, taxi company cards. Glancing around at the normality of a life interrupted, I wondered if she'd had any family, any parents who were on their way to see their daughter's dead body in the mortuary.

A clattering at my feet pulled my attention away from the inside and I looked down to see a petite little cat appearing through the cat flap. Mostly tortoiseshell, its front left leg was ginger tabby and looked as if it had been grafted on from another cat entirely. The tips of its toes were painted with little patches of white.

"Hello," I said as it emerged fully, the little door rattling as it closed.

The cat meowed and looked up at me with its piercing green eyes as if I should understand what it was trying to say. It wrapped itself around my legs, rubbing its head against each of my shins in turn. I crouched down and stroked it as it leaned its forehead into my hand.

I stood up and peered once again into the kitchen. By the sink, to one side of the room, an empty food bowl stood on a plastic mat. I looked down at the cat. "Are you hungry?" I asked it. I was pretty sure it said yes. "Hang on," I said out loud, pointing my finger. "I'll be back soon." And I turned to go down the side of the house.

The cat gave a plaintive meow as I left it, seemingly thinking I was abandoning it with its empty tummy. I walked up the road to a little corner shop where I selected a couple of sachets of food and some dry biscuits and then I made my way back to the house. The cat was nowhere to be seen.

I opened up one of the packets, and the little cat re-emerged through the back door and started wrapping itself around me, looking up at me and chirruping, seeming to understand what I was doing. "Sorry I don't have a bowl," I apologised, emptying the contents of the packet onto the pavement by the wall of the house.

The cat sniffed at the food and then looked up at me with an air of disdain as if to say, 'Is that the best you can offer?' and it lifted its tail high into the air and went into the house.

"Huh! Charmed I'm sure," I said as the last inch of tail disappeared. I tipped a pile of dry food next to the contents of the sachet and left the rest of the food in a little pile in case anyone else came round and found the cat in need of a meal. Then I took another look around the garden, went back to my car and drove home.

## 29

I had a couple of hours before I was due to go round to see Judith Ryan so I quickly made myself a sandwich and a cup of coffee and took them through to the living room, where I spent some time revisiting the statements of family members and trying to piece together who was where and at what time during the evening of Margaret-Elizabeth's death. I wrote down a timeline with names and positions, starting from when Jonathan Scraggs and a few of the others had run out into the garden and finishing when they received the phone call that Margaret-Elizabeth had been declared dead.

My mind was dragged from that summer evening ten years ago to the present by the ding-dong sound of my doorbell. I pushed all my notes to one side and hobbled to the door, my foot aching from having been stuffed underneath me for too long without moving. I removed the walking stick from its new home against the door, and opened up. Several feet beyond the door, with his back towards me and his arms folded, stood Sam Charlton.

"What are you doing here?" I asked, my mouth suddenly dry and my heart pumping faster by the second.

He turned round and took a few steps towards me. He held out his hands, palms upwards and tilted the corners of his mouth downwards. "I thought you might be upset."

"Upset?" I shouted. "Why on earth would I be upset?"

He took a few paces back towards the gate and then swung round and took a couple forward, running his hand over his head. "Look, Verity, can we go in? It's probably best not to have this conversation on the doorstep."

"Fine," I snapped at him and stood back, holding the door open to let him in.

He headed straight for the kitchen and leaned against the counter. He was wearing jeans and a long-sleeved ribbed top. He pushed the sleeves of his top up almost to his elbows and folded his arms across his body.

I stood on the opposite side of the room, glaring at him expectantly. "Well?" I said. I'd wanted it to sound demanding, in control, but I couldn't keep my voice from shaking. I clenched my jaw and looked at the floor, taking in a deep breath to try to steady my heart.

He moved over to me and held his hands up as if he were about to touch my shoulders but I lifted up my arms and pushed his hands away from me before he had the chance. I surprised myself with the violence of the action, my wrists crashing into his forearms.

"See, you are upset," he said, throwing his arms in the air and turning back towards the counter, resuming his position leaning up against it.

"I am not upset."

He flung his right arm towards me. "You're doing a bloody good impersonation of upset," he said, curling his lip and running his hand back and forth across his head.

"I am not upset," I repeated, emphasising the words and looking him directly in the eyes. Fury snatched at my chest, threatening to bubble over and I stared him down whilst struggling to maintain my composure. Memories of the silky soft voice taunted me and I glared over at him, wiping away the visions stabbing at my brain. "You want to sleep around, who am I to stop you?" I hurled my hands into the air. "What you do in your spare time is completely up to you, isn't it?" And I pointed towards the front door in an attempt to encourage him to leave.

"Look," he said, holding one hand up, a note of conciliation in his tone. "I've driven all the way up here because I thought you might want to talk about it." He folded his arms again and looked at the ground, shuffling his feet.

Rage boiled up inside me and poured out in my words. "You thought *I* might want to talk about it," I shouted. "What's it got to do with me? You're the one who can't keep his dick in his pants, not me." I pursed my lips and stared at him, raising my eyebrows.

Any conciliatory tones vaporised, his voice getting louder, the pitch higher. "You were the one who said you weren't ready for a relationship, Verity," he shouted, one hand on his hip the other wildly gesticulating above his head. "What did you expect me to do, take a vow of chastity?"

"Urgh," I growled and turned to face the other way.

"You can't call all the shots," he said to the back of my head. He took in a deep breath, slowed his pace down, his voice less harsh. "You can't have everything your own way."

I stayed silent, staring at the wall like a petulant teenager.

"You can't say you don't want a relationship and then get angry when I sleep with someone else."

"I am not angry." I bared my teeth as I turned back to face him.

"Well you're doing a fine job of acting as if you are." His eyes opened wide and he jutted out his jaw.

"Well I'm not. Why the hell should I care what you get up to when we're not together?" I folded my arms and stared at him, then threw them out wide. "Feel free to fuck whoever you like. Whenever you like. And as often as you like. There, you have my permission. Go ahead."

"That's really grown up."

"At least you know now. Go ahead and do whatever you want. Behave however you like. Go shag as many women as you can find."

"You said you didn't want a relationship," he snapped. "You said that. Not me." He stabbed his finger towards me through the air, punctuating the words.

"I didn't ask you to come up here, Sam."

"I came because I thought you'd be upset."

"Well, there you have it. That just shows that you don't know me at all. I'm not in the slightest bit upset."

He sighed, and leaned back, his hands against the counter. "Do you want me to leave?"

I bit my lip and looked across at him. I didn't want him to leave. I wanted him to stay. I wanted him to take me in his arms and say sorry. I wanted him to scoop me up, to kiss me, to take me to bed, to hold me. I wanted him to tell me that everything would work out alright. I wanted him to make love to me, and put his arms around me like he had before, linking his fingers with mine and whispering in my ear as we fell asleep. I looked down at my feet.

He asked me again, "Do you want me to leave?"

"Yes," I said, without looking up at him, and he walked out of the house without saying another word, slamming the front door behind him as he left.

## 30

By the time I pulled up outside Judith Ryan's house I'd managed to regain my composure. After some not inconsiderable time prevaricating, I'd turned my phone off to prevent me caving into the temptation to ring Charlton and ask him to drive back. I'd put some make-up on to hide my puffy eyes and red cheeks. Then I'd spent some time sitting cross-legged on the living room floor doing breathing exercises and focusing on the matter in hand. The more I concentrated, the less time I gave my brain to think about Sam Charlton and lost opportunities.

I smoothed down my clothes, took a deep breath, arranged my face into what I hoped looked like competence, then rang the doorbell. Judith Ryan appeared and ushered me into the front room. She looked uncannily like her sister, and I couldn't tell if she was the older or younger of the two. The similarity ended with their looks, though, with Judith oozing an air of old-fashioned hippy, her hair falling about wherever it landed and her baggy ill-fitting clothes hiding a much slimmer body than her sister's.

I stepped over discarded shoes, walking boots and dog toys on my route across the cluttered room and sat down on a sofa covered in hand-crocheted blankets and dog hairs. Judith sat down opposite me, shooing a shaggy-coated dog off the sofa before she sat down. The dog sloped off and curled up in a dog bed in the corner of the room and then continued sleeping as if it hadn't ever been interrupted.

"Thanks for seeing me," I began.

"No problem," said Judith, tucking her legs underneath her on the sofa. "Happy to help. Well, I'm really not sure if I can help, but I'll do my best. Fire away."

"Tell me a little bit about Margaret-Elizabeth," I suggested. "What was she like?"

"Vivacious," Judith said looking up and smiling. "Precocious. A little spoiled, maybe. She was the apple of her parents' eyes and nothing would convince them that she wasn't the perfect child. Even more so now."

"What do you mean?" I asked. "Even more so now?"

"Well," she said, looking out of the window into nothingness. "How can anyone compete with a dead child? In their eyes, she'll be forever perfect. The paragon child. The most adorable, beautiful, talented child. With no faults at all."

"You mean, she's been put on a pedestal?"

"Exactly," said Judith, punching the air with a loosely clenched fist, as if she were banging a drum with a drumstick. "Any other child is going to be slower, stupider, uglier, more rebellious, more trouble. They don't have to say it all the time, but you can see it in their eyes. They look at other children hitting adolescence, teenagers, taking their first awkward steps as adults—I'm talking especially about their nephews and nieces here—and you can see them thinking 'Margaret-Elizabeth wouldn't have done that'."

"She'll forever be an innocent eleven year old."

"Yeah," she said, running her hands through her unruly hair. "She wasn't that innocent either."

"How do you mean?"

"I don't mean anything sinister by that. I just mean that she got into trouble from time to time, the same as any other eleven year old does. I remember Nicole being furious with her for lying one time, a week or two before she died. Margaret-Elizabeth had done a spelling test at school, one the children all marked themselves, and had told the teacher she'd got top marks. She hadn't, she just didn't want to admit that she'd made a mistake. The teacher found out and told Nicole. But try telling Nicole about that now, whoa." And she held her hands up as if she were trying to stop a speeding train.

"So Nicole and Matthew look back with rose-coloured glasses?"

"Hmmm...Nicole more than Matt, but yes they both tend to do it. I guess, they can't imagine what having a teenager is like. Or having a slightly awkward child. Jake Johnson, for example. I didn't really know the Johnsons so well, but our paths crossed at parties, birthdays, you know?"

I nodded.

"He was always a little socially inhibited," she carried on. "He always found it harder than most to make small talk or just any kind of talk. Unless it was about his favourite video game. But Nicole could never just accept that he was a bit different. That that's how he was."

I thought about her comment that he'd always been a timid boy.

"She was forever telling Theresa what she should do to 'bring him out of his shell'. And our son, George, he was

193

diagnosed with autism not long after Margaret-Elizabeth died and Nicole just snorted when I told her and said he was just socially inept. Socially inept! Can you imagine saying that to a parent? He was seven at the time. But, of course, if you tried to counter what she was saying, or disagreed with her, she'd burst into tears and it all became about her grief. I don't know, it just seems that they froze in time when Margaret-Elizabeth died and she'll forever be a version of herself that she never actually was when she was alive." She looked down at her hands.

Sibling rivalry was alive and kicking, I thought. I changed direction. "Tell me about the night that Margaret-Elizabeth died."

She sighed and stared through the window into the sky. "It's all a bit of a blur. You know how it is. You just do things, you just get on, you go into survival mode, but it all went by so quick and then you have to try and unpick it afterwards." She paused, tugging at her trousers and pulling them straight. "We got the call from Matthew and we just went straight round."

"What time was that?"

"I guess it was about 11.15 in the evening, maybe a little later. We were just about to head upstairs to bed."

"What did he say? When he rang."

She looked back out of the window, gazing into nothing-ness. "I answered the phone. He wasn't making sense to start with. He just kept saying 'she's gone, she's gone'. I thought he meant Nicole. I thought they'd had a row and she'd left him. But then he said something like 'we came home and she wasn't in her bed' and I realised he meant Margaret-Elizabeth."

"And you went straight round?"

"Yes. Karl drove. I'd had a glass or two of wine. Well, Karl had had a couple of beers but what can you do?" She shrugged.

"What about George?'

"Luckily my mother-in-law was living with us at the time so she stayed here with him."

"So tell me what happened when you got there," I said.

She clasped her hands together, then ran both of them through her hair, making it even more dishevelled than it had been. "Nicole and Matt were there in the front room, pacing, crying and shouting. Shouting at each other."

"Was there anyone else there when you arrived?"

"No, we were the first. Jonathan and Chrissy got there seconds after we did, and the Todds came a couple of minutes after that." She paused, and I waited for her to carry on. "Jonathan kind of took charge. He shouted for people to follow him. No one in particular, he just sort of looked over his shoulder as he ran out of the room and said, 'follow me'."

"Who ran after him?" I asked, scribbling in my notebook.

"Karl did, definitely. And David. All the men I think, they all ran out into the garden."

"Matthew too?"

"No, he didn't go into the garden. I'm not sure. I can't remember exactly how it went. Chrissy said she'd go out the front in case Margaret-Elizabeth had wandered out there. I don't know why, I don't think there was any way she could have got out the front without anyone knowing. She wasn't very tall and there was a bolt across the top. It made more sense that she'd gone out through the patio doors. But I think Chrissy just wanted to make sure."

"So you and Nicole were still in the living room. And what about Marion Todd? And her daughter, err…"

"Diane."

"Yes, Diane. Where were Marion and Diane?

"I think they went to make some tea." She looked up and rolled her eyes. "Typical, isn't it. In a crisis someone always makes a cup of tea." She tutted. "I don't think anyone actually wanted tea, but I think Marion probably wanted something to do."

"So there was just you and Nicole in the front room, then?"

"Yes, we sat on the sofa and Nicole was just sobbing. She was saying 'I can't cope, I can't cope'. I said to her, 'We'll find her, we'll get her back. She'll have wandered off'. She'd sleep-walked before," she said looking across at me. "But Nicole kept saying, 'no, no, she's not coming back. She can't come back'."

"She can't come back?"

"She knew. She knew Margaret-Elizabeth was dead. Mother's instinct, you know?"

I nodded, although I didn't know. I'd never had children so I couldn't really imagine how you'd know something like that, but I took her word for it. "How long were the two of you alone in the front room?"

"Not long. Well, it didn't feel very long. Marion came running through shouting, 'Jonathan's got her', and Nicole was gasping for air. Then Jonathan arrived with Margaret-Elizabeth and laid her on the floor. He was yelling to call an ambulance. Not at anyone in particular, just yelling it out into the room. So I grabbed my phone and called them and told them what had happened. She looked lifeless, Margaret-Elizabeth. She looked dead."

"But they told you to try to revive her?" Before she had

a chance to answer, my attention was caught by something flashing past the window. I leapt to my feet, my reactions heightened to any unexpected movement. The nerves up my arms jangled like barbed wire scraping in my veins as I peered through the window.

## 31

"What is it?" Judith said, getting to her feet.

"I thought I saw someone in your garden. Looking in, or maybe running past the window." As I said it I was doubting myself. I was on edge, that was for sure. We stared out into what looked like an empty garden.

She peered through the window, looking this way and that. "I can't see anyone. Maybe it was a bird flying past," she suggested.

"Could have been," I said, unable to keep the doubt out of my voice. I sat back down, sneaking the occasional glance to my right, hoping I might catch sight of a face. Or hoping I wouldn't. I couldn't decide which would be worse. "I'm sorry," I said. "I'm a little on edge, I had a break in the other night."

"I heard, yes."

"You were saying…when you called for the ambulance?"

"They said to keep trying, they were shouting instructions down the phone. It was hard to hear because Nicole was screaming and crying and leaning over Margaret-Elizabeth and touching her, stroking her. I think it was Diane who took her away. She had to drag her. Maybe someone else helped her, I can't quite remember."

"So who tried to revive Margaret-Elizabeth?"

"Jonathan to start with, but he gave up after a while and Diane took over. I think Marion must have gone out to keep Nicole company. Nicole burst into the room at one point shouting at us to bring her back. 'Bring her back to me' she was shouting. But it was useless."

"How long before the ambulance arrived?"

"God it seemed to take forever, but it wasn't that long. Diane was pumping Margaret-Elizabeth's chest when they arrived and then they took over. But we all knew it was no good."

"So who was there in the room when the ambulance people arrived?"

"Um, me and Diane. Nicole and Marion came in just as they arrived. Then Karl and David came in from the garden. They'd run through the woods but couldn't find the man that Jonathan had seen. Chrissy had come back at some point, I can't remember exactly when. I remember she got halfway to saying there was no sign of Margaret-Elizabeth out the front, but then she saw what was going on and just sat down quietly in a chair."

"So, you went off with Nicole to the hospital?"

"Yes, we went in the ambulance. They tried all the way there to revive her. They must have been driving fast because it only took seconds to get there. Then in the hospital they wheeled her off, but they soon came back and said there was no use keep trying. Nicole was begging them. Begging them to give it another go. But the doctor just kept shaking his head and saying sorry."

"Was Matthew at the hospital?"

"He arrived with David. I think they'd followed in the car. They got there just before the doctor came out and said that there was nothing they could do."

"What happened then? After they declared Margaret-Elizabeth dead."

"Well, you can imagine, Nicole didn't want to leave the hospital. She kept saying she didn't want to leave Margaret-Elizabeth there. It was awful. They gave her some sedatives to take home and I said they could come and stay at ours. Nicole couldn't face going back to the empty house, so David dropped us all off at our house. Karl came back later. He brought some clothes with him, but Nicole had fallen asleep by then. I was actually really surprised the next day when Matthew and Nicole wanted to go home. I really thought they'd never go back. Their house had been turned upside down by the police, apart from anything—they'd been through everything."

A noise somewhere near the back of the house sent a fresh shockwave pulsing through me. I jumped up and ran across the front room. Judith pushed herself onto her feet. As I reached the door I turned back towards her. "Stay here," I demanded, confining her to her own front room, and she lowered herself back onto the sofa. Then I ran uninvited through her house towards the kitchen. Another bang. This time it sounded like a door slamming shut. I crashed through the door into the kitchen and hurtled across the room, leapfrogging discarded coats, wellington boots, and dog food bowls on my way. I yanked open the door and rushed out into the cold, late afternoon air.

I scanned the small garden, just catching sight of a trainer disappearing over the fence at the boundary. Running as fast as I could, I reached the fence where I'd spotted the shoe and peered into the wasteland beyond. The Ryans' garden backed onto the edge of Boultham Park and on the other side of the fence trees, bushes, brambles and weeds combined to form a thick cover. I scanned through it, but there was no movement. The fence was about a metre or so high, with the horizontal planks of wood on the park side, so no foot holds to help me. I grabbed the top of the fence and pulled myself up, my feet scrambling against the fence to try to gather some momentum from below. I'd been attempting to jump up and sit on the top, then swing myself over and drop down on the other side. But I misjudged and tumbled over the fence, falling head-first into a tangle of brambles and nettles.

Snapping twigs and the sound of dry autumn leaves being crushed under running feet made me temporarily forget the pain of the thorns scratching at my bare flesh, and I dragged myself upright and gave chase. I dashed under low branches, and leapt over clumps of nettles, slipping on patches of damp ground where the light hadn't reached for many a month. The faint autumn light, the overhead cloud and the canopy of trees clinging onto their remaining leaves combined to create a darkness that meant it was impossible to see further than a few feet.

Still, I ran on regardless, pushing the branches to one side, my breathing loud and laboured. It only took me a minute or two before I emerged from the thicket into the open space of Boultham Park. I glanced around. It had been a pleasant afternoon for the most part and a few families sauntered towards the lake; a couple with two children and a baby in a sling, an elderly pair holding each other up, a woman with a whole gaggle of dogs. Nobody who looked suspicious. Nobody lurking, or skulking. Nobody running away. I leaned my hands on my knees and caught my breath, peering back into the little area of woodland from where I'd just emerged. Nothing. Whoever I'd been chasing had just disappeared into thin air.

I sprinted back to the Ryans' house the long way round, skirting around the clump of woodland and removing thorns from my skin and twigs from my hair as I went. The temptation to scratch the nettle stings on my face was almost overpowering, but I managed to resist. As I ran, doubts crept into my mind. Maybe I was so on edge I was imagining things. Had I really heard a noise? What on earth would Judith Ryan think of me suddenly running out of her house? And coming back covered in scratches and stings. I approached the front door, took in a deep breath, and decided I wasn't going to take any chances.

"I've had a break-in, I've been chased in my car, Jake Johnson is dead and so is Jade Griffiths," I said to a wide-eyed and open-mouthed Judith after I'd sat her down. "And I think this is all somehow connected to Margaret-Elizabeth's murder."

She just stared at me.

"When is Karl coming home?" I asked.

"Err…um…he'll be here soon," she stuttered, her brows knitted together with concern.

"Okay, I'll wait till he gets here. Then I want you to lock all your doors, lock all your windows. Make sure no one can get in. And if there's the slightest thing, call the police. Okay?"

She nodded, but still said nothing.

## 32

I left the Ryans still fretting over their door and window locks. They'd already rung their son George to get him to go home, and I ran out into the street. I'd brought the battered hire car with me, rather than my own as I wanted to get in position for Marcus leaving work. I'd decided that my best course of action was to get some more pictures of him with the mystery woman and then go to his office tomorrow to confront him. It was taking too much of my time and I wanted it to be over so I could concentrate on Margaret-Elizabeth. I was also rather hoping that if I showed him the evidence, he'd confess to Collette and then it wouldn't be me who'd have to tell her that she'd been right and that her husband was, indeed, a rat.

There was a good hour before Marcus would be leaving work, so I drove down to Branston and parked up a little way along the road from the red brick house to wait for him. I fished out my notebook and started reviewing some of the notes I'd taken, but my heart wasn't in it and I pushed it back into my handbag. I peered at my face in the rear-view mirror, the stings pock-marking my cheeks and forehead, and some angry red scratches creating deep marks on my nose and chin. My hands and forearms were itching like crazy from nettle stings and I was still finding bramble thorns deep in the flesh of my palms.

On an impulse I grabbed my phone. I stuffed my handbag and camera under the passenger seat, and got out of the car, pushing my phone into the back pocket of my jeans as I did so. The street was deserted—I imagined most of the occupants were at work. I walked up to the house and mimed knocking on the door, just in case anyone was watching. After waiting for a few seconds, I moved down the side of the house, peering in through the windows as I did so. The house looked empty.

A wooden side gate led into the back garden, and as luck would have it the bolt on the other side wasn't thrown shut. The gate and surrounding fence were about six feet high so provided good cover and I pushed the bolt shut quietly behind me to prevent anyone from following me through. The small garden consisted of a recently mowed lawn and some neatly kept borders, with French windows at the far end of the house. An eager-looking sparrow pecked at a bird feeder hanging from an elaborate feeding station that took centre stage in the middle of the lawn. I walked up to the kitchen window and took a tentative look through. There was no sign of life, so I put my head to the window, my hands cupped around my face, and peered around the room.

An open-plan kitchen diner took up the entire back of the house. It wasn't a large room. There was just enough space for a small dining room table, which was placed in the middle of the dining area by the patio doors. Beyond that, a modern sideboard leaned against the far wall with a comfy-looking rocking chair nestled next to it. A book lay on the sideboard with a bookmark two thirds of the way through and I imagined the blonde-haired lady sitting in the chair with the doors open, reading the book and watching the birds in the garden. Appliances covered the counters at the kitchen end of the room, making it look cluttered and busy, although this was more due to lack of space than untidiness.

I moved along the house to the patio doors and pushed my head close to the glass to take a good look around. I tried to see what the book was that someone had almost finished but the spine was turned away and I couldn't quite see. A few photos were placed on the top shelf of the sideboard and I squinted to try to see what was in them, but they were too small and too far away. One appeared to show the Golden Gate Bridge with somebody standing in the foreground but I couldn't make out who. A couple of the others had a child running along a beach and playing in the snow, but it was impossible to see what age the child was or whether it was the teenager I'd seen Marcus with the other day.

A wedding photo hung on the wall opposite the doors, with a bride resplendent in her long white dress, a veil flowing down her back. She was standing with, perhaps, the matron of honour and a page boy, but I was guessing. I strained to get a better look but just as I was trying to decide whether the bride was the blonde lady I'd seen Marcus with, the kitchen door handle started rattling. I shot back, away from the glass, listening intently.

From within the house came the sound of the kitchen door opening and closing and I flattened myself hard against the wall. Noises I couldn't quite place filtered through the windows. Maybe a kettle boiling, a fridge opening, a toaster being pressed down. A flutter of movement caught my eye as someone crossed the room and walked around the dining table. I took a furtive glance as I inched myself further along the wall so as not to be seen if they turned around.

A woman stood, with her back to me, rummaging through one of the drawers in the sideboard. But this wasn't the blonde lady; this was someone else, someone shorter and stockier with short, spikey dark hair. She pulled something out of the drawer and shouted out loud, "I've got it!" and held up a piece of paper.

She began to turn around, and I slid along the wall, towards the kitchen, lowering myself under the kitchen window and praying that no one was going to come through the door into the garden.

"Great," shouted a voice I recognised. Marcus was in the house.

I glanced at my watch. *Shit!* What was he doing here at this time? And who was this woman?

"We need to get going!" The words came from an agitated voice that I didn't recognise, but from the tone I was pretty sure this was the teenage boy. Certainly a teenage boy, if not the same one I'd seen the other day. The woman was different, why not the boy? I couldn't assume anything.

"Give me five minutes," the woman shouted back from the dining area, and then she said something in a quieter tone that I couldn't quite catch from outside.

Marcus' shape appeared beside her and he stroked the woman's shoulder. I craned my head to the side, whilst squashing myself tight against the wall. I held my breath and remained as still as I could, not wanting to do anything that might attract their attention. They spoke in muted tones. Marcus and the spikey-haired woman moved back towards the kitchen and sounds of cutlery on crockery filled the air for a couple of minutes. I imagined someone hastily eating a slice of toast, maybe after a busy day of work and no time for lunch. Then there was quiet and I strained to hear what was going on, not daring to peek into the room. Through the silence, a slamming door caused me to jump and I let out an involuntary gasp as my body jerked forward. Now sounds were coming from around the side of the house. Voices, keys rattling, car doors opening and shutting. I bolted upright, glancing through the window into the empty house and then ran for the side gate.

Marcus' car stood empty on the road but as I ran up the path towards the front of the house, a little yellow Toyota was pulling out of the road. As it turned the corner, I sprinted to the hire car, blipping the locks as I ran. I leapt into the car and gave chase, fastening my seat belt as I pulled up to the junction.

## 33

I pulled out of the housing estate just in time to see the yellow car turning right onto the main road, heading towards the city centre. A stream of traffic held me up and I rapped my fingers against the steering wheel as I watched the yellow car disappear round the bend into Branston village. Taking a more aggressive approach than I normally would, I sped out across the oncoming traffic, ignoring the shaking fist of the closest driver, and slotted into the traffic heading through the village. Marcus and his fellow travellers were several cars ahead, but thankfully the colour of their vehicle stood out against the greys and blacks and it wasn't too hard to keep track of.

We headed northwards; down Canwick Hill, past the city along Broadgate, and up the steep incline of Lindum Road. Then at Pottergate Arch, the little yellow car veered off towards the left and they led me onwards, past the Lincoln Hotel and along Nettleham Road. By this point, there was only one car between me and them and as they indicated and turned left into the private hospital I swept off into the hospice car park on the opposite side of the road. I waited a few minutes and then drove across the road and into the hospital grounds. There was the car, parked at the far end, its occupants nowhere to be seen. I presumed they'd gone inside, so I drove to the opposite end of the car park and parked as far away from them as I could.

Luckily the hospital was small, with one main entrance, and I had a clear view from where I was sitting. I slunk down low in my seat and waited. Whilst I sat there, I Googled the hospital to try to see if I could find any hint as to what they might be doing, but short of a list of cosmetic surgeons I didn't come up with much. GPs and various specialists offered private clinics but if I was honest, it could have been anything. I started looking at which specialists offered clinics on a Thursday but ended up confused. Some came to the hospital every other week, some once a month, some at various other intervals and without knowing where they started counting it was impossible to narrow it down. I sighed and gave up.

I unzipped my camera from its cover and fired off a few shots of the main door. I zoomed in on a squirrel running across the tarmac and up a nearby tree, then scanned back to the door. I focused through the camera on some of the windows, behind which I assumed were patients and doctors, but I couldn't see anything.

There was still no sign of Marcus or the others so I gave the Ryans a quick ring, and was reassured that there had been no further disturbances in or around their home and that George was safely in his bedroom, studying for an upcoming assignment. Or playing on his Xbox, they weren't really sure. But he was there, which was the main thing.

The light was fading and I had completed several sudokus on my phone by the time the party emerged through the hospital doors. I picked up my camera and fired off a burst of shots, watching them through the viewfinder. The spikey-haired lady had her arms around the teenager's shoulders and Marcus was bending low, leaning in towards the boy, close to his face, saying something and nodding. The teen got into the back of the car, and Marcus moved around to the passenger side of the car, staring out across the car park. I clicked away, Marcus apparently staring straight at the camera lens, although I was sure he couldn't see me or, hopefully, the camera.

Hanging well back, I followed the group as they made their way to Branston and the little red-brick house. As they huddled on the door-step, kissed and waved, I fired off a round of photographs, then snapped Marcus as he got back into his car and turned one last time to blow a kiss. I followed him back to his home, where we arrived not long after his normal time, which I was sure he'd be able to write off to Collette as traffic delays. She'd be left thinking that he hadn't been anywhere after work at all. I ached, a physical pain in my chest, at the thought of Collette being cheated on. Her life would crumple if her marriage broke down. But why was there a different woman in the house today? And what on earth had they been doing at the hospital? I sat there snapping Marcus walking through his own front door, no further forward in my understanding of what was going on than I had been before.

## 34

After showering and coating myself in Savlon I made myself a quick dinner, then I sat in my living room preparing for my visit to Anthony Bridges the following afternoon. I wasn't sure whether he'd answer my questions, but he'd agreed to see me and that seemed positive. The walking stick was back in position leaning against the front door. The chair had been wedged once again under the door handle at the back. Every blind and curtain in the house was pulled and each window had a trap of some sort beneath it; bottles made of thin glass that would crash to the ground if the window was opened, Christmas bells attached to handles that would ring and fly off if disturbed, ball bearings balanced so that if anything moved they'd crash into saucepans below. I was pretty sure that if anyone managed to unpick the window locks they wouldn't be able to get in without creating something of a commotion. Even so, I had to stop myself from walking round the house and checking everything for the millionth time.

I'd hidden the kitchen knives back upstairs, although I

kept one close to me. Just in case. And I'd put another one in my handbag. I was sure it wasn't strictly legal to go around carrying a knife in your handbag, but it was a chance I'd have to take.

I settled back down in the front room and reviewed my notes from the day. Colin O'Gorman had been convinced that Anthony Bridges hadn't been capable of murder, yet everything I'd heard or read about him indicated that he was a thuggish man with a penchant for young women and girls. He'd been in the woods that night. But O'Gorman was right; that didn't make him a murderer. There had to be something more concrete.

I went back over and over the pictures on my laptop, pictures of notes and interviews, statements, screenshots. Nothing stood out. My eyes scratched with the effort of staring at the screen for so long and I lay the laptop to one side and went into the kitchen to get a glass of wine. I leaned my elbows against the worktop and ran a hand across my face. Maybe I should relax. Give my brain a little time to think. I grabbed the glass of wine and went back into the living room, deciding to watch something on tele that required no thought at all. John used to call it 'brain-wipe TV' for the effect it had on him after a hard day's work.

I flopped down onto the sofa and flicked the remote at the television. I went from channel to channel, unable to find anything of interest. A soap, a reality programme, a James Bond movie I'd seen several times, another soap – same story, different accent, an old episode of Columbo. I scoffed. He'd have this wrapped up in no time. He was pacing about a room with his raincoat flapping open, a cigar in one hand, and tapping his head with the other, figuring it all out in less than an hour.

I settled eventually on some kind of reality show. People were locked away in an apartment block, communicating via an internal social media channel. This was their only method of talking to one another and they could project whatever image they wanted to the other participants. They could tell the truth, lie, or pretend to be someone else entirely. It seemed that the point was to get the other participants to like you, or the version of you that you chose to present them, so that they'd vote for you at the end of the show. It all appeared utterly pointless, but I began to get drawn in by the sheer mendacity of the contestants, lying and cheating in an attempt to manipulate the others. I found myself rooting for the few who were being truthful, although that was probably nowhere near as effective, and the other contestants were no more likely to believe what they said.

The messages zipped from one contestant to another, to groups who'd formed little cliques, to other groups surmising what the first group was doing, the bickering and factions deepening as the programme progressed.

I was losing interest—not only was the arguing, the divisions and the infighting getting the better of me, it was the way the contestants presented themselves as well. Even the ones who seemed to be being honest had a vision of themselves that didn't come close to the reality.

"On social media," the commentator droned, "behind the smokescreen of your computer, you can be whoever you want to be."

A smokescreen.

I fired up my laptop again and took another look at the messages on the book club Facebook page. I read through everything I'd photographed right from the start, not just skimming this time, properly reading. It took me a long time, and I had to keep re-reading as the messages were uninteresting and repetitive. It did appear that there were messages being sent from one member to another at times. It wasn't clear from the info that I had whether these were private, but I guessed they were.

There were a few messages from Angela Thompson to Theresa Johnson, mostly along the theme that she didn't like the books that Matthew Ellison had chosen for the book club, or asking why he always got to choose what they read. Theresa's replies were non-committal but she appeared to agree that there was an imbalance of power.

Several of the group messages spoke about re-reading books that they'd read before. Perhaps that was why Angela Thompson didn't like it, if Matthew Ellison was making the group read books they'd already read. But the messages suggested that the group had enjoyed the books so much that it would be good to revisit certain parts and have a further discussion about them. So, where was the harm in that?

It was then that I noticed the date of the last message. I checked again. I went back to my notes and the details of the night Margaret-Elizabeth had died. There was no doubt about it, despite what Mary Walker had told me earlier, the Facebook group had been wound up two weeks before Margaret-Elizabeth had died.

# FRIDAY

## 35

I'm wandering round my house holding the walking stick aloft, checking the traps I've laid. Except it isn't my house and I can't find my way to the front door. I know I have to get to the front door because I have to go and see Anthony Bridges, but I keep getting lost. There are too many rooms, each one leads to another and it takes me further away from where I want to be. I'm beginning to panic. I'm going to be late. There's a staircase, and I can see my garden out of an open door at the bottom, but as I turn a corner on the stairs I'm taken down a landing and back round to a big bedroom and dressing room where dancers are getting ready for a stage show. Someone thrusts a sequined dress at me and a headdress with feathers, and I shake my head. I don't know the dance, I don't know the song. There's a crowd cheering in the background and I'm carried along with the other dancers towards the stage, fighting against all the bodies to stay backstage. As I break free of the dancers I start to run but a tortoiseshell cat saunters across the hall and I fall, fall into a dark vacuum, tumbling down into nothingness.

The jerk of my head threw me from the dream and I scanned around, momentarily disorientated. As I reached full wakefulness, a piecing pain in my back drove its way into my consciousness and I realised that I was bending over my laptop. My head was pressed against the screen, the laptop resting on my legs, which were tucked underneath me, my back bent almost double. I uncurled myself, taking my time to unwind my back and stretch out my muscles. I wasn't sure how long I'd been in that position but the stiffness of my torso and limbs indicated that it had been quite a while. As I stood up and stretched, the glowing light of dawn was taking hold across the sky and I decided the best thing I could do would be to go for a walk.

I didn't really intend to, but after meandering around absent-mindedly, I somehow ended up back at Jade Griffiths' house. The sun was creeping upwards, painting the sky with fiery red and orange swathes, and I pulled my coat in tightly as the cold air licked around me. I wandered around to the back of the house and peered in through the kitchen window. The little tortoiseshell cat was asleep on one of the kitchen counters; she opened one eye and gazed up at me.

"I bet you're not allowed to sleep up there," I admonished.

She jumped down and pushed her way through the cat flap, purring and meowing and rubbing round and round my legs. She'd eaten all the food I'd left yesterday. Well, it could have been another cat, or a fox even, but the food had all gone so I opened another packet and placed it on the floor for her. This time she looked a little more gracious and started to eat some of the wet food and some of the dry. I should have brought some water, I thought, but when I looked into the kitchen there was a little left in her bowl. Maybe I'd call back with a bowl and a bottle of water later if I had the time.

"What's your name, gorgeous?" I asked, and the cat glanced up at me, then resumed eating without letting on.

She really was a pretty cat, with her one incongruous ginger leg. I sat down on the back doorstep while she finished eating her breakfast. Then she came over and jumped onto my lap, rubbing her head on my chin. Maybe she was grateful that I'd brought her some food. Each time I stopped stroking her, she'd turn to look up at me, then nudge my hand with her head as if to say, 'who said you could stop?'. After a few minutes of kneading my legs with her paws she settled down, curling into a tight ball and purring deeply as she fell asleep. I stroked the top of her head and leaned against the door, looking round the garden and wondering who would come and claim her.

The cat leapt up, clawing at my thighs, startled by the sudden ringing of my phone. It was barely eight o'clock and I had no idea who'd be calling at that time. It was Mike Nash.

"Verity, hi," he said, sounding way too jovial for that time of the morning.

"Mike, what can I do for you?"

"Are you around to meet? I'd like to catch up with you if possible, before I head into work."

"Yes, sure. Do you want to talk now? I don't have much on until I go and see Bridges later." I gave the cat a rub under its chin, then it wandered off and finished the last few dry biscuits.

"Not now, no. Not right now. I'd rather meet if that's okay?"

"Okay," I said, a little unnerved by his caginess. "Where do you want to meet, Mike?"

We settled on a chain café to the south of the city as that was easiest for Mike to access on his way to the police station. I called a cab, gave them Jade's address and gathered my things together.

"Sorry, Peg Leg," I said to the cat, but she didn't seem to care.

She disappeared through the cat flap and I watched through the kitchen window as she jumped back onto the counter, turned round three times and then curled up and went back to sleep. I looked around the kitchen, hoping she had enough water to last. The vision of everyday domesticity I was looking at caught me off guard and I shuffled uneasily as I peered into the sheer normality of an everyday life that would never be resumed. I held up my phone and took a few pictures of the scene; the notes on the fridge door and the keys in a bowl. I wasn't sure they'd be any use, but it couldn't do any harm.

I stood back, tipped out another sachet of food onto the path, and then dipped back under the police tape, around to the front of the house and waited for the taxi to arrive.

## 36

Nash gave a cheery wave from across the café. I indicated that I'd get myself a coffee and joined the queue. The place was busy, presumably with commuters making their way to work, but the baristas worked through the orders with a precision speed and it was only a few minutes before I was sitting down opposite Mike in a seat by a floor-to-ceiling window.

"Now then," he said, rubbing his jaw.

"Mike," I blurted out, before he had chance to speak. "I'm really sorry if I got you into trouble when I told DC Shepherd you'd let me know about Jake Johnson's suicide not being a suicide."

He held up a hand. "Nothing I can't handle there, Verity, nothing at all. But, I will ask you not to repeat anything I'm about to tell you. Not to anyone."

I nodded.

"You understand?" he asked. "It's not about me getting into trouble." He paused. "Although, that is obviously a factor—"

"I understand, yes," I interrupted. "I was stressed. I

wouldn't say anything to harm your reputation." I took a sip of my coffee and tried to squash down the guilt that was threatening to push its way to the surface. Although he was saying it hadn't been a problem, I was convinced that it had caused him more trouble that he was letting on.

This time he held up two hands. "Like I say, like I said before, it isn't a problem. Really. But, I shouldn't be meeting you now. I shouldn't be telling you anything. That's why I didn't want to discuss it over the phone. These are ongoing investigations and I'm really not allowed to discuss them with anyone outside the force." He picked up his tea pot and poured himself a cup of tea, stirring in the milk, then the sugar with a meticulousness that was as frustrating as it was slow. Round and round his spoon went, clanking against the cup. "The thing is," he carried on at length. "The main thing is, that I'm concerned about what's going on."

I shook my head. "What do you mean, Mike? What do you need to tell me? I absolutely promise that I won't tell a soul."

He looked down into his teacup, like a fortune teller studying the messages it held. "Well, first thing, the first thing is that we found your file," he said at last.

"My file? You mean…"

"The file on Margaret-Elizabeth. Yes, the one that was stolen from your house."

"You found it? Where was it?"

"In Jake Johnson's bedroom."

I stared at Nash open-mouthed, furrowing my brow. A weight took hold of my chest, pulling at me as my brain scrambled for anything that would help to make sense of what he had just told me.

Nash nodded. "I know. It's odd. What would Jake Johnson want with the file?"

I thought back to the conversation we'd had when Jake had first been found dead. "We did wonder if his death was connected to Margaret-Elizabeth's," I reminded him. "But what would he take the file for? And why would somebody want to kill him? After he'd taken it…" I rubbed my forehead, ironing out the deep creases that had appeared, and pulled my mouth to one side. "Nash, what does that mean, do you think? That Jake Johnson had the file?"

He shook his head and raised his eyebrows, his eyes closed, as he gave a deep sigh. "I don't know, Verity, I really don't know. If he'd stolen it and someone killed him because they wanted it from him, then why was it still in his bedroom?"

"And why would anyone want it anyway? Especially given that the vast majority of it is still available in the archive on the Herald's website."

"They're stealing information that they could have got without stealing it, you mean?"

I thought about this for a while, grasping at thoughts that came and went like bits of fog in my brain, disappearing as soon as they arrived. "Mike, I've been over and over and over the contents of that file and I can't find anything in there that's incriminating. You know, I'm not sure that anyone really wanted it."

He looked over at me. "What do you mean? Are you thinking the file is a diversion? A red herring?"

I nodded, then thinking aloud I said, "I wonder if the purpose was just to frighten me. To put me off. I mean, there's definitely something that someone doesn't want to come to light. But I don't think it's in that file." The pumping of my heart was getting louder in my ears as I spoke my fears out loud.

"So whoever it was, thought that a burglary would

make you hold your hands up and say 'whoa, this isn't for me'." He opened his mouth wide and laughed, lightening the moment a little. "Then it was someone who doesn't know you very well, Verity. Someone who doesn't know you at all!"

"Yeah, well." I shrugged. "What else is there to do but keep looking? If there really is something new to be found, then that just makes me more determined to get to the bottom of it. And, Mike"—I looked at him—"if they're that desperate, then it's probably something worth keep looking for."

We both sipped our drinks. I cupped my coffee with my hands, deep in thought while Nash poured himself another cup of tea.

After a minute or two I said, "What else was there, Mike? You said 'firstly' before you told me about the file."

"Ah, yes. Well, that's maybe a little more delicate." He began the methodical stirring of his tea once again.

"C'mon, Nash, spill the beans."

He rested his spoon on the saucer. "Well, you may get a call. Correction, you will get a call, later, from DC Shepherd. She'll want you to go to the station and talk to her again." He looked across at me. "The ballerina statue you found?"

I nodded. "Yes?"

"You said you didn't touch it when it was in your bin, apparently."

"I didn't. I had my rubber gloves on." I held up my hands to illustrate.

"Well, what I overheard – it's not my investigation, but...well, you know—"

"Nash! Just tell me," I snapped, the worry getting the better of me.

"The ballerina was covered in fingerprints. But just one set." He paused. "Yours."

"But, how…? I didn't touch it. I swear I didn't." I shuffled in my seat, the growing agitation leaving me unable to sit still.

"I guess the question is, the main question is, if you didn't touch it when it was in your bin, how did it come to have your fingerprints all over it?"

I was rendered speechless for the second time in less than half an hour. I looked at Mike to give me an answer.

"The ballerina was used to hit Jade Griffiths. It's what caused the great cavity in her forehead. So, the question DC Shepherd will be wanting to ask is how your fingerprints got to be on a statue that was used to hit her over the head with."

I opened my mouth and shook my head, unable to find any words. My heart was upping its rhythm, my palms clammy with sweat. I clenched and unclenched my hands, staring wide-eyed at Nash. "I—I never saw the ballerina until she turned up in my bin," I stuttered, running both hands through my hair.

"What DC Shepherd will be asking you about is what happened from when you got to Jade's house until you woke up and called the police."

"I don't know, Nash. I was out cold." I tried to keep my voice level, not wanting to attract the attention of the other customers, but desperation was clawing at my throat. How could they ask me about something I had no recollection of?

Nash held out a hand across the table, patting the air between us. "I should add, Verity, I really need to add that the ballerina was not what killed Jade. There are strong indications that she was strangled well before she was hit over the head."

"Nash!" I exclaimed, banging my hand down on the arm of my chair and causing several people in the café to turn round and stare. "Nash," I repeated in an agitated whisper. "You might have prefaced your story with that piece of information." I clutched at my chest as if I might be able to still my heart from the outside, and I took in a deep breath. "For fuck's sake, I thought you were telling me Shepherd thought that I'd murdered her!"

"Well, I don't think she's completely ruled that out yet," Nash said, not helping the process of slowing my pulse, or easing my laboured breath. "But it's looking very unlikely."

"Very unlikely!" I said through clenched teeth, practically hissing at him across the table. "Nash, she was dead well before she called me." I tipped my head. "You know what I mean."

He nodded and held up his hands. "I'm sorry, Verity, I'm really sorry. I'm not trying to alarm you."

"You could have fooled me," I said, widening my eyes and holding my hands against my head. "She was cold, Mike. When I tried to take her pulse she was cold. Really cold."

"What I hear, what I'm hearing, is that she had been dead for several hours before the phone call was made from her phone to yours."

"They wanted me to go round there," I said almost to myself.

"And the depression in her head was caused after she died. Sometime after, apparently."

I took in a couple of deep breaths, my heart returning to something approaching a more normal pace. I closed my eyes and sucked in my lips. Then I looked Nash directly in the eyes and said, "So, what are you telling me? That someone killed Jade, called me from her mobile a few hours later, knocked me out and…what? Made me hit her on the head whilst I was unconscious?"

"I'm imagining they hit her on the head themselves, wiped the ballerina clean and then pressed your hand all over it. Then they must have dumped the ballerina in your bin whilst you were at the police station."

"So someone's trying to frame me?"

"If they are, they're doing a very amateur job of it. Your movements are well documented, and you were nowhere near Jade's at her time of death. The doctor very quickly established that she'd been dead some time when she was hit with the ballerina, and the fact that there are only your fingerprints on it would be a bit suspicious in itself. It's all a bit clumsy."

"Maybe they're just upping their efforts to put me off. To try to stop me looking any further into things. Or to slow me down."

Nash looked at the floor. He lowered his voice. "I'm telling you this, Verity, because I think you need to be very careful. Whatever's going on, two people are dead. I don't want any more adding to that list. And I certainly don't want it to be you."

"I'm not giving up."

"No. I wasn't expecting you to. Just be careful, Verity. Be very careful." He paused. "And maybe think about staying somewhere else for a few nights, eh?"

I bit on my bottom lip, visualising all my intruder traps. "I'll think about it, Nash. I will. But I don't want to get anyone else involved if it's not necessary. Someone's been following me and if I stayed over at a friend's…well, I don't want to take any risks. I don't want any of my friends involved in this."

"You could check into a hotel for a few nights?"

I thought about it. I had enough of the Ellisons' money to allow me to do that. I nodded at Nash, "I'll think about," I said, but I knew that I probably wouldn't.

We stood up to leave, walking together to the exit. Nash's car was parked right outside and he blipped the locks open. He pulled open the driver's door and then looked over at me. "Take care, Verity," he said. Then he tapped his finger against his nose and added, "And when DC Shepherd calls, act surprised, won't you?"

"I'll be winning an Oscar," I promised.

## 37

I was walking back home when my phone rang. I looked at the unknown number calling and as I answered I steeled myself for an uncomfortable conversation with DC Shepherd.

"Hello," I answered, adding a breezy tone to my voice to try to convey an air of carefreeness; of someone who hadn't caved in a stranger's head.

"Is that Verity Spencer?" said a female voice I didn't recognise.

"It is, yes. How can I help?"

"I'm Angela Thompson. You left me a voicemail a couple of days ago. Sorry it's taken me a while to get back to you."

"No worries," I said.

It turned out that Angela Thompson had moved out of Lincoln a few years ago, into one of the villages nearby. She was heading into town to do some shopping and wondered if I'd be free to meet up.

"I can meet this morning," I offered. "I have an appointment this afternoon, but I'm free right now."

After some prevarication we arranged to meet in just over an hour, in a café in the Bailgate area of town, uphill, not far from where I lived. Angela said that she was used to parking not far from the castle and that would make it easier for her, so we agreed on the venue and said our goodbyes.

I sauntered along, watching the city waking up as I went. Workers busied themselves unlocking shop fronts, setting out tables and chairs, positioning A boards that advertised their wares. A small queue of people waited outside one of the banks, tapping their feet and checking their watches. Early shoppers rushed past, heads bowed, bags in hand. As I made my way to the foot of Steep Hill, I pulled my coat up to protect my neck, the chill wind wrapping itself around my body like a snake. I paused to window shop but didn't really take in what I was looking at. My mind was elsewhere. I couldn't shake the image of Jade from my head. In a repeated pattern, the memories kept invading my brain; waking up, finding Jade, the coldness of her wrist, the wound in her head, that stray hair in the corner of her mouth, then back to waking up again. What *had* happened between me arriving at Jade's and me finding her body?

I went over it again as I made my way up the hill. The light in the front room, the television broadcasting to an empty space. Both had been turned off by the time I'd been standing at the front of the house later that evening. What else? A half-drunk cup of tea. The light on behind the little window in the side of the house, which was suddenly turned off as I approached. Tripping over, falling against the doorstep. Rolling over into the garden. Then what? My brain was trying to rescue a memory, trying to hook onto something, but it was refusing to be caught.

I surprised myself as I looked around. I was halfway up Steep Hill, lost in thought. I hadn't even noticed the gradient. I glanced at my watch; I was early for Angela Thompson, but it wasn't worth going home, so at the top of the hill I took a detour through the grounds of the castle. I'd come out the other side and double back along the road to the café where we'd agreed to meet. As I entered through the stone arch, the low sun dipped in and out of clouds, forming patches of light and dark green across the lawn. Shadows raced across the grass that disappeared over the walls and into the streets beyond.

Away across the castle grounds, to the side of the Gothic style courthouse, a group of workmen were laying stone flags, cutting them with an angle grinder and bashing them into place with rubber mallets. A man held a hammer aloft; I was unsure what he was about to hit but it stopped me in my tracks. As he lifted the hammer high above his head a memory shot into my head like a high speed train; I was lying on the grass at Jade's house and someone was looming over me, holding something, bringing something down towards my head. That was when it had all gone black. That was when I'd lost consciousness.

I stood there, staring, watching the men working; cutting, placing, hammering, tapping. There was something about the memory that was niggling, something that my mind was keeping from me. A piece of the picture was firing sparks, but they were going nowhere, fading and dying like the embers of a spent firework.

Children ran out of the Victorian prison building, skipping across the lawn, followed by harassed-looking parents. The children circled their parents like tiny screaming vultures, tugging at jumpers and hands, begging to be allowed to walk round the ramparts. I watched as they span and tumbled up the stone stairs, running around the ancient walls and gazing over at the cathedral opposite. Whatever was pulling at my brain would have to wait. It was time to go and meet Angela Thompson.

I didn't have time to go through the castle grounds and along the road. Instead I doubled back, left the way I'd gone in and headed straight for the café where I'd agreed to meet Angela. She was there when I arrived, a statuesque and striking black lady. She wore a scarf around her hair and a smart tweed suit coupled with flat black shoes. Even with no additional elevation she must have topped six feet and as she stood up to shake my hand she towered above me. She stared down at me with piercing blue eyes that seemed to sparkle against her dark skin and I was captivated by the unusual contrast.

After ordering coffee, I thanked her for returning my call and double checked against my notes the names and ages of her children.

"Hannah," she said. "She's twenty-one now. She still lives in Lincoln. When we moved to Fiskerton a few years ago, she wanted to stay in the city. She moved in with her boyfriend, Alex. We gave them a couple of months, but they've proved us wrong. That must have been three years ago now and they're still together. Planning on getting married next year."

"We?" I asked. "Sorry, that sounded a bit blunt. I mean, in all the reports I've read you are described as a single parent."

"No worries," she said. "Yes, it's true. I was. I met Michael about five years ago. That's why I moved. We'd both been single for some time; both single parents. We wanted somewhere new. Somewhere that was ours, with no memories of other halves."

"That makes sense." I paused. "So Hannah is your eldest?"

"Ah, yes and then there's Callum. He's twelve now. He spends term times in a special school; he's got, well, certain difficulties. He lives there during the term and comes home for holidays." She looked down at her hands, her face betraying a vulnerability that was at odds with the strength of her build. "Mind you, I think he's happier at school if I'm honest. He loves the routine. He loves the teachers and his carers. I like having him home though. While I can. I think there'll come a day when it isn't possible, but not yet."

"So he would have been, what two or three when Margaret-Elizabeth died?"

"About that yes. Hannah was about eleven or twelve."

"Was she friends with Margaret-Elizabeth?"

"Yes, they were great friends. They were at different primary schools, but they were due to go to the same secondary school in the September. I think they'd been to one induction day, or an introductory session or something. They were really excited to be going to the same school." She rummaged around in her handbag and pulled out her phone, scrolling back through the years until she found a photo of Hannah and Margaret-Elizabeth together.

She passed me the phone. Hannah was tall like her mother, a good head and shoulders taller than Margaret-Elizabeth, with paler skin than Angela but the same piercing blue eyes. The two girls stood side by side, grinning into the camera, Hannah with her right arm around Margaret-Elizabeth's shoulders.

"Do you think Hannah might talk to me?" I asked, handing her back the phone.

She sprang back in the chair and looked at me, her brow furrowed and her mouth set straight. "What would Hannah be able to tell you?" she asked. The change in her demeanour was stark. I'd touched a nerve.

"It doesn't matter," I backtracked, not wanting to lose any momentum.

"I can't see what Hannah has to do with anything."

"No, no. It doesn't matter. I just thought it would be nice to hear about Margaret-Elizabeth, from a friend of hers. A different perspective." I shook my head and leaned forward, trying to reconnect with her. "It really doesn't matter."

She bit her bottom lip, then took a sip of the sparkling water she had in front of her. "Sorry," she said. "But Hannah was hit hard by Margaret-Elizabeth's death, and I really don't think she'd want to rake over old ground."

I switched tack. "The night Margaret-Elizabeth died, you were at the Walkers' with the others?"

She nodded.

"It was book club night and you were all there together?"

She nodded again, looking up at me without lifting her head.

"What book were you reading?"

She blinked rapidly, leaning back in her chair. "I really can't remember. Why on earth would it matter?"

"I was looking through the messages on the Facebook group and it isn't really very clear what book you were reading at the time. It's just that the group seems to have been closed down a couple of weeks before Margaret-Elizabeth died."

She opened her mouth, but said nothing.

"I'm just trying to set the background for myself. You know, for what happened that night."

Angela Thompson stood up, picking up her handbag.

She pulled herself to her full height and looked down at me, sitting in my chair. "I thought you were going to be asking me serious questions," she said. She didn't wait for a response. "But I can see that this is going to be a complete waste of my time." She threw me a withering glance, turned on her heel then marched out of the door, slamming it behind her.

"Well, that went well," I said to what I thought was an empty café, although I heard a stifled sniggering from behind the counter somewhere. I drank up my coffee, paid for both drinks, then headed home.

## 38

When I got home I leaned against the kitchen counter looking at the photos I'd taken of Jade's kitchen. The little cat appeared in a couple and I wondered how she was, hoping she'd have enough water to last her. I presumed someone knew about her and would go round and take her home, or at least to a rehoming place before too long.

I zoomed in on the photos and scanned around Jade's kitchen. An uneasy sense of over-intrusiveness stung at my conscience; picking over a dead person's intimate life didn't sit well, especially as I couldn't see that there would be anything of any use. Still, I carried on scanning, the unease not strong enough to stop me. I guessed I'd already taken the pictures so I might as well look at them.

The kitchen had all the features of modern domesticity; a built-in oven and microwave, an under-counter washing machine, appliances filling the corners of the counters. Next to the sink, a cup stood upside down on the draining board, a teaspoon next to it, a plate resting against it. The ordinariness of it all was heart breaking. I went back to the picture that showed the fridge-freezer. It stood against the far wall, next to a door that I assumed went through to a hallway. Various notes and business cards, photos and lists formed a haphazard pattern and I studied them all methodically to make sure I didn't miss anything.

A couple of the photos showed Jade with another young lady. The blonde lady oozed confidence, her radiant smile lighting up the photo. Jade appeared a little more reserved, her smile muted in comparison. The pair appeared to be on holiday somewhere, the mountainous backdrop and crystal blue sky not indicative of a British landscape. In another photo, Jade stood in front of the Eiffel Tower, a road bike held in front of her, her fist held aloft, and I took this to indicate that she'd ridden the bike there. The Let's Kill Cancer logo on her T shirt suggested that this might have been a charitable ride.

I moved along the fridge door, past a taxi card held in place with a Miss Piggy fridge magnet. Various muppets kept other assorted items in their place. Kermit guarded a shopping list: milk, coffee, potatoes, cat food. The Cookie Monster, a recipe for chocolate brownies. Beneath Bert and Ernie was a list of phone numbers. I zoomed in as far as I could, moving the zoom back and forth until I was close enough to see the numbers but before they became blurred. There were three phone numbers on the list and I started to scribble them down. The first and second number were clear and visible but the paper was turned up at the corner, obscuring the last two numbers of the third. I wrote it down nonetheless, in case I ever had the inclination to try out the hundred different combinations to figure out what the last two numbers were.

Grabbing my phone, I tapped in the first number. It just rang and rang. No one picked up and there was no option to leave a voicemail. I tried the second one. This one rang about six times, then the click of a voicemail came and a male voice said,

*"Hi, you've reached the voicemail for Jake Johnson, you know what to do. I'll get back to you soon."*

I rested my phone on the counter and stared at the photo. In amongst all of Jade's personal photos, shopping lists, the daily normality of everyday life, was the phone number of someone who had been killed just a day before she was.

Without really thinking, I grabbed my car keys and jacket then headed for the door. I wanted to get into jade's house and try to find out why she had Jake Johnson's number. By the front door, I stopped myself, thinking that I'd need a good excuse in case anyone saw me, especially given the police tape strung across the garden. I also needed some tools to try to get through the door. I'd heard about people breaking into houses by using their credit cards. In case it wasn't that simple, I took a few other items with me; a knife, a coat hanger, a thin plastic spatula. Then I found a bottle of water and a bowl to leave for the cat, and with that I headed straight out of the door and back to the house.

The cat came flying out of the cat flap, rubbing round and round my legs and meowing plaintively.

"Hello, Peg Leg," I said. "Don't try telling me you're hungry, I was here not long ago so I know you've got a full tummy."

I looked at the back door. It was closed with a typical mortice lock. I stared at my ragtag collection of breaking and entering implements and thought that they were going to fall well short of the mark. As I was walking round to the front of the house, the next-door neighbour looked up from clipping the edges of his impeccable lawn and caught my eye.

"How d'ya do?" he said.

"Hi," I said, smiling and wishing that he would go inside. He didn't, he carried on clipping the lawn. The front door was secured with a yale lock, much easier to squeeze something round and open it up, but Mr Nosey was still there, clipping away. I scouted around under plant pots and rocks, behind bushes and in flower beds trying to see if there was a spare key anywhere but there was nothing. I imagined if there had been the police would have found it and taken it away. As I stood up and glared at the lock, wondering whether my thin plastic spatula would have enough strength to push the snick of the lock back, a voice interrupted my thoughts.

"Are you okay there?" the neighbour asked, peering over the hydrangea that I'd thought had given me some cover.

I stood up and flashed him a wide grin. "Err...hello!" I said, smoothing down my clothes. "Hi."

"Can I help?"

"Well, the thing is," I said, desperately scrabbling in my brain for an excuse that sounded marginally plausible. "I'm Jade's cousin."

"Oh," the neighbour said, resting his arms on his long-handled shears. "I'm really sorry about...you know. Lovely girl. Such a shame." He looked to be in his seventies and his weather-beaten face took on a defeated appearance, his jowls drooping as he leaned his chin on his hands. He shook his head. "I don't know what the world is coming to," he said. "I'm really sorry for you, I am."

"Yes, I...err...thank you," I said. "I, well, my mum,

that's Jade's aunt, asked me to come round and feed the cat." I pointed to the water and the bowl as if that would give a little more weight to my paper thin cover story. "It's just that she said Jade left a spare key in the garden, but I can't find it." I pointed to the police tape still fluttering to the back of the house. "I wonder if the police might have taken it. I put some food out the back, but I need to get in and…" I grasped for a reason. "Empty the litter tray. Mum doesn't want the house to smell." I smiled.

"Okay, well I don't think she ever left a key in the garden, I think your mum's got the wrong end of the stick there. She was quite security conscious."

"Oh, okay," I said, eyeing up my tools out the corner of my eye and wondering how long he was going to be in the garden.

"But she gave me a spare key. I can let you in if you like. You won't be long will you? it's just…" he trailed off so I wasn't quite sure what his reasoning was, although I suspected he was a little wary.

"No, no," I said. "I just need to sort out the cat, I'll be in and out in five minutes."

He tipped his finger to his forehead and headed into his house, before re-emerging a couple of minutes later with the key in his hand. And I added breaking and entering on the list of things I'd need to discuss with DC Shepherd when she rang me later.

"Lovely girl, Jade," he said, as he let me into her house. "Were you close?"

"Yes," I lied. "Yes, although she was younger than me, but our families are close."

"I'll just let you go in, then," he said, hovering by the front door. "I'll wait here."

I scooped up the water and the bowl and stuffed my makeshift tools into my handbag, hoping that the old man hadn't seen them. I walked through Jade's house and into the kitchen. The neighbour loitered by the front door and I pushed the kitchen door a little so that it didn't appear that I was being rude, but obscured me from his view. The cat came clattering through the cat flap and stood expectantly by her food bowl.

"Now you're pushing your luck," I told her.

I went through Jade's kitchen opening all the drawers. Cutlery, tea towels, a drawer of oddments. I wasn't sure what I was looking for, but it wasn't knives and forks. Or stray screws.

"Are you local then?" the question drifted down from the front door.

"Yes," I shouted back, opening a cupboard filled with plates and bowls.

"So I guess you helped Jade move in? I thought I'd seen you before."

"Yes, that was probably it," I said, thinking it was more likely he'd caught sight of me being loaded into a police car the other day.

I sneaked past the half-closed kitchen door, stealing a glance down the hall. He was standing in the open door-way, looking out into the garden. The dining room was adjacent to the kitchen, so I tiptoed past the door into the hallway, pushing it almost closed as I crept through. This was clearly a room that wasn't used very often. A fold-down table was pushed against one wall, but no chairs were evident. Some stacking plastic crates stood in one corner, neatly labelled; 'books', 'winter boots', 'Christmas decorations'. A dark wood chest of drawers was placed on the wall opposite the table, piled with empty boxes and packaging, I assumed in case the purchases needed returning. I wished that I was as well organised.

"That would have been, let me think, how long since Jade moved here?"

I was stumped, I had no idea. I looked around thinking that the house looked as if it had been occupied a while. Jade must have been in her early twenties, so it could have been anything from a few months to a couple of years. "Gosh," I shouted back. "Time flies, I can't remember."

One by one, I went through all the drawers, peering over my shoulder every few seconds to check that the neighbour hadn't crept in and seen me. There were files with payslips, energy bills, bank statements, insurance documents. Jade's whole life neatly arranged before me. I rummaged through some old diaries, barely filled in, some unopened toiletries.

"Are you nearly done?" the neighbour's voice pierced my thoughts once again as he closed in on me down the hallway.

I slammed the drawer shut and ran through to the kitchen, bumping into him in the doorway. "I'm sorry," I said, and I hung my head low, rubbing my eyes with the cuff of my sleeve. "I'm sorry. This…is…so…hard." And I took in a gulp of air and feigned a sob.

"Hey," the neighbour said, resting a hand on my elbow. "Don't worry, take your time. I just have to get going soon."

"I'll be two minutes," I said through my hands and heaved another great sob.

The neighbour moved towards the front door, and I shot back to the chest of drawers, picking my way through appliance manuals, guarantees, rental agreements. I sat on the floor. There was nothing here. And I couldn't go through the entire house, not with the neighbour standing over me. I bent forwards and rested on my hands, shouting out to the neighbour, "Almost done, I'll be right there." As I went to stand up, I leaned on the chest of drawers for support, pushing it and moving it a fraction. Something fell to the ground. Something had been stuck behind the drawers and the wall. A slim blue notebook. I wondered if the cat might have pushed it off the top. I reached under the drawers and picked it up, flipping through the pages. On the first page, an intricate doodle spelled out the words 'Jade's Lincoln Japes Blog'. I stuffed it into my handbag and ran through to the kitchen.

"Just finishing," I shouted out to the man. I scanned around the kitchen and as I passed the fridge freezer I pulled the list of phone numbers from underneath the Bert and Ernie magnet and placed it between the pages of the notebook.

"Need any help?" the neighbour asked, lumbering back down the hallway and opening the kitchen door fully. He laid a sympathetic hand on my back.

"No, I'm good." I nodded, his gesture of kindness in the face of my lying, catching me off guard. I said nothing, just looked at him and smiled.

"Then let's go," he said, thankfully not appearing to notice that there was no trace of a litter tray to be seen.

I let him get halfway to the front door. "One sec," I said and ran back into the kitchen. Glancing over my shoulder to check that he wasn't looking, I grabbed the key out of the back door and rammed it into my pocket. You never knew.

I was just heading back towards the hallway when I heard the old man saying, "Oh, hello. I thought you'd finished here."

That was followed by the voice of DC Shepherd saying, "Just a few things we need to tie up."

*Shit! Fuck!* DC Shepherd already had me down as a potential murder suspect. This wasn't going to help. I tiptoed over to the fridge freezer and slid the list of numbers back under the Bert and Ernie magnet, then crept to the back door.

DC Shepherd was asking the elderly neighbour what he was doing, lingering there in the doorway.

"I just let Jade's cousin in, you know. She's sorting out the cat."

I looked at the empty bowl of food and swore again. I grabbed one of the packets off the counter, ripping it open and tipping it into the food bowl. Then I rammed the empty packet into my pocket. It oozed liquid cat food all over my jacket.

*Keep her talking, keep her talking,* I repeated silently as I made my way, once again, to the back door. I pulled the key out of my pocket, dripping now with cat food and fumbled with the lock.

"Thanks, sir, you don't need to stay," DC Shepherd was saying.

"But, the young lady—" he protested.

*Good, good, keep talking.* I twisted the key in the lock, holding it tight, trying not to make a sound. I inched the door open.

"Don't worry, we'll take care of that."

*Fuck!* I didn't have time to escape. I left the door as it was, then crept back into the house, scanning around me for somewhere to hide. I made for the space under the sink, there'd be nothing of interest there and it had no shelf. I could squash in there. I opened the door and slid inside, pulling the door shut with a tea towel hook.

It was tight. I had my knees up to my face, pushing into my cheeks and a bottle of bleach digging into my side.

There were footsteps now in the kitchen, clip clopping across the tiled floor.

"What we looking for?" a male voice said.

"Anything that ties Jade to Jake Johnson," DC Shepherd's voice replied. "You look in there and I'll look in the front room."

"I thought SOCO had been all over the house."

"They have," DC Shepherd said. "I'm not sure we'll find anything, but let's have a quick look around. Anywhere she might have some paperwork."

There was silence for a few seconds. Then DC Shepherd's voice crossing the kitchen floor. "I'm not sure what that old man was doing. Look, the cat's bowl's full." A pause, then her voice again, from the direction of the door this time. "There's no one else here, no one in the garden either. I reckon he was feeding it himself, didn't want to say he'd let himself into the house. He's left the door open though." The back door closed, then there was the sound of a key turning in the lock.

I strained to hear. Footsteps walking away from me; drawers opening and closing in the next room. I held my breath, clinging onto the tea towel holder to keep the door closed. I wished they'd hurry up. A sharp cramp stabbed into my calf and I bit my lip as I struggled not to react. I couldn't stretch my toes out, there wasn't room; I clenched my teeth and bit through the pain until the cramp subsided.

Eventually I heard the clip clop sound of heels on tiles and DC Shepherd's voice once again. "Anything?"

"Not in here," the male voice replied.

"C'mon," DC Shepherd said. "Let's have a quick look upstairs. You take the back bedroom I'll have a look in the front. Then we're out of here."

I held my ear against the door, breathing as shallowly as

I could. Stairs creaked, muffled voices now from afar. I inched the door open and unfolded myself from inside the cupboard, hobbling uncomfortably towards the door. Biting on my lips, I turned the key little by little then pulled on the door until it was open enough to slip through. I shot out, sliding it shut behind me, unable to lock it. I hoped DC Shepherd, if she checked it, would just assume she hadn't locked it before.

I slid along the side of the house, edging forward, creeping towards the front. The coast was clear. My heart leapt into my mouth as the old man appeared around the corner of Jade's front wall, peering down and staring straight in my eyes. My legs almost gave way as our eyes locked, me creeping out of the house. My mind thought of a hundred, equally implausible reasons I could give to DC Shepherd as to why I'd been in Jade's house, and why the neighbour had thought I was her cousin. I froze, mid-step, barely breathing, the blood in my body appearing to have stopped pumping. Everything had ground to a halt.

The old man froze too, staring me in the eyes.

I put my fingers to my lips, nodded my head in the direction of the house and then drew a finger across my throat. Heaven knows what he thought I was doing, sneaking out of the house like that, and he had no reason at all to help me. He must have had some empathy for my situation though, because he glanced at the front door and touched the side of nose. He held his left hand up a little, palm towards me. After several seconds he moved his hand and started to beckon me forward. Crouching in a half-upright position, I ran along the side of the house, past the wheelie bins, towards him.

"Quick," he said in a stage whisper.

The coast was clear. "Thank you," I whispered as I tiptoed past and leapt into my car.

As I completed a hasty three-point turn in the road, the elderly neighbour stood in his front garden, his long-handled shears once again in his hands and he touched his forehead with his finger before resuming his clipping.

## 39

---

I should have been preparing for my meeting with Anthony Bridges. I had less than two hours before I'd be sitting opposite him. But Jade's notes were fascinating.

In the thin blue notebook, there wasn't a huge amount written down, but the doodle in the front of the book related to a blog that she'd been writing online. Jade's Lincoln Japes Blog, the doodle replicated in electronic format. The blog had a very amateur feel about it, there was nothing sophisticated. It looked as if it had been written on some free software with no additional frills. There were a few posts, an introduction and a couple of short blogs.

The introduction was dated a few months ago.

*Hi I'm Jade. Welcome to my life. I live in Lincoln and I work in a local charity shop. I've decided to write this blog as a catharsis. It's no secret that I've had therapy for several years. I was assaulted on my way home from school when I was a teenager and it affected me quite badly. I guess the fact that the same creepy guy went on to*

*murder a little girl really did my head in. That could have
been me. Anyway, here I am. Still alive. Still coping, just.
And I thought it would be good to just write down my
thoughts in a blog.*

*So, here goes. As I say, welcome to my life. I'm going to be
posting things about how I'm feeling, up days and down
days, what works for me. So any tips for relaxation,
support and so on, please leave a comment. Or DM me if
you want it to be private. Please get in touch if you've had
a similar experience, any kind of assault or abuse. If we
help each other it makes it easier. Let's get through this
together!*

The blog page informed me that the introductory post
had had fifty-seven views and six likes. There were no
comments.

A few weeks later, there was another short post.

*Hi folks! Well, here's my latest update. I'm doing okay,
thanks for all who asked and I guess my blog touched a
nerve as I've had some messages from people who'd like to
get support from, and give support to, other people who've
been through similar experiences. Thank you, guys! I
don't want you to leave comments on here because it's an
open forum for everyone to see, but maybe we could have
an online closed group or a get-together for the local folks,
if you like.*

*So, here's what's been happening for me. I've been doing
some research into the guy who assaulted me. He's a far-
right politician it seems. I don't know why I want to find
out more about him. I can't explain it. Nobody in my life
thinks that it's a good thing to do, which is why I'm telling
you guys, I think you'll understand. And I know you'll*

*offer support. I guess I want to try and find out what his motivation was.*

*So people out there, get in touch! I'll post a few photos and pictures and stuff soon! Love ya, Jade.*

There were a couple of comments on this post. Two people saying they would send Jade a direct message, another from @FranDan said:

*Hi Jade, looking forward to reading your blog, I totally get why you want to find out about the man who assaulted you. You want to get in his head. Eww…not nice, but I so understand that. Good luck, looking forward to reading more on the blog.*

The blog post had been seen by forty-seven people and three had liked it, although there was no way of knowing who those people were.

Following that, there were one or two posts that mentioned places Jade had visited in Lincoln, bars and restaurants, some recommendations, an offer from a local shop. Nothing of interest. The last entry made me sit up though. It had been posted a couple of weeks ago.

*Hi my friends! Well I've had an interesting few weeks. Great to meet some of you and talk to others virtually and on the phone. I think we are developing a great idea about how we can support each other in the future, which is amazing! We are stronger together and can get great comfort from knowing that we are not alone and are supporting each other.*

*In other news, I don't want to sound like a conspiracy theorist, but listen! I can't reveal sources and I don't want to say too much yet, but there's been a real twist in things. You all know that I've been looking into the guy who assaulted me, don't you? You all know that this is the guy that is supposed to have murdered Margaret-Elizabeth Ellison. Well, from conversations I've been having with certain people, certain people who don't want to be named I should say, I think there was something else going on. Something dark and worrying. And the whole Margaret-Elizabeth thing is just a diversion. Folks, I think the accusation of murder against Bridges is just a smokescreen.*

A smokescreen.

## 40

I stood outside Lincoln prison and smoothed down my skirt. After reviewing Jade's blog posts I'd run upstairs and changed into something that I hoped made me look business-like and authoritarian. I was wearing a wool suit, with a straight pencil skirt and a tailored jacket, a floral silk scarf around my neck. All I needed was a pair of horn-rimmed glasses and I'd have had the librarian look nailed. I'd bought the suit years ago when I'd given a speech at a conference in front of hundreds of college lecturers on the impact of childhood trauma on adult learning. For the most part it seemed to have fallen on deaf ears, although a few people came up and engaged in debate after the event was over.

Was it the right look for a prison visit though? I had no idea, but I'd been through a dozen outfits prior to this one. And here I was. It would have to do. I stepped over the threshold into a reception area, where I gave my name and the name of the person I was visiting, and then I waited with several other visitors until the appointed time had been reached. Everyone else wore some kind of lanyard round their necks, or name badge on their lapel. Everyone else looked as if they'd been here many times before. Several greeted each other, as well as the guards. There were no family visitors here, I guessed there must be separate visiting hours for family and professionals. I didn't feel very professional. I felt like an imposter. I thought someone would point me out and ask me to leave at any moment. I sat in a corner, picking at my nails. To keep my nerves from getting the better of me, I rehearsed my questions over and over until a guard arrived and called us.

The guard led us through an open courtyard and we headed for the main prison building, where he unlocked the door and ushered us all through. We were instructed to wait in a hallway, clinically white and with barred windows high up near the ceiling. He locked the door behind us before walking to the far end and unlocking that door, which was also promptly locked as soon as we were all the other side of it. I followed along behind the others, hoping that I looked as if I knew what I was doing. All our bags were searched by a guard and then scanned by an x-ray machine. Once we were all given the okay, we were ushered as a group through another series of secured doors before we reached the visiting room. It had the appearance of an old-style school gym, set out for an exam. Desks were placed at intervals of several metres, with a chair either side. I was directed to a particular table and told to sit to the left of it and wait there.

All the visitors took the seats they were directed to and we sat in silence for several minutes. The sense of being unable to leave unless someone else let me out was strangely unnerving. Several locked doors lay between me and the outside world and the sensation was weird and unpalatable. Again, the windows were barred and so high you couldn't see out of them. They should bring youngsters here on school trips, I thought, scanning the room around me and taking in the men standing guard, the locked and armoured doors; if this didn't put them off committing crime, nothing would.

I glanced up at the sound of another door unlocking, this time at the far end of the room. Prisoners wearing orange vests filed into the room, heading straight for certain desks. I recognised Bridges from his photos the minute he walked through the door, his bald head bobbing as he walked towards me. His thick, rubbery lips curled into a smile as he approached. He pulled out the chair and sat down opposite me without any formalities or introductions.

"Thanks for letting me come to see you," I ventured.

Bridges pushed his chair back a few inches and spread his knees out wide, tilting his head to one side and pursing his lips. He clasped his hands and let them rest in the gap between his legs. "So," he said, "you're working for the Ellisons?"

I swallowed, smoothing my skirt and repositioning myself in my seat. I looked up at him; he was leaning back, his feet splayed out under the table, an air of untouchability about him. "I'm reviewing all the information about Margaret-Elizabeth's death, yes."

"And?" he asked. "Have you come to any conclusion yet?" His top lip formed into a sneer.

"I just wanted to ask you a few questions, if that's okay," I said, ignoring his goading.

He spread his arms out wide. "Ask away," he said. "I can't guarantee that I'll answer, but you can ask."

I sat up straight and tucked my feet under my chair,

crossing them at the ankles. "The night that Margaret-Elizabeth died?"

He nodded, slumping further into his chair. He put his hands back together, resting them against his lower abdomen.

"You were there. In the park. In amongst the trees. What brought you there?"

"I heard shouting. I went to see what was happening. I saw something on the ground, bent down to see what it was, realised it was a child. And then someone called out and I left them to it. That's it. That's the sum of my involvement."

"You didn't stay to help?"

He shifted in his seat, pushing his legs out to the side of the desk. "No."

"You didn't try to revive Margaret-Elizabeth?"

"No."

"Had you followed Margaret-Elizabeth home from school before?"

He looked away. "No."

"She said you had."

He licked his lips. "Maybe I did, then."

"Wasn't that what you'd done before? Followed schoolgirls and then exposed yourself to them?"

He scoffed. "If you say so."

"What were you doing in the woods that night?"

"I was on my way home." He unclasped his hands and used them to push himself up in his chair. "Are you going to ask me anything that I haven't already answered?"

I took a breath. I could see why people found him intimidating but I wasn't going to allow him to rattle me. "Where had you been?"

"Why is that important?"

"Well it might give you a good reason to have been there that didn't involve murdering a child."

He sat upright, shuffled forward in his seat, propped his elbow on the desk and pointed his finger towards my face. "It's none of yours or anyone else's business where I'd been, but I'll tell you something. I did not murder that child." He leaned back. "Now, any sensible questions?"

"Tell me about Pure Britain."

"What's to tell?" he asked, spreading his arms wide. "It's a political party. That's it."

"It's got some quite extreme views."

"Depends what you're comparing them to." He turned his hands palm up. "We have plenty of supporters."

"Do you use the money that people donate through PayPal for your own ends?" I asked.

"I use it to further the aims of the party."

"Does that include your own living expenses?" I looked around me. "I mean, obviously, when you have living expenses."

He glanced off to one side, running his tongue over his teeth. Then he stared back at me. "What I spend my money on is none of your business."

"Did you set up a charity to bring Asian families to Lincoln? To house them and find them jobs?"

"Have you read the aims of my party?"

I nodded.

He pointed at me. "The problem with this country is too many fucking foreigners coming over here, thinking it's a cushy number. Thinking we'll feed them, house them, give them jobs." He pointed to the barred windows as if there might be hordes of refugees out there.

"Wouldn't it be a great way to prove that you were right? Wouldn't it help you to prove your point? Bring people into the city so that you can poke your finger at them?"

"Give it a rest. You're off into the realms of conspiracy theories now. Next you'll be telling me the holocaust didn't happen." He opened his mouth wide and gave a guffaw. I wasn't sure if he was suggesting that, in all likeliness, he believed that to be the case. But I was in no mood to explore that one with him.

"Okay. Let's go back to the night Margaret-Elizabeth died. Tell me what you were doing in the woods that night."

"Walking home."

"From where?" I asked. "A pub? A friend's?"

"Yeah, probably."

"Which?"

"Take your pick," he said and sighed, crossing his arms across his chest.

"Fine. Tell me what you know about Jade Griffiths."

"Who?" he said, an air of nonchalance in his voice, but he sat up and leaned forward, his body language not matching his tone of voice.

"Jade. You know, the young girl whose breasts you groped on her way home from school."

"What about her?"

"She was doing some research into you, recently. Why do you think that was?"

"How the fuck should I know?"

"You know she died a couple of days ago?"

He looked across at me, his tongue between his lips but he said nothing.

"Yeah," I said, trying to sound as casual as I could. "Murdered. In her own garden."

"Why would I know anything about that?" He gesticulated around him, indicating the locked doors and barred windows.

"You have friends. People. Some powerful people."

He pointed his finger at my face, inches away from me. His warm, salty breath puffing into my face. He stared at me, but said nothing.

I kept my position. I wasn't going to move back or give any indication that my heart was pumping so fast and hard that I worried he'd be able to hear it. "So?"

"So? So fucking what. You think I have enough influence that I can order a murder from my prison cell? You've been watching too many movies, sweetheart."

I leaned in towards him. Both our elbows on the table, our faces inches apart. A guard twitched in the corner of the room. I leaned in closer. "Don't call me sweetheart," I hissed at him across the desk, my finger almost touching his face. "Tell me what you know about Jade's murder."

We glowered at each other for what seemed like a lifetime. I set my jaw hard and stared into his eyes, unblinking. He sat back and looked away.

He stared back at me, puckering his lips into a lopsided sneer. "I. Fucking. Know. Nothing," he said. "Shitting hell. I've spent the last ten years with one murder accusation against me. Now you're trying to pin another one on me. What gives you the idea that I know anything about it?"

"She was writing a blog," I said. "She was researching you and your history."

"And?"

"She thought you were hiding something."

"What, precisely?"

"She didn't elaborate."

"Tell me about this blog," he said, sitting back in his chair and folding his arms.

"Her last entry was only a couple of weeks ago. She said she'd discovered something. She said she was fairly convinced that the accusation of murder, that you'd murdered Margaret-Elizabeth, that it was a smokescreen. A smokescreen for something darker."

"What did she say exactly?"

I fished out my notebook and read it out. "That the accusation of murder against Bridges was just a smokescreen."

"I think she was probably right," he said, tilting his head to one side, a smile spreading across his face.

"How do you mean?"

"You're barking up the wrong tree," he said. "You think I was trying to hide something?"

"Well, if not, what did she mean?"

"You need to start looking closer to home, my dear. What if it was convenient to blame me? What if accusing me was a smokescreen for someone else?"

"What are you suggesting?"

"I'm not suggesting anything at all," he said, rubbing his chin with his hand. He pointed towards me. "You're the fucking investigator, you join the dots."

Our time was up. The guards indicated that we needed to wrap up. My brain was whizzing, parts of the puzzle were shifting, some things that had made sense seemed no longer to make sense, and other things that hadn't made sense had a new light shining on them. Pieces were moving like one of those puzzles where you moved squares one at a time until the picture became clear. The picture was far from clear, but several more pieces were sliding into place.

I stood up and looked down at Bridges. "Thanks for agreeing to see me," I said. "It's been really helpful."

He glanced up at me. "You know," he said. "I've done some stuff in my life that I shouldn't have. I've done things that I'm not proud of. But"—and he stood up—"I'll tell you one thing. I didn't fucking murder that child."

I turned to leave. And I had to say, I was beginning to believe him.

# 41

I spent most of the evening sitting cross-legged on my sofa, poring over all my notes. A bag of crisps and a bottle of wine sat by my side in lieu of dinner. I was adding to my timeline, from the earliest date I had, which was when the Facebook group had been established, some years before Margaret-Elizabeth's death. I wrote everything down, cross referencing and double-checking the interviews as well as all the notes I had in my notebook.

My timeline ended up with arrows and stars and lines all over it, insertions and crossings out clarifying where there were discrepancies. What began to puzzle me the most was the timeline of the night of Margaret-Elizabeth's murder.

The babysitter was clear that she had checked on Margaret-Elizabeth at around 10.30pm, just after News at Ten had finished, and that the Ellisons had arrived home a few minutes before eleven.

They all agreed that they had spent a couple of minutes chatting before the babysitter had gone home, then Nicole had tidied around for a minute or two and it was then that she'd gone upstairs and had noticed that Margaret-Elizabeth was not in her bed. So that gave a window of less than half an hour for someone to enter the house and take Margaret-Elizabeth away, murder her and leave her in the woods. Although, I guessed she could have still been alive when they'd first realised she had gone. Maybe someone was in the woods, strangling her with her dressing gown belt as they frantically searched the house and garden, as they called their family for help.

Judith Ryan had said that she was called at about 11.15pm, which meant that the Ellisons had spent fifteen minutes searching for Margaret-Elizabeth before calling their relatives. The relatives all agreed that they had arrived at the house within minutes of each other and that Jonathan and the others had gone out into the garden to search.

There was some confusion about who was where during the next hour, which was understandable. Everyone agreed that Jonathan had reappeared carrying Margaret-Elizabeth and that this was about fifteen or twenty minutes after he'd ran out into the garden. That sounded about right – they'd have been searching the garden, running around, spotting Bridges over the fence and then Jonathan Scraggs would have run across the lawn, jumped over the fence and carried Margaret-Elizabeth back into the house. Karl and David had chased after Bridges and hadn't come back until another twenty minutes or so had gone past.

Christine, Scraggs's wife, had run out to the front of the house, everyone pretty much agreed on that, and Judith had stayed with Nicole in the front room. Marion and Diane Todd seemed to have gone from room to room making tea and trying to calm things down.

It was Judith who had then called for the ambulance and

barked instructions to various people to try to revive Margaret-Elizabeth whilst they'd waited for the ambulance.

According to the records, the ambulance had been called at 11.49pm and had arrived at the house at 12.01am. The paramedics had worked on Margaret-Elizabeth for a little while, before leaving the house at 12.08am.

In Matthew Ellison's interview with the police he stated that he had searched for Margaret-Elizabeth out the front of the house, alongside Chrissy Scraggs. She corroborated this, stating that she had gone one way down the road and Matthew had gone the other. The Ellisons' house was almost at the end of a cul-de-sac and Chrissy had reached the end of the road fairly quickly, searching gardens and driveways, then had returned to the house only about twenty minutes or so after she'd left. But nobody saw Matthew Ellison again until the ambulance was about to head off to the hospital. I guessed it might have taken a while. He would have had more to look at than Christine Scraggs, in and out of gardens, perhaps going around the back of houses, calling for his daughter. Still, I was unable to place him with certainty on my timeline from the time the relatives had arrived around 11.15pm or thereabouts, until the ambulance had left the house almost an hour later on. And that was frustrating.

# SATURDAY

## 42

On Saturday I downloaded all the photos of Marcus onto my laptop so that I could take a good look at them. I had no idea what was going on, but it seemed that there was enough here to confront him with. He was most definitely hiding something from Collette and it was causing her some considerable stress. I'd have to wait till Monday now. Marcus wouldn't be at work until then, and there was no way I could go round to their house, not with the girls there, to challenge him.

I chose a dozen or so of the photos and saved them onto a card so that I could take them to Boots or somewhere and get them printed out. I had discovered over the last year that it was much more powerful to present people with actual, printed photos rather than just show them the evidence on the camera, or on a laptop. Having real, undeletable material pictures seemed to bring it home to people more and I'd found they were much more likely to confess that way.

I spent the rest of the morning in the hire car reception with a very unhappy representative, explaining the damage to the car. I span them a barely believable story about having an accident. I told them about a driver who had crashed into me and who hadn't stopped, which was indeed true. I said that they'd disappeared before I could get their number plate, and that it was in the countryside well away from CCTV cameras. That was also true. The trouble was that the damage ran all down one side and across the back of the car. It was very clearly more than one collision. The man behind the reception desk had led me out to the car park, pointing out the different areas of damage.

"I'm terribly sorry," I said. "I must have banged my head or something because I really can't remember the exact circumstances. Maybe I hit a tree after the other driver hit me?"

He peered at me over the top of his glasses, raising his eyebrows in what I took to be disbelief.

Thankfully, I'd taken the full insurance, and after some considerable time they let me go. I didn't think they'd be wanting to hire me another car anytime soon though.

Before I set off to get the pictures printed I sent Robert a quick text:

*In town, fancy a coffee?*

It was only a couple of minutes before a reply came back.

*Coffee?! It's past midday and it's Saturday. See you in The Steam Hammer.*

I picked up all the paperwork from the reception desk, stuffed it in my handbag then headed across town towards the city centre. I went to The Steam Hammer first, and peered in through the full-length windows. There was no sign of Robert and Keith so I carried on down to Boots and printed off my photos. I'd brought an envelope with me and I slipped the pictures inside so that they didn't crease and then walked back towards the pub.

By the time I arrived, Robert and Keith were halfway through their first pint. I waved at them through the window and Keith pointed towards a glass of red wine waiting for me on the table.

"Thanks for the wine," I said as I approached them. "Although I think I might start with a coffee." I went and ordered coffee then took it back to the table.

"Bring back the real Verity," Keith implored, looking at the sky as if I'd been abducted by aliens and replaced with a more sober version of myself.

"Don't worry, I'll get onto that in no time," I reassured him. "How are plans coming along for the gala?"

He discussed the problems he was having with some of the contractors, sorting out the menu, deciding what drinks should be complimentary but, generally speaking, it all seemed to be coming along smoothly. After a little while I decided to take the bull by the horns. "Sam isn't coming," I said, pushing my empty coffee cup aside and taking a sip of my wine.

Robert tilted his head to one side and said, "What did you do?"

"I didn't do anything," I protested. "I rang him up and he was in bed shagging someone else. So he's uninvited."

They both grimaced. "Oops," Keith said. "That must have been awkward."

"Well, he wasn't actually shagging when I rang." I paused. "Well, maybe he was, I don't know."

"See," Robert said. "That's better than the last call you had with heavy breathing. At least you knew who it was this time."

I glared at him over the top of my wine glass. "At least I didn't decide to video call," I said, trying to be flip about the whole thing but not really managing.

A little while later, Keith asked, "How's the investigation going?"

I sighed. "Slowly. I don't know, something isn't adding up. There's something that someone is trying to stop me finding out but I have no idea what it is."

"Cryptic," Keith said.

"They seem to be doing okay then," Robert quipped.

"How do you mean?"

"Well, if you have no idea what it is they don't want you to know…"

"Oh, yeah. I see. Yes, they're doing a very good job as the more I dig, the cloudier it all becomes."

"How close are you to spending all that money?" Keith asked.

"Nowhere near," I said.

"Just keep digging then. Something'll come up."

I'd just finished my second glass of wine when my phone rang. It was a number I didn't recognise. "Sorry," I said, pointing to the phone as I left the table and headed out of the door. "Hello?" I said into the phone.

"Hi," a female voice said. "You rang this number. I was just checking whether you were going to try and sell me double glazing. In which case I was going to block you. But, I'm also waiting for a call from someone about my masters, so I thought I'd best check."

"Oh," I said, surprised. "Well, actually I'm neither of those. Can I ask who's speaking?"

"It's Charlotte," she said. "Charlotte Jones."

"I'm sorry," I said. "When did I ring you?"

"Hang on," she said. There were a few clicks and whirrs down the phone, then a pause. "Hi?"

"Yeah, I'm here."

"It was yesterday afternoon."

My head was spinning. The only calls I'd made yesterday afternoon were to the numbers in the list I'd got from Jade's fridge door. The list that had had Jake Johnson's number on it.

"Okay, yes, thanks for calling back. My name's Verity Spencer. I was ringing to ask you about Jade Griffiths."

"Who?"

"Jade Griffiths."

"I don't know anyone with that name."

"She may have been calling to ask you about Anthony Bridges," I suggested.

"I'm really sorry," she said. "I don't know any of these people. Maybe you rang the wrong number?"

"Anthony Bridges is the guy who allegedly murdered Margaret-Elizabeth. Have you heard his name mentioned?"

"Oh, yes. Now I know who you mean. Jade. Jade's Lincolnshire Japes. The blog. I gave her my number in a direct message. But she never called."

"Listen, Charlotte, thanks for calling me back. It's just that I found your number on a list that Jade had. If I send you her number can you check if she ever rang you? Maybe you missed her call as well?"

"Yeah, sure," she said. "Text it to me and I'll check."

I went back into the pub and sat down. Another glass of wine had appeared whilst I was gone and I admonished

Robert and Keith, although I didn't refuse it. I searched my phone for the call I'd received from Jade's phone the night I'd been lured round to her house and I texted it to Charlotte Jones. It was about twenty minutes later when a reply came back.

*Hi Charlotte here. I've checked the number you sent. No calls or texts from that number. Sorry I can't help.*
*Charlotte*

"What was Jade doing with Jake's number?" I said out loud.

"Eh?" Keith said.

"Jade Griffiths. She was the young lady that Anthony Bridges assaulted. She was doing some research into his background. In her kitchen she had a list of numbers. Jake Johnson, who is now dead, and this lady, Charlotte"—I pointed to my phone—"were both on it. But Charlotte says she never received a call or text from her."

"So, that suggests she'd only just got the numbers," Robert said.

"Hmm…and didn't get round to ringing them, maybe? Charlotte said she gave Jade her number because of the blog, but why would she have Jake's on the same list?"

"He could have seen the blog too, maybe?" Keith shrugged.

"I guess."

"What was the blog about?" Robert asked.

"It was about her life, generally. She mentioned being assaulted by Bridges and I think a few people got in touch to support each other. In her last blog she mentioned getting together, or something, like a support group."

Keith took a swig of his beer. "So, could this Charlotte have been assaulted too? By this guy, or maybe by someone else? Maybe she wanted to join in the support group?"

"Yeah, could be," I mused. "But that doesn't explain why Jade had Jake Johnson's number. Does it?"

## 43

L ater on that afternoon, I held onto Robert's arm as we staggered up the hill towards Steeple Lane. It was slow going. They had suggested calling in at another pub on the way to my house, but my head was already light so I'd declined.

"You two," I said as we weaved up the hill. "You two are like those Irish things."

"Pints of Guinness?" Robert offered.

"No, silly. Trolls."

"I'm pretty sure trolls are Scandinavian," he said, grabbing my arm as I stumbled on the cobbles.

"The green things."

"Clover leaves?"

"No! The little nasty things. You know, like evil little gnomes."

"You mean, leprechauns?"

"Yes, they're the things. You're like them. You two. Both of you. You sit on my shoulders saying, 'go on, just one more', and look how I end up." I stumbled again, clutching for Robert's arm to steady myself. With that, my phone rang, so I pulled it out of my pocket and aimed my finger at the answer button. "Hellooo," I said.

"Verity Spencer? It's DC Shepherd."

"DC Shepherd, hi!" I said, trying to sound as sober, and free of worry, as I could. "How can I help you?"

"I need you to come in and answer some more questions," she said, getting straight to the point.

"Absolutely. No problem at all," I said with an enthusiasm I thought might be a little too fervent. "Any particular reason?" I asked, hoping I sounded as if I had no clue at all.

"There's just a few things we need to clarify, that's all."

"Well," I explained, wagging my finger in the air. "I don't think it's too good this afternoon, I've been in the pub."

"Uh-huh. Probably best not now then."

After some deliberation, I agreed to go in on Monday afternoon and answer her questions. Once I'd hung up, I stood for a while clutching the phone in my hand. I formed a small O with my mouth and exhaled through it, relieved that I seemed to have played the innocent well enough, and certain that I hadn't come across at all tipsy. Then I missed my pocket and dropped my phone on the ground and it bounced down the hill, Keith running after it and retrieving it for me.

When we reached my house we lounged about for a while. I found Robert and Keith a bottle of wine. They were both a good deal bigger than me and their bodies could take a lot more alcohol. I got them to make me a strong cup of coffee and then I curled up on the sofa, cup in hand.

"The thing is," I said later as I put my empty cup down on the coffee table. "Why would they close the Facebook group?"

"I imagine they didn't want to carry on after Margaret-Elizabeth had been murdered. Perhaps reading seemed a little trivial after that," Keith said.

Robert added, "And didn't they stop holding their book club anyway? They wouldn't have needed the Facebook group if they weren't having book club meetings."

"Well, yeah, that's what I thought. But I've double-checked the date, and it definitely closed two weeks before Margaret-Elizabeth died."

"Maybe it had run its course. Maybe they were going to close the book club anyway, so they shut down the Facebook group," Keith said, pouring the last dregs of the wine into his glass.

"Yeah, could be that the children were getting older. Perhaps it was harder to get together, finding babysitters for older ones, I don't know."

The conversation moved away from Margaret-Elizabeth and we sat putting the world to rights until the wine was finished and the sun had long gone down.

# SUNDAY

## 44

---

Not unsurprisingly, it was quite late when I woke up on Sunday morning. I sloped down the stairs in my pyjamas, made a cup of coffee then took it back up to bed with me. It was almost midday by the time I felt the inclination to actually get out of bed. The weather had turned very autumnal again, cold and wet with a frigid grey sky and not a hint of blue on the horizon. It was the perfect day for snuggling on the sofa in pyjamas watching black and white movies.

Instead, I sat in my pyjamas peering at the photo that I'd taken of Jade's fridge freezer door, the photo that had Jake Johnson's phone number on it. The final number in the list had the last two digits missing and I tried to figure out if there was a hint as to what either of those missing digits were, but there was nothing. So, I took out my notebook and made a list from 00 to 99—one number for each line—and I started to work my way through the list, adding each combination in turn to the existing numbers that I had.

I managed to tick quite a few off the list before I paused for another cup of coffee. It was amazing how many numbers gave the unobtainable call. Some rang but weren't answered, and some went to voicemail. Where the call went to voicemail I made a note of the name, if people gave one, but didn't leave a message. My plan was to go through all the numbers first, talking to people who answered and crossing off those that were unobtainable. Then, if I didn't locate the mystery person the first time round, I'd do a second sweep of those numbers that had rung but not been answered.

The first person to answer was number 09, who snapped up the phone after only half a ring.

"Yes," a male voice said, a note of impatience clear in the tone.

"Hi, my name's Verity Spencer and I'm—"

"You're not selling anything are you?"

"No, I—"

"Well that's good because I'm not buying anything. I'll put the phone down."

"Err, no. I'm not selling anything, I promise. I'm investigating a crime."

That seemed to pique his interest a little more. "Oh yeah? What have I got to do with it?"

"Well, I don't know." I explained about the incomplete number and that I was trying to find the phone with the last two mystery digits. "The number was in the house of someone who'd been writing a blog. Jade's Lincoln Japes? Have you heard of it?"

"I've never read a blog in my life."

"I think she might have been trying to draw some kind of support group together. I mean, she was based in Lincoln, but I guess the blog could be read anywhere so it might have been virtual, I suppose."

"Well, I live in Kent so…"

"Does the name Anthony Bridges ring any bells with you?"

"Nope."

I sighed. "Do you remember the murder about ten years ago of Margaret-Elizabeth Ellison?"

"Remind me."

"She was eleven. She was murdered in Lincoln."

"Doesn't ring any bells, no."

"Okay, well thanks for your time. If you do think of any reason your number might have been on a fridge in Lincoln, let me know."

And so it went on. Gradually I had a page of numbers with ticks, crosses, and the occasional name, but I wasn't getting anywhere. I was on my third cup of coffee by the time I'd worked my way through every combination, number ninety-nine being another unobtainable tone. I sat and totted up; I'd crossed just over half the numbers off the list, either because the numbers were not available or because I'd spoken to the owners and ruled them out. I turned to a fresh page in my notebook and wrote down all the remaining numbers and started from the beginning again, dialling all the phones that had rung and not been answered, or had gone to voicemail.

This time a few more people answered. Mostly people were willing to listen and answer questions, but nobody could explain why their number had been on the door of a fridge in Lincoln. I only got through a few of the numbers when I felt the need to stretch my legs and have a change of scenery, so I ran upstairs, got dressed, and headed out to feed Jade's cat.

"Hello Peg Leg," I said as she clattered out of the cat flap.

She was less than impressed that I hadn't been round

the day before. I picked her up and stroked her and she buried her head deep into my chest, purring with the pleasure of being fussed over. I put her down and opened a packet of food.

"I'm seeing the police again, tomorrow," I informed the cat. "I'll let them know you're here. I'm sure one of Jade's family will come and get you and take you home. Mind you," I added, "don't let on I was here the other day. I'm already in DC Shepherd's 'suspicious' book."

I left her alone to eat her dinner. I sat on the back doorstep for a while and after she'd eaten she jumped up and fell asleep on my knee. The garden looked exactly as it had when I'd left it, the bucket of weeds, the boots, all still unmoved. I wondered if Jade had any family.

I set the cat down on the pavement and said goodbye, stroking her head and promising to come back and feed her the next day, if she hadn't been claimed by then.

When I got back home, the sun was going down. I poured a glass of wine, hair of the dog I thought, before going to change back into my pyjamas. I resumed my position on the sofa, my legs folded underneath me, and started again on the list of numbers.

After some time, I'd eliminated a few more numbers. I reached out and stretched my arms, pulling my back tight. I'd just hit the sixties on my list and I was getting stiff from huddling over the notebook. I took a little exercise – to the kitchen for more wine – then settled back down to ring the remaining numbers.

It was number seventy five that came good. A young man called Callum answered. I'd explained about the number being discovered in Jade's kitchen and then I mentioned the name of the blog.

"Oh, yes," he said, and my heart leapt in anticipation.

The hairs on my neck and down my back prickled as they stood to attention, waiting to hear what he had to say. "You recognise the blog?"

"I sent a message. I used the contact form on the blog. She said she wanted to set up a support group and, well, I've struggled a lot. You know, I tried university but I couldn't hack it. I tried a job, but I thought people were looking at me weird. I'm a little different and it's like people can see through me and tell that I'm not the same as them."

"So you contacted Jade to join the support group?"

"Yeah, she was looking at two I think, a virtual one online and a meet up one. I thought I'd prefer the meet up one. I don't like interacting over the Internet, well I like texting and stuff but not talking to people. I don't really like meeting people much but I thought the others might understand, you know?"

"Do you live in Lincoln?"

"I live in Navenby, it's not far away."

"When did you send Jade the message?"

He let out a low, thinking-style, hum. "I guess it was just over a week ago. It was the middle of the week, a Wednesday I think. Maybe Thursday. But it definitely wasn't over two weeks ago, so it'll be just over a week, yeah."

"Did you hear back from her?"

"She sent me a message, a reply to my contact on the blog. I think it might have been an automated thank you."

"But she didn't ring you?"

"No, I don't think so."

"You don't have a voicemail, might you have missed the call?"

"I guess so."

"If I send you her number, can you check your missed calls?" I asked.

"Sure, I'll check."

"Thanks. Oh, and, Callum?"

"Yeah?"

"I'm sorry to ask you this, but, the support group? It was for young people who'd been assaulted, yes? Sexually assaulted, like Jade."

"Not really, it was for all survivors. I know Jade had been assaulted by that guy on her way home from school. And I think a couple of comments were from people who'd had that happen to them, well, something similar. But others, like me, hadn't been attacked in public like that. I was abused at home. By my grandad. For years. When my parents went out…you know."

"I'm sorry, Callum, that must have made life really difficult for you."

"Yeah, well…"

"Thanks for your help."

I put the phone down and texted him Jade's number, just as I had with Charlotte Jones. But this time the answer was different.

*Hi, yes I did have a missed call. She rang me on Tuesday but I missed it.*

Tuesday, the night that Jake Johnson had died.

Jake Johnson had been on a list of people who'd contacted Jade through her blog. A blog she'd set up to support survivors of sexual abuse.

I finished my glass of wine and headed off to bed, although I struggled to sleep. Thoughts of abuse, broken adults needing support, ballerina statues and car chases raced through my head, one after another, thought after thought. Dreams flitted into my brain as I drifted in and out of sleep, the reality mingling with the subconscious. I couldn't stop, I couldn't let it go. I wouldn't let it go. For the sake of Margaret-Elizabeth and now for Jake and Jade, I would not give up.

# MONDAY

# 45

I needed to talk to people who had known Jake Johnson as a child.

The only people I could think of were the other children of the book club members. But I didn't have any of their contact details. I looked again at the list of parents and children, reviewing all the notes I'd recorded about them in my notebook and on my laptop. Rereading all the transcripts of their statements to the police gave me no further clues, but I kept coming back to the messages on the Facebook group. The television programme I'd seen had shown how easy it was for people to pretend to be something they weren't. I flicked back in my notebook to my record of the meeting I'd had with Paul Hardy when he'd told me all about using codes.

Although I almost knew the Facebook messages off by heart now, I reviewed them one more time. There were definitely repeating patterns; when you looked at it as a whole, the same phrases, the same book titles, repeated over and over again. On the face of it, it looked like a normal conversation but the patterns were there, just like on the site Paul

Hardy had shown me. No wonder I hadn't been able to notice a difference before. Matthew Ellison usually started the threads off.

> So this week we'll be revisiting Catch 22, we read that a few weeks ago and everyone seemed to enjoy it, especially chapter ten.

There would be a couple of innocuous replies but peppered among them, the words would repeat.

> Chapter ten was great.

> Catch 22 is one of my all time favourites.

> We got a bit stuck on page forty-four. Lol.

> Page forty-four. That was a fun read.

> Can we re-read Chapter nine? I preferred that to Chapter ten.

On first glance it wasn't obvious, but in each thread many of the replies referred to specific chapters, specific pages. Matthew Ellison would refer to a particular book, one they had allegedly already read and the replies followed a similar pattern.

> Chapter six wasn't such a good read last week.

> Page seventy was fun though.

> The whole of that book was fun.

As I read it now, the words leapt out at me 'fun', 'chapter', 'good read', the page numbers, over and over in the replies, scattered amongst other more innocuous comments. I leaned back on the sofa, a mixture of triumph and confusion swirling through my brain. I had no idea what they'd been doing, but I was pretty convinced that it hadn't involved reading books.

The rain was pelting against the windows, lashing down onto the garden and bouncing off the path. I looked again at the list of parents and children. Many of the children had left home now. I had no idea where they were, and I couldn't ring their parents to ask them. But Sebastian Walker was at Lincoln University. And that just so happened to be where I needed to go and confront Marcus before my date with DC Shepherd later. A plan was formulating in my mind. And the meeting with DC Shepherd was perfect timing. If I could talk to Sebastian Walker before my appointment, I might just be able to give her a motive for Jake Johnson's death, and by extension Jade's, even if I had no idea who it was who had actually done the deed. But then, she was the detective, I'd leave it in her hands. And it might ease her suspicions about me.

By lunchtime the rain had eased a little, but I decided I'd take the car down to the university anyway. I had to get over to the police station after I'd seen Marcus and the weather app on my phone assured me that there would be intermittent heavy showers over the next few hours.

I parked up in the car park and waited for a lull in the rain, wishing I'd prepared for this a little more thoroughly. I'd been so focused on finding Sebastian Walker that what I was actually going to say to Marcus hadn't really entered my head. I grabbed the envelope with the pictures and ran into the university. The main building had been the first construction when they'd started building on this site, and it was several floors high, with the first few arranged around a large atrium. Students milled about, backpacks on their shoulders, rushing to lectures, eating in the café, reading notices, huddled over in discussions. I'd been to Marcus' office once before and remembered that it was on the first floor. I leapt up the stairs two at a time and turned towards the row of offices. The corridor was open to my right, overlooking the atrium, the noise of students going about their business drifting up and echoing off the walls. I ran along, scanning the doors to my left, skimming the names but none of them were Marcus' so I took the stairs up to the next floor, running back the other way. Confusion was setting in; I couldn't find his name. I needed to confront him before I went to my meeting with DC Shepherd. Apart from not wanting to string Collette along any longer, I had to find Sebastian Walker, and Marcus was my only connection to him.

A grey-haired man emerged from a lift at the end of the stretch of offices, his suit the same shade as his hair. I ran up to him and called, "Excuse me."

He span round, raising his eyebrows.

"I'm looking for Marcus Smith's room," I blurted, sounding more desperate than I'd hoped. I lifted up the brown envelope, hoping that he might think I was on official business.

The man surveyed me from head to toe, but obviously decided I seemed harmless enough as he pointed me to a room at the end, near a break-out area with tub chairs and a coffee table.

"Thanks," I said and ran over. I looked over my shoulder as the man disappeared down the corridor, then I pushed Marcus' door open.

"Hey—" Marcus started to say when the door opened without an announcing knock. "Oh, err…Verity…" His voice rose as he saw me. "To what do we owe this pleasure?" He smiled at me, but he rushed over and shut the door behind me, then hovered near the entrance, eyebrows raised in expectation.

"Can I have a word?" I asked.

"Sure, sure, come in. Sit down," he said, indicating a chair to the side of his desk.

I sat on the appointed chair, wondering how on earth I was going to explain why I was there, and feeling like a complete traitor.

He sat behind his desk, resting his forearms on the surface and clasping his hands together. Once again, his eyebrows moved upward and he tilted his head, waiting for me to explain why I was there.

"Okay," I said and looked down at the envelope in my hands. This was going to be harder than I'd thought. I took a deep breath. "Okay…Collette asked me to follow you."

He sat back. His top lip curled up to one side, his brow shot down and he spread his hands wide. "She asked you to do what?"

"To follow you."

"And you agreed?" His voice was high, the tone rising as he spoke. "How professional is that? Verity, you're supposed to be our friend."

"I know, I know. I tried to refuse, Marcus, I really did. But you know how she can be." I swung my head from side to side.

He mirrored the action. "Well, yeah," he agreed. "But why on earth would she want you to follow me?"

I swallowed. "She thinks you're having an affair."

"She what?" he spluttered. "She's been listening to way

too many tales of your escapades. What could possibly make her think I was having an affair?"

"To be honest, Marcus," I said, gathering a little momentum, "and cutting to the chase, you have been sneaking around and seeing other women." I held up the envelope. "I followed you. I followed you to the house in Branston."

He held out his hand. I passed over the envelope, and he tipped out the contents onto his desk. He sifted through the photos; him walking up the path of the red brick semi, kissing the blonde lady at the door, waving goodbye later the same day. He shuffled through them, picking out the photo of him getting into his car, the blonde lady in the passenger seat, the boy in the back. Then he moved on to the one showing the spikey-haired lady climbing into the little yellow car, Marcus clearly visible in the passenger seat. He paused, his elbow on the desk, his fingers resting against his mouth. He studied the picture of the three of them emerging from the hospital, him leaning in and saying something to the boy. He said nothing.

I looked up at him, and he met my gaze, a tear working its way down his cheek and landing on the face of the teenager.

"Marcus?" I said.

He pulled in his lips, closed his eyes, sat back in his chair. He clutched his hands together in front of him. "I was going to tell her," he started. "I was. I just didn't know how. And…" He paused. "The time never seemed right. I'd get home and she'd be tired, or full of what had been going on with the children, and I just never found the right time."

"How long has it been going on?"

He shot a glance at me, his eyes wide. "I'm not having an affair, Verity. That's not what this is." He indicated the photos spread out in front of him. "Look, there are two

294

different women here. Do you really think I'd be having an affair with two different women?" He tuned his gaze away, then back towards me. "I mean, do you really think I'd be having an affair at all?" He threw his hands in the air.

"Then what's going on, Marcus?"

He studied his hands, opening and closing his fingers. He clenched and unclenched his teeth, his jaw twitching as he did so, then he stared out of the window and sighed.

"Marcus?" I said.

He turned back to me, sucking in his cheeks. After some time, he took in a deep breath and said, "The boy is my son."

"Your son?"

He nodded.

"How? He must be fifteen."

Marcus nodded again. "He's seventeen." He looked up at me. "I'd just finished university. One of the people on my course, Janet, was a good friend. And, well anyway, we stayed friends...for a while." He swallowed. "She had a girlfriend, still has, that's Carol in the pictures," he said pointing to the spikey-haired lady. "Anyway, when they moved in together they were desperate for a baby. They paid for IVF treatment but it didn't work and they couldn't afford to go through it all again." He glanced up, then straight down at his hands. He shuffled the photos about on the desk. "They...um...they asked me if I'd help."

I leaned forward, and stared at him, but he kept his eyes firmly on the photos. I said nothing, just let him take his time.

"I was moving away, you see. To here, actually, where I met Collette." He looked up at me, his forehead ridged with deep lines, his cheeks red, and he blinked and brushed away a tear that was threatening to fall from his eye. "I didn't know her then. I hadn't met her."

I nodded. "Okay. It's okay." I reached out across the desk and touched his arm.

He swallowed again. "Um…well I went round at the, er, at the right time of the month and, well you know, Verity, I went in the bathroom and Janet was in the bedroom and Carol was the go between. And well, Luke was the result."

"Luke," I repeated, scrutinising him in the pictures.

"Yeah. And well, then I moved away. I never met him. I didn't want to. I mean he was their son, not mine. Janet did let me know when he was born and I did think about him sometimes over the years, but mostly…you know…mostly I didn't, actually."

"So how come they're here?"

"They tracked me down. They used old networks, and Facebook, other social media and got in touch."

"Why, Marcus? What did they want? And why are you sneaking round hiding it from Collette?"

"Luke has kidney failure." He looked up at me. "He needs a kidney transplant and Janet isn't a good match. Apparently the wait for a donor through death is too long… um…for him. He doesn't have long enough. His kidneys are failing too fast. And the best chances of success with a live donor is with a blood relative. So they tracked me down and asked if I'd be tested."

"And?"

He nodded. "Yeah, I'm a good match. So, er…I agreed to do it, and they rented the house and they all moved down here to be close to me for a while, so that he can have the transplant." He stopped trying to prevent the tears falling, and I leaned over and moved the photos across the desk out of the way. Marcus bent over and rested his forehead against the wood. "I'm sorry," he whispered.

"You're going to donate a kidney? Is that okay? Is that something that is okay, to give away a kidney?"

He sat up, wiping his cheeks with his palms and nodded. "Yeah, yeah it's okay to only have one. And I think your body adjusts, so..."

"You need to tell Collette, Marcus."

"I know, but well where do you start? 'By the way, honey I have another child'? Or 'I'm going to give someone one of my internal organs'?"

"She'll understand I'm sure."

"Eventually, maybe. When she's got over the whole, you kept this secret from me for all these years, perhaps."

"Yeah. Well, you did keep it secret from her."

"I just... It just wasn't part of my life, you know?" He shrugged. He looked up at me, a weak smile spreading across his face. "He's such a great kid, Verity. I don't think I'd be as calm in the face of potential death."

"Kids can be very resilient."

He nodded, reaching across and picking up the photo that showed him leaning into Luke.

"You have to tell Collette, Marcus."

"I will, just not now."

"You have to. You have to go home and tell her, right now."

"I can't, Verity. Not right now."

I stood up, hands on hips. "You need to go home, Marcus, and tell her." And I pointed to the door in case he wasn't quite sure which way to head.

But he sat firm in his chair, shaking his head. "Give me a day or two."

"I will not," I demanded. "She thinks you're having an

affair, Marcus. She's been in pieces. She'll be relieved that she's only losing one of your kidneys not the whole of you."

He snorted. "I have to go for more blood tests and stuff. I have to get my own head around this."

I wagged my finger at him. "You'll need Collette to help you. You're going to need her to be supportive, to be there when you have the operation."

He didn't move.

"Jesus, Marcus, how are you going to explain being away overnight and coming back with a scar in your tummy? Or back. Or wherever they get your kidneys from."

Silence.

"Marcus she's in bits. You have to tell her. You have to put her mind at rest. You're torturing her."

He nodded. "Give me tonight. Give me tonight to think about it. I mean, to think about how I'm going to put it to her."

I sat down again. "Give me something in return."

His head shot up, his eyes probing my face. "What do you mean? What do you want? Money?"

"Oh, don't be ridiculous. I'm not blackmailing you. I don't want money. I just want you to give me a phone number, a student's phone number."

"I think you'll find that's still blackmail, Verity." He shook his head. "You know I can't do that. That's confidential information."

"Okay, you're choice. I'll head off and find Collette and tell her myself." I stood up and started gathering the photos together.

Marcus shot out of his chair and put his hand on mine. "Please, Verity."

"Then give me the phone number."

"I can't." He sighed and sat in his chair, turning towards

the computer monitor where he clicked the mouse and tapped at his keyboard. "You know I absolutely cannot give you any personal information about a student. I'd get the sack."

"Fine," I said, stacking the photos and returning them to their envelope.

Marcus got up, moved around the desk and went to the door.

"Where are you going?"

"I'll be back in five minutes," he said, looking over his shoulder. "I imagine you'll be gone by then."

"Yeah, to tell your—"

But he'd gone. He left the room, shutting the door quietly behind him. I slumped in the chair, disappointment raging through my body as I sagged down, sticking my legs out under the desk. As I looked up, I noticed that Marcus had left his computer screen on. *Careless*, I thought. But then I realised that, not only had he left it on, but he'd left it open on a spreadsheet. I stood up, moved around the desk, and sat in the chair Marcus had just vacated to take a closer look. The title of the spreadsheet was '*Student Contact Information*'. The information was arranged alphabetically, with the surname, first name, home address and other details in columns stretching off the screen. Each letter had its own tab and I scrolled through them until I got to W and clicked on that. There it was, several names down, Sebastian Walker.

## 46

"Thank you, Marcus," I whispered to the room. "I'll give you till tomorrow." I took out my phone and tapped Sebastian Walker's number into it and let it ring as I gathered up my things and left Marcus' office.

I moved over to the breakout area and sat down in one of the tub chairs. I was just about to hang up when a breathless voice heaved through the phone. "Yes?"

"Sebastian?"

A few heavy breaths and then the voice said again, "Yes."

"It's Verity Spencer, I'm not sure if your mum or anyone else mentioned me, I'm looking into—"

"I'm scared."

"Sorry?"

"I'm scared," he repeated.

Not without reason, I thought. "Where are you?" I asked. "Are you at the university?"

He said that he was. He said that he was in a friend's room at the uni. "I'm not going home." His voice was shaking, the fear palpable even through the crackle of the phone signal.

"Can you come here?" I told him where I was and that I'd wait for him.

I didn't have to wait long. Within ten minutes, Sebastian appeared, accompanied by a young lady. She appeared to be another student, a backpack slung across her shoulder and a notepad clutched in the crook of her arm. Her long black hair fell almost to her waist and she chatted as she walked, glancing up into Sebastian's face every now and again as if she were reassuring him. He slunk along, his head bowed, his shoulders hunched over, looking as if he had the weight of the world on them.

As they approached I stood up and held out my hand. "Verity Spencer," I said. "Thanks for coming over, Sebastian."

"Err, Seb, please. And this is Maria." He indicated the girl at his side.

"Let's sit down," I said, pointing to the tub chairs. "Does anyone want a drink?" I asked, signalling the café below with my thumb.

They both shook their heads so we sat down. Sebastian stared at his hands and shuffled in his seat. He shot me a glance with his pale grey eyes but returned his gaze to his hands without holding the look. He ran a hand through his unkempt ginger hair and then rubbed both palms on his tracksuit trousers.

"Sebastian," I said, leaning towards him. "Seb. What is it that you're scared about? I need you to tell me." I fought the urge to look at my watch. I knew I didn't have much more than an hour until my appointment with DC Shepherd, but I couldn't push him. I needed him to trust me.

Whatever he'd been holding in for all these years was bursting to be told; I could see that from his demeanour. But he wouldn't open up if I tried to force it from him. "I know it's hard, but we need to make sure that you're safe. I'm meeting the police this afternoon. I can help you, Seb."

He rocked in his chair but said nothing.

"I understand that you might be scared. I know what's happened to Jake and Jade." I paused to look at him. He was biting his lip and tugging the cuffs of his sleeves so that they covered his hands. "But I need you to tell me why."

Silence.

I had to get his confidence. I needed him to tell me what had been going on at the book club. He was my only link to both Margaret-Elizabeth and Jake Johnson. I switched tack; something a little less uncomfortable. "Did you know Jade, Seb? Jade Griffiths?"

He shook his head.

"Did you know that Jake had contacted her?"

A nod. He pulled his cuffs completely over his hands and pushed them into the side of his head, as if he was trying to squeeze the thoughts out of his brain.

Maria leaned over and gave him a hug, pulling him to her. He lifted his hand up, still clutching at his cuff and laid it on her shoulder. It was an awkward gesture, from someone who seemed unsure how to respond to such a sudden display of kindness and support. He pushed her back, and returned to his position, rocking back and forth in the chair, his head nodding forward a little, back a little.

"Jade was setting up a support group for survivors of abuse," I said, more of a statement than a question.

Another short nod.

"And Jake contacted her."

Seb opened his mouth but nothing came out.

The connection hit me. I didn't know why I hadn't seen it before. "This is all to do with the book club isn't it?"

For the first time he caught my eyes, the nod of his head so tiny it was almost imperceptible. He turned back to his hands, picking at his thumb nails, the tension etched across his forehead. He pulled his mouth to one side and resumed his gentle rocking, back and forth, back and forth.

"Seb, I want to help you. But I need to understand what's been going on."

He looked up again and pulled his lips in. Maria patted his knee, leaning in towards him.

"Did Jake talk to Jade about the book club?"

He shrugged. "I don't know."

"The book club," I said again. "Tell me about the book club. What were they doing if not reading books?"

I let the silence stretch between us, desperate though I was for him to answer. I needed to get to my appointment with DC Shepherd and I needed to be able to give her all the information. I watched Sebastian rocking, picking at his nails. Periodically his tongue appeared in the corner of his mouth. He brushed a hand through his unruly hair. I couldn't rush him.

Eventually he looked up at me, his eyes slanted down, his brows knotted above them. "Abusing us," he said in a voice so quiet it was almost inaudible.

"Abusing you?"

He nodded.

"You and the other children?"

Another slight dip of the head.

A million questions flooded into my head, but I had to take it slow. "The books they mentioned in the Facebook group then, they were code? For what?"

"I don't know." His voice was still so quiet I had to

strain to hear what he was saying. "I don't know about that. I was only a child." He looked up at me, his big eyes imploring, although I wasn't sure for what.

"Okay," I said. "Can you tell me what happened? What do you remember?"

He bit the inside of his cheek. He took a deep breath and then the words started to come, little by little, with pauses and gulps for air, his methodical rocking not letting up for a second. "When I was little, I remember it. They used to get together, usually at Margaret-Elizabeth's house. Sometimes it would be at our house and sometimes other houses, but usually Margaret-Elizabeth's. The other kids would come round then, when I was small. After a while that didn't happen but it did in those days. They used to make us play games. They made us do Simon Says and things like that, like it was a party and when you lost you had to take something off. Then when you had no clothes on there'd be forfeits and stuff." He swallowed. "After a while we'd all have no clothes and then..." He clasped his hands together, the knuckles whitening with the tension. "Then they'd make us do things to each other."

"And the babies?"

He looked across at me and held my gaze. He pulled his mouth full over to one side, biting on his bottom lip. "Yes," he said. "The babies too."

Maria took hold of his hand, and he briefly looked up at her, but then he took his hand back and stared at it, as if there might be traces of her still left on it. The silence stretched between us.

"So, the other children would come round to yours? And you'd go to their houses too?"

He nodded. "When I was little yes. It kind of seemed

normal, you know, like play dates and stuff. You don't know what other people do, do you, when you're small. You think it's okay. Especially if your parents are saying it's okay."

"Yes. Absolutely," I agreed, trying to give some affirmation to this destroyed young man. "Seb, did it happen often?"

"I can't remember. When I was little I think it was more often. When we used to go round to the others' houses, but maybe that's just how I remember it, I don't know. But then later, it was only when they came to ours. All the adults would be there, watching."

"But by that time, the other children didn't come?"

"No, it was just us."

"You and Isabella and Jasmine."

"Yeah."

"And what happened then? With the three of you?"

"Stuff…" He shuffled in his seat. "Between us. They made us…touch each other and stuff, other stuff."

"And the adults? Did they do anything to you?"

He nodded, but said nothing. Maria patted his knee.

"Seb, I just want to clarify that I've understood you properly, okay?"

Another brief nod.

"What you're saying is that when you were little, all the families got together and you played games that involved gradually taking all your clothes off?"

"Yes."

"And then you were made to do forfeits, inappropriate forfeits that involved touching each other?"

"Yes. And other things."

"And other things, yes."

He shook his head. "And I don't want to talk about that now."

"That's okay," I said, aching to do something, anything, and reeling in the knowledge that there was absolutely nothing I could do. "And, also, you said the adults touched you?"

He nodded and hung his head low into his chest. "It wasn't just touching, you know? It was other stuff too. Worse stuff. Much worse. I'm not telling you. I'm not telling anyone."

"Okay, that's okay. Seb, did any of the adults ever take photos? Or videos?"

"I don't think so no," he said shaking his head. "I don't remember that." He was hunched over, almost into a ball, his hands clasped together in front of him. Still rocking.

"Do you think the books they mentioned in the Facebook group could have been code for the things they made you do to each other?"

He looked up at me. "I guess," he said.

"Did you talk to the other children about the games?"

"I think I said something to Hannah once when we were at a birthday party and we were playing a party game and I said something... I can't remember exactly but I said something about taking all our clothes off and I'd win cos I had the biggest, you know...willy." He coughed. "Um...and the mum of the boy who was having the party overheard and told my mum. She laughed it off at the time, but she was furious when we got home."

"What did she say?"

"Something about private games stay private and I shouldn't tell people about our special games." He stretched his fingers, then clenched them back into tight fists. "I think it was after that when we stopped having other children round. And we stopped going to other people's."

"And you never told anyone about it?"

He shook his head. "I don't know why, not then. Just that it seemed private. Maybe they said things to us back then, I don't know I can't remember. Then, after..." He trailed off.

I looked at him. "After? After Margaret-Elizabeth?"

"Yes, after Margaret-Elizabeth died they told us that the bad man had killed her because she'd told someone. Told someone about our private secrets. They never said it, but I knew. I knew that if one of us said anything that he would come and kill us too. And now, and now...Jake, he was going to tell someone and look..." His rocking had picked up a pace, back and forth, back and forth, faster and faster.

"And did it stop then? After Margaret-Elizabeth died?"

He nodded. "The abuse? Yeah, it stopped. But the threat was always hanging over us. Whenever I heard of a child murder I always wondered if they'd told someone a secret and that was why they'd been killed. And now I'm older, look, it's still there. Jake... What's going on? I mean...." He looked into my eyes, his face contorted, tears tumbling over his cheeks and falling onto his clasped hands.

I reached over to touch him, I wanted to calm him, although I wasn't sure how. As I reached out my hand, my wrist buzzed, the watch springing to life with the beginning of a text message. I reached with my finger to dismiss it, not wanting to appear distracted to the distraught young man in front of me. But as my finger approached the watch, the first line of the message caught my eye. In capital letters someone had written;

*WANT TO SAVE HIS FAMILY? GET HERE IN…*

I couldn't see the rest. I tapped on my watch but I couldn't get the whole message to appear.

"I'm sorry," I mumbled and reached for my phone. "I'm so sorry. One moment." I stared down at my phone, black spots swimming in front of my eyes, air fighting to reach my lungs.

*WANT TO SAVE HIS FAMILY? GET HERE IN TWENTY MINUTES. NO MORE OR THEY'RE DEAD. TELL THE POLICE AND THEY'RE DEAD STRAIGHT AWAY. DON'T BE STUPID, NO POLICE. NO ONE ELSE. HOLDING A KNIFE TO HER THROAT NOW, DON'T MAKE ME SLIP. GET HERE NOW.*

The phone fell from my hand, bouncing onto the carpeted floor. Seb and Maria both turned to look at me. I shook my head at them. "I'm, I'm…sorry," I stuttered, looking up at them. "I have to go." I scrambled for my phone and stood up. As I grabbed my coat and handbag I turned to Maria and pleaded. "Call the police, get them to make sure that Seb is safe." I moved my gaze to Seb, crouching down in front of him and looking up into his eyes. "You have to tell them, Seb. You have to tell the police what you just told me. Okay?"

He nodded. Maria stood up and looked across at me, puzzlement wrinkling her forehead

I stood up and ran towards the stairs, pointing and shouting over my shoulder as I went. "Don't leave him on his own until the police get here, okay? Stay with him. Don't leave him, okay?"

"I won't," Maria said, the first words she'd spoken since they'd arrived. "I'll stay here." She reached for her phone, punching it three times as I picked up my pace and leapt down the stairs, almost falling over myself in my haste to get to my car.

# 47

Thank God I'd brought the car. I sprinted across the car park, unsure how I was staying upright. With each step I took, the shaking reverberated from my feet and up through my body, my legs threatening to crumple and hurl me to the ground. I jumped into the driver's seat without bothering to take my handbag off my shoulder, then thrust the car into gear and headed out of the car park towards the house in Branston. Someone had followed me there the other day. Someone knew where Marcus' other family lived and I had to get there as fast as I could. Looking around me for any signs of police cars, or traffic cameras, I put my foot down, willing cars to get out of my way, and taking liberties with the highway code to get there as fast as I could. At this time of day I could probably get there in ten minutes if I didn't pay any attention to the speed limits.

My tyres squealed against the tarmac as I turned sharply left at the end of Branston village and into the housing estate, before careering round corners and pulling up outside the house with a screech of tires. I fled the car and sprinted to the front door, rattling the door handle, but it was locked.

I banged on the door with the side of my fist, although I didn't wait for an answer. I scurried over to the front room window and peered inside. The room was empty. There was no sign of anyone. Hurrying round to the back of the house, I banged my knuckles against the back door and tried the handle, but this door was locked too. I shot across to the patio doors and stared into another empty room; everything was in place, just as it had been when I'd been here the other evening. I ran my hand through my hair and rushed to the back door again, banging my fist against it. Why were they not answering the door?

My wrist vibrated.

*TEN MINUTES. DON'T YOU CARE ABOUT YOUR BEST FRIEND?*

My heart hammered into my throat, and I lurched forwards into the wall, sinking to my knees. I stared at my watch, the breaths coming too fast to take any oxygen in, and my head began to spin. They were at Collette's. *Oh my God, Collette.* I'd been there the other day; someone must have seen me. As I staggered to my feet I looked at the time. I wasn't going to get there. I wasn't going to get there in time. A sense of dread tore through my chest as I ran up the path and back into the car. I flung open the door of the car and leapt back inside, before reversing up the road and hurtling round the bend, back up to the main road.

Horns blared as I pulled out into the stream of traffic without even looking, trying to keep hold of the steering wheel with sweaty, clammy palms. I grabbed my phone, and hit the call button, putting the phone on speaker and holding it against the steering wheel as I drove. I sped along at a good deal more than the speed limit, breaking so many traffic laws in one go that I couldn't keep count. My phone started to ring. I shot through a traffic light that was about to turn red, swearing as I overtook a slow van on the junction. Then I pulled sharply in front of an elderly couple, their mouths opening in unison as I almost clipped the wing of their car.

Someone answered the phone but said nothing.

"I'm on my way! I'm on my way!" I shouted to the phone, balancing it in one hand as I pulled up behind a queue of traffic waiting at the junction ahead. "I'm coming. I'm nearly there. The traffic is a nightmare."

"Hurry, then. Hurry," said a voice I recognised, and in a rush the pieces started falling into place like a winning game of Connect 4. In the background, a soft whimpering indicated that Collette was there. Still there.

"I'm fucking hurrying!" I screeched down the phone.

The phone went dead as I turned onto South Park Road, driving as fast as I dared past the police station. I was leaning forward, right over the steering wheel, willing the car to go faster. I shot up the High Street, heading away from where I needed to be and cursed the lack of bridges over the river. Bile rose in my throat as panic threatened to overwhelm me. Thoughts of Collette kept me concentrating on what I was doing, desperately trying to keep myself under control. The car lurched across the road as my foot slipped off the accelerator, the shaking making it hard to judge exactly where I was placing it. My knuckles whitened as I gripped the steering wheel and I pushed the peddle down as far as it would go, spinning round the corner into Boultham Park Road and racing down towards Collette's house. "Faster, faster, faster," I screamed to the car, drumming my hands against the steering wheel in an effort to speed it up. A man stood expectantly by the zebra crossing ahead, placing one foot on the road. I blared my horn at him and he leapt back onto the pavement, his mouth agog, his fists flailing after me, hopefully too stunned to take down my number plate.

I screeched round the corner into Collette's street, the tyres spinning against the road. Pulling up sharply outside her house, I yanked the handbrake on then ran from the car without bothering to close the door. I barged through the front door and down the hallway, crashing into the kitchen, where nothing could have prepared me for the scene in front of me.

## 48

Cutlery and broken crockery littered the floor. Pans covered the counters where they'd been knocked from their display on the wall. Upturned appliances littered the work surfaces. And in one corner of her own kitchen, Collette sat crumpled against the cupboards. A scarf had been tied around her head and it was pulling her mouth into a monstrous smile. Her knees were pressed up against a cupboard door to one side of her body and she clutched her arms against her chest, her wrists lashed together with a cable tie. Streaks of mascara ran down her face, mingling with tears and snot, giving her the appearance of a grotesque clown. And crouching above her, holding a long bladed knife to her neck was Nicole Ellison. My knees buckled at the sight of my best friend looking so frightened and helpless.

As I staggered into the room Collette whimpered around the scarf and tried in vain to pull her skin away from the knife. I yanked my handbag off my body and threw it to one side as I ran across the room towards her.

"Hold it!" Nicole said, jabbing the knife towards

Collette's neck as I approached, her face contorted with an emotion I couldn't read.

In the living room, a television blared out, an over-enthusiastic children's presenter reading out letters from young viewers, and I attempted to peer in.

Nicole appeared to read my thoughts. "Don't worry," she said, an arc of saliva spitting out of her mouth as she forced the words out. "The little brats are next door with the neighbour."

Collette wiggled her hands and shuffled on her bottom, attempting to say something around the scarf. Nicole ignored her.

I held up my hands in supplication. "What do you want? Why are you doing this?"

She turned her attention away from Collette and approached me, the knife pointing out towards me as she closed in.

I leapt straight in, trying to wrong foot her. "I know about the book club, Nicole. I know what you were doing."

She carried on towards me, making stabbing motions with the knife. "You don't know anything," she said, her top lip curled back, baring her teeth.

"What do you want? Tell me, Nicole. Why are you here?"

"What do I want?" she demanded, thrusting the knife into the space between us. "You stupid fool. You know what I want."

"Tell me," I said. "Humour me. What do you want?"

She said nothing, but she crept forwards with the knife held out in front of her.

I stood my ground, my hands still held out towards her. I was weighing up my options. Could I kick out her legs from underneath her? Or maybe reach out and snatch the knife? I moved my weight from one foot to the other like a feint from a footballer, deceiving the opposition. As I pulled my foot behind me in preparation to kick at Nicole's ankle, Collette began to shake her head and cry out as best she could around her gag.

My feet were swept from underneath me, a great kick from behind taking me completely by surprise. I tumbled onto the floor, my knees crashing onto the cold tiles, followed by my hands. As I rolled over, the figure of Matthew Ellison loomed above me, and the flashback to Jade's garden took on a new clarity – the torn parka, the hands aloft. As he bore down on me, I pulled my feet into my chest and sprang them at his body. He lurched back into the kitchen counter. Collette attempted, once again, to get to her feet and Nicole rushed over to her, the knife pointing this time at her ribs.

I leapt to my feet and held up my hands "Whoa, whoa, hang on!" I shouted.

Matthew Ellison reeled forwards, his hands outstretched, and I dodged out of his way at the last minute, spinning round and kicking him in the back, sending him flying into the counter opposite.

"Now hang on!" I shouted at the top of my voice. "What the fuck is going on here?" I glared from Matthew to Nicole and back again. "Tell me," I demanded. "What the fuck do you want?" I stood there with my jaw set firm, daring either of them to make a move.

Matthew turned around and stood with his back against the counter. He glanced across at Nicole, then down at Collette, who was whimpering on the floor, and then back up at Nicole.

Nicole started to shake her head. "No," she said to him. "No, I'm not giving up. We can do this."

When Matthew failed to reply, Nicole moved the knife, jabbing the point into Collette's neck, and prompting a stifled scream of anguish from Collette. A trickle of blood began to drip down her neck, joining the tears and saliva falling off her chin, rolling over her chest and disappearing beneath her blouse.

"What do you want?" I directed the question this time to Nicole.

She curled her lip but said nothing.

"Come on, Nicole. What is it? You want me to pretend to the world that you didn't murder your own daughter?"

Collette gave a gasp around the scarf and her face crumpled as she stared at Nicole out of the corners of her eyes.

"I want you to stop," Nicole demanded. "I want you to stop your investigation. Nobody has to know, nobody has to know what happened."

I shook my head. "It's gone too far, Nicole. Even if I stop, the police are only a step behind. It's only a matter of time."

She jabbed the knife at Collette's neck again, grabbing hold of Collette's hair and yanking her head back to expose more flesh. "You want your friend to stay alive?" She held the knife against her neck as if she were about to slit Collette's throat and images of Jade's dead body played around my head.

I held my hand out towards her, trying to keep it from shaking, trying to give off an air of authority; to appear in control as fear threatened to spin everything away from me. I looked at Collette, her features squashed into a tight mess, her eyes pleading for help, and I forced myself to remain calm. Measured. Composed. "Nicole, you're not going to achieve anything by killing Collette. You're just going to make things worse for yourself."

"Worse?" The word shot out of her mouth as if it were poison, and Collette gave a silent sob behind her gag. "How could it possibly be worse?" She kept hold of Collette's hair, but jabbed the knife forwards towards me. "This is all your fault. You fix it. You fix it, now. Or you'll have another life on your conscience."

"My fault?" I gasped. "How on earth is this my fault?" I said the words with care, trying not to allow my voice to quiver, trying not to allow the unnatural rhythm of my heart to seep through. I took in a deep breath to ease the hammering, the thumping against my ribs as if my heart was trying to break free from my chest. It didn't work. My composure crashed into pieces on the floor around me, and I struggled for breath, heaving as I attempted to regain control.

Matthew seemed to notice the beat in my voice and stepped forward, pointing at me as he progressed. "You just wouldn't fucking leave it alone. Would you? We sent you a warning and you just wouldn't fucking leave it. Jake wouldn't have died if you'd dropped it, but oh no Verity Spencer had to keep digging, digging, digging."

I gathered my thoughts together. I needed to maintain control. I couldn't let anything happen to Collette. At the very least I had to get her out of here. "I told you the first day I met you that I don't give up."

"You know why we hired you?" Matthew asked his lip curling up at one side. "We hired you because you're a woman. A woman we thought who would be easily scared off. When our friends raised the money, we had to be seen to spend it and why not just let a woman fritter it away. Anyone else would have strung us along and spent the money on themselves."

I tilted my head. "Well, yeah, you picked the wrong

person then," I said, with a cockiness I wasn't feeling. "So, Matthew." I looked directly at him, turning my body so that I cut Nicole out completely. "Tell me, what you hoped I'd achieve. That I'd review all the information and conclude that everyone was right. That Bridges was guilty, but there just wasn't enough proof?" I took a step back. "I tell you what," I said, picking up pace, getting into my stride, "I probably would have." Over near Collette, Nicole let out a gasp, but I didn't acknowledge that. I carried on. "You told me Bridges had some dangerous friends. Then you persuaded Jake to break into my house, didn't you? You thought that would scare me. You know what? It made me realise there was something to hide. It made me more determined to get to the bottom of it." I carried on. "You got someone to try to run me off the road." I paused and looked at Nicole. "Or was that you? Whilst your husband was out hanging Jake from a tree."

"It was supposed to scare you," Matthew yelled, slamming his fist down on the counter.

"Well it just made me more strong-minded." I spat the words back at him.

Matthew slumped against the cupboard. Red flushes blazed across his cheeks. Nicole yanked Collette's head back again. For a moment, the silence was only broken by the tinny music drifting in from the television in the next room.

"Tell me about that night," I said in a low, soft voice, my hands held out in front of me. "Tell me what happened with Margaret-Elizabeth."

Nicole let out a whimper, but she maintained her position. Matthew shuffled uneasily. They exchanged a glance, but neither of them said a word.

"Okay," I said, folding my arms. "Let me tell you how I

see it." I paused and took a deep breath, glancing from one to the other. "You couldn't take it anymore." I stared at Nicole. "The abuse. Your beautiful daughter. I imagine she was popular, no? I bet she was the most popular of all the girls."

Nicole bit her lip. She looked down at Collette and pushed the knife against her throat again. I needed to be careful. I had to strike a balance between pushing her enough, but not so far that her rage would take over while the knife was that close to my best friend.

"You'd already had enough hadn't you? You'd already persuaded everyone to wind up the Facebook group." I was putting two and two together as I spoke, spinning a story out of the scant facts that I knew. "What happened? Did you realise that it wouldn't be enough? That the abuse would still carry on?"

Nicole let out a low growl, yanking Collette by the hair.

I thought she was about to thrust the knife into Collette's neck so I rushed forward, looking her directly in the eyes. "You came back from your book club that night and you went up to see your little girl. Remember what you said to me, Nicole? Remember, when I came to see you? You said when you were at the hospital you just wanted to have your time again. You wanted to go into Margaret-Elizabeth's bedroom and see her sleeping and stroke her hair and everything would be okay this time." I paused, looking at them both in turn. "But you couldn't could you? You couldn't unring that bell. You couldn't turn back time."

I looked at Matthew. "When did you know? Did she tell you straight away that she'd permanently stopped you all from being able to abuse your precious daughter? Or did you go up and find your wife with the dressing gown cord around Margaret-Elizabeth's neck? Did you shout at

Nicole? Try to revive Margaret-Elizabeth? Or did you just carry her dead body to the woods?"

He span round sweeping everything off the counter with both arms; bottles, glasses, mugs and containers shattering onto the floor. "You have absolutely no idea!" he screamed, spit showering the broken shards.

"Then tell me!" I shouted back at him. "Tell me what it was like to find your wife murdering your daughter. Tell me what it was like to have to cover it up for the last ten years, playing the victim, pretending your grief was because you didn't have the answers and not because of the guilt you were carrying." I stamped my feet and moved across the room, stabbing my finger towards him. "Did you deliberately call your family because you knew the evidence would be messed up? Or was that just a lucky extra?"

He straightened up, trying to back away but there was nowhere to go.

I was right on top of him, poking into his chest this time. "And what about Bridges? Was he just a convenient stooge? In the wrong place at the wrong time?"

He looked at me for a split second and then swiped with his right arm, landing his forearm against the left side of my head with a thud that hurled me to the ground. Collette shouted out around her gag, her whimpering growing louder and more agitated. I lay on the ground and Matthew leaned over me, reaching down to grab my shirt but I lifted my head up and smashed it into his nose. He reeled to one side, clutching at his face, blood pouring through his fingers. Pain ripped through my forehead, clouding my vision, but I wasn't about to let that distract me.

Nicole shot across the room, the knife in her hand, leaving Collette shivering in the corner. As Nicole ran across the room, I swept my feet up and kicked at her hand, but she managed to keep hold of the knife and she turned towards me, lifting it up high. I scrabbled out of the way, clawing my way across the kitchen floor, kicking back at Nicole with my heels. Matthew flew down, grabbing hold of my ankles, and dragged me back across the tiles, the shards of broken crockery digging into my body as he pulled me across the floor. I wriggled one of my ankles free from his grasp and shot my heel back into his jaw, narrowly missing his bloody nose. He staggered back, tumbling into the cupboards as a peal of children's laughter came through the open door of the living room. Nicole rushed forward once again, pulling the knife up high above her head and plunging it down towards me.

I rolled out of the way as the knife stabbed into the hard tiles, the reverberation causing Nicole to call out and drop the knife, which shot across the floor. In the adjoining room the voices of the television presenter pierced the air. "...*and a very happy birthday to Fabian from Exeter, look at this amazing picture of Minecraft that Fabian has sent us...*"

I leapt to my feet and hurtled across to where the knife had fallen, bending over to pick it up, but just as my finger-tips reached the handle Matthew's foot made contact with my ribs and shoved me into the cupboard door. I crumpled to the floor, a piercing pain ripping through my side. Nicole darted in, scooped up the knife and held it high above her head. I had no time to move out the way, so I arched my spine like a cat and sprang backwards at her, pushing into her chest and sending her plunging onto the tiles. Blood spurted from my arm as the knife flew past me, slicing into my flesh through the fabric of my shirt. Any pain I might have felt must have been blunted by the adrenaline my body was producing because the sensation barely registered. I used my momentum to leap to my feet, snatching a fallen frying pan from the counter just as Matthew lurched towards me with his blood-soaked hands outstretched. His nose sat horribly out of line and I brought the frying pan crashing into his face, teeth scattering onto the floor as I did so. My guts lurched as Matthew fell, straight down like a felled tree, face first onto the floor with a sickening crunch as more bones were broken in his face.

Nicole let out a roar, still clutching the knife, and barrelled into me with a rugby-player tackle, forcing me against the wall. Once again she lifted up the knife, but I grabbed her round the neck, pushing her away so that the knife was beyond the reach of me. I tightened my grip of her, the blood oozing from the cut on my arm, and shoved her backwards across the kitchen. A tinny, trilling theme tune started in the adjacent room, kids singing about different families, as I manoeuvred her back towards the counter on the far side of the room.

Nicole clutched the air with her left hand, and thrust the knife uselessly with her right. I gritted my teeth and growled as I drove her back, the knife falling from her hand as I smashed her into the worktop. I dug my thumbs into her throat and shook her, screaming into her face, "How long did you think you'd get away with it? Hey?"

Her head shot forwards and backwards as I pulled her this way and that.

She held up her hands in defeat, pleading for me to loosen my grip. I relaxed my hands, but kept them round her throat. "What did you think? You could get away with this forever? And keep killing anyone who got close to the answer? What about Jake? What did he do?"

Nicole gasped for air. She reached up and tried to pull my hands from her neck, but I squeezed them harder and she held hers up again. When I released her windpipe once again, she inhaled deeply, opening her mouth wide.

She nodded, a brief tip of her head, then screamed at me, "He'd spoken to that bitch. She was putting ideas into his head. Telling him Bridges wasn't guilty." For a moment she just stood there, her head hanging low, and I thought she might be feeling remorse.

I dropped my hands to my side, lowering my guard. Nicole seized the opportunity, pushing me to one side and swooping in to pick up the knife, which she thrust at Collette. Collette slumped down against the wall, the knife pushing against her throat and looked up at me, her face twisted in anguish.

I stepped over Matthew's unconscious body and crouched down beside Nicole and Collette. "Nicole," I said in a hushed voice. "Nicole. This is not going to help. This isn't going to bring Margaret-Elizabeth back, is it? More death, more pain."

She flicked her eyes up towards me and I held her gaze. She just stared back at me, her forehead furrowed into a deep frown.

"It's understandable," I said, my tone gentle, trying to gain her confidence. "She was your baby. Your precious baby."

Nicole let out a sob, but didn't loosen her grip on Collette, or move the knife away from her neck.

"I guess it started as something daring, maybe fun, with the book club, I don't know. But it turned into something else. Maybe you enjoyed it at the beginning. But as Margaret-Elizabeth grew, you started to think it wasn't right, perhaps you thought it needed to stop?"

She nodded a small, brief nod. "It got out of hand," she said. "I'd spoken to Matthew but he wasn't listening. He said I was the only one, and if I didn't like it I could leave him, leave the group. I couldn't," she said through laboured breaths. "I couldn't leave him. But I couldn't stand it anymore."

I looked her directly in the eyes. "That night, Nicole, when everyone was looking for Margaret-Elizabeth and trying to revive her. Where was Matthew?"

She glanced up at me, her brows knotted in puzzlement. "I don't know," she said, shaking her head.

"Tell me," I said. "You strangled Margaret-Elizabeth with her dressing gown cord, then what happened."

"He took her to the woods, laid her down."

"And the cord?"

She shook her head. "I don't know," she said. "I don't know."

"So you called your family, had them find Margaret-Elizabeth and try to revive her all the time knowing she was dead."

At that, she stabbed the knife towards Collette. She bared her teeth, snarling like an animal. "I was distraught!" she shouted. "I wanted them to revive her, I wanted it to work. I wanted my baby back, she wasn't supposed to *die.*"

"Then all these years you've played the victim."

"I am the victim!" she yelled. "I lost my daughter. No one can understand how that hurts. I am the victim."

"You killed her, Nicole."

She grabbed Collette's hair, yanking her head back with a force I thought would crack Collette's neck. Collette let out a horrified screech, muffled by the scarf in her mouth, her eyes filled with terror as her gaze momentarily locked with mine.

Nicole's mouth contorted into a wide grimace. "Stop this!" she screamed at me. "You can stop this. You can tell them. That awful man, he did it. He deserves to be in prison. Tell them he did it, or I'll slice your friend's throat right now." She tilted the knife again, holding the blade flat against Collette's neck. Then she drew her hand back and prepared to cut my best friend's throat.

I only had a split second. I sprang to my feet, kicking out at her arm, and the knife twisted up into the air, catching Collette's cheek as it left Nicole's hand. I grabbed her by her lapels and shoved her onto the floor, leaving Collette holding her face with her tied hands. Nicole took hold of my hair and jerked my head down, thrusting it towards the floor but I managed to yank it back before it made contact. She threw me to one side and I rolled onto my back, pulling her with me, then I rammed my knees into her chest and sent her backwards onto the floor. We both leapt to our feet, circling each other until finally I shoved her and she hurtled into the cupboards.

"You have to be stopped, Nicole. You can't keep this up any longer."

She looked at me, a fleeting expression coming over her face. Perhaps it was defeat. She opened her mouth to answer me but instead of speaking she grimaced, pulled her arms back and thrust me away with the palms of her hands. I crashed to the floor, the pain jarring up my spine, and I rolled back, yelling out in agony. Nicole lurched forwards, stamping her foot down onto my chest. I clawed out at nothing with my hand, all the air gone from my lungs, willing my diaphragm to work. My lungs seared with fire as I grappled for some oxygen, and I thumped at my chest with my hands to try to shock them into action.

A flash of movement caught my eye and Collette staggered into view, her mascara-smeared face contorted into a monstrous mask as peals of laughter drifted through from the television in the adjacent room. Nicole pulled her leg back to kick me in the ribs, but Collette rose behind her, the knife in her bound hands. I'm not sure where she was aiming, but she plunged the knife down into the base of Nicole's back, deep into her glute muscles. Nicole turned her face upwards and screamed, clutching at her back and sinking to her knees, the knife buried up to the handle, blood oozing down her legs.

"Bitch!" she shouted, her arms flailing as she reached for the knife.

"Don't pull it out," I yelled at her, the force of the sudden intake of air ripping my lungs apart. "You'll make it worse," I gasped through laboured breaths, leaning my arms on the floor for support whilst my diaphragm steadied itself back into a normal rhythm.

But she ignored me and yanked at the knife, gritting her teeth and ripping it from her body. Blood gushed out from the wound, pumping down her leg. I ran over to Collette and untied the scarf from around her mouth, then pushed Nicole to the ground and pressed it hard onto the wound. "Call an ambulance!" I yelled at Collette.

Nicole flung herself round, the bloodied knife in her hand and thrust it wildly in the air. Collette leaped back, her legs escaping the slashing blade. Nicole bared her teeth and hurled herself at me, stabbing the air with the knife as she approached. I kicked up at her, but missed her hand and the blade sliced across the surface of my lower leg. She lunged forward again. This time I was prepared and I slammed the sole of my shoe towards her face, making contact to one side of her nose. Her mouth and cheek contorted sideways as I thumped my foot against her head and she landed on the floor beside her husband.

Collette fell to the floor, quivering and crying, her shoulders heaving. I picked up the blood-coated knife and sliced through the cable tie holding her wrists together. Then I took her in my arms and held her close to me until her sobbing had subsided. On the television, an animated presenter was announcing something, introducing children, some kind of swashbuckling nonsense. I rocked Collette in time to the music drifting through and gently stroked her head.

I leaned away from her. "I better call the police," I said, surveying the damage to the room, and indicating the two unconscious people on her kitchen floor. "They'll be wondering where I am. I'm late."

"Huh?" she said, examining her hands, and rubbing the blood off with the hem of her top.

I found my phone and sat back down next to Collette. We both leaned against the wall, our legs pushed up against our chests. I stroked her knee. "There is some good news," I said.

"Wha...?" Collette said, wiping her face with her sleeve.

"Marcus isn't having an affair," I said, dialling the emergency number into the phone.

## 49

DC Shepherd eyed me with suspicion, as the Ellisons were loaded into an ambulance with a police escort. Paramedics had examined both mine and Collette's wounds and declared them superficial. We'd been cleaned up, had some steristrips applied and been given the okay. Several police officers milled about Collette's kitchen after having picked up and bagged the knife, as well as all of Matthew's teeth.

A little while later, in the midst of all the chaos, Marcus arrived, bursting through the door his mouth flapping open, his forehead ruckled and creased. A police officer held him back as he ran into the kitchen.

"Take it easy, sir," the police officer said.

"Take it easy!" Marcus bellowed as he pointed across the room and wrenched himself from the officer's grip. "That's my wife." And he ran over to Collette, scooping her into his arms where she once again dissolved into a fit of sobs.

I walked over to DC Shepherd. "Sorry I missed our appointment," I said, indicating the kitchen by way of explanation.

She was examining the messages on my phone. A police car had been sent to the house in Branston, just to check that the occupants were all okay and safe. After several minutes, her walkie-talkie sprang to life, an officer's voice crackling into the kitchen.

"Go ahead," DC Shepherd said, leaning down towards the speaker.

"All clear. Two adults and a minor. All safe. Confirmed no other occupants in the house."

I breathed a sigh of relief and, looking around me, it seemed as if everyone else was doing the same. DC Shepherd looked across at me. "You will still have to come down to the nick to give another statement," she said. Then she quickly followed that up with, "Although not now. It can wait." She looked me up and down, my blood splattered clothing telling a story all on its own. "I think you might need to go home and get cleaned up. And have a rest." She reached out her hand and patted me on the arm. Perhaps she was softening up a little.

A little while later, I walked over to Collette and Marcus, huddled in the corner on the sofa cuddling each other. They sat back as I approached, and Collette looked up at me. Her neck bore an angry red stripe where the knife had cut into her throat. "Hey," I said. I looked at Marcus. "Did your wife tell you that she's a demon at fighting?"

"Uh-huh." Marcus nodded. "I'm staying on her right side from now on, that's for sure."

I nodded and started to walk away.

"Verity," Marcus called after me.

I turned round.

"Thanks," he said. "Thanks for coming to see me." He looked at his wife. "I've explained things to Collette. It's a lot to take in, what with all this." He indicated the room around him. "But we're good."

Collette nodded and glanced up at Marcus. Then she lifted her eyes back at me. "I don't know what to think," she said. "But I just want a clean slate. A start again." She shifted her gaze back to Marcus. "And soon, I think I want the girls to meet their half-brother. Once we've got it straight. It'll take a while to get my head around, but, yeah, thanks."

"Good," I said. "I think I'm done with following friends though. Next time I'll pass." I rolled my eyes to the ceiling and held my hands up.

Police milled about, roaming from room to room. Collette and Marcus sat in a huddle on their sofa, presumably trying to make sense of the last few days. Thankfully, someone had turned the television off.

After some time, DC Shepherd's walkie-talkie once again crackled into action.

"Got it," a male voice called down the line.

DC Shepherd and I had spent some time earlier scanning Google maps. In the aftermath of Margaret-Elizabeth's death the area surrounding the Ellisons' house had been searched. Police had looked in rubbish bins, outhouses, all through the woods. Mostly they had followed the route that Bridges would have taken back towards the city centre. The dressing gown cord used to murder Margaret-Elizabeth had never been found. In the confusion, with all the family there and people coming and going, nobody had noticed Matthew Ellison slip away. He'd told police that he'd been out the front, and Chrissy Scraggs had always corroborated that yes, they'd gone out to the road; she'd gone one way up the street and he'd gone in the opposite direction. But Matthew had been gone for almost an hour.

We'd searched the map to see where he might have gone. The church that the Ellisons used was about a twenty-five minute walk; quicker if you were running with a murder weapon in your hand desperate to find somewhere to hide it. There'd been other possible locations in the direction he'd set off that night, away from the city centre; some business premises, school outbuildings. Officers had been dispatched to them all, although it made sense to me that he'd have chosen somewhere he was familiar with.

"You have it?" DC Shepherd responded.

"Hidden in a crevice behind the font in the church," the voice explained.

DC Shepherd turned to me and smiled. "Thanks," she said, then with a brief nod she turned away and headed off to talk to her colleagues.

"Verity!" a voice boomed across the room and Mike Nash appeared in the doorway. Collette's house seemed to contain more police officers than the police station.

"Mike, hi," I said, walking over to him. "Did Sebastian Walker get in touch?"

"He did, Verity, he certainly did. He gave a very clear statement to the police and, well, there'll be an investigation into his allegation of historical sexual abuse."

"And the book club parents?"

"Well we're trying to get hold of the other children, see if any of them will give statements to corroborate what he says."

"He was quite compelling."

"Indeed, he was, very compelling. And the book club members will all be arrested and interviewed."

"Do you think they'll be charged?"

"That's hard to say, Verity, very hard to say. It'll depend

a lot on whether the other young people are prepared to say anything."

"It looks as if Jake was about to try and get help. Hopefully if the others have been affected...well. Let's hope, hey." I looked up at him. "The Facebook group?"

"Yes?"

"The messages. I'm pretty convinced they were coded. Clearly they weren't actually reading books. I think the books referred to something else that was going on. Perhaps particular types of abuse, or things they were getting the children to do. I don't know, but you might find some evidence there."

"I'll take a look. I'll certainly take a look." He leaned in and whispered in my ear, "And I'll let you know how we get on, but—" And he leaned away again, putting his finger against his lips. Then he tapped the side of his nose whilst darting a quick glance towards DC Shepherd.

# THE FOLLOWING SATURDAY

# 50

I looked at myself in the mirror on the back of Robert and Keith's spare room door. The cut on my arm was fading fast; I didn't think anyone would really notice it. I was wearing a full-length, dark blue silk evening gown. The tucks to the side of my body emphasised my waist and the fit glossed nicely over my lack of bosom. Sequins covered the bodice and they glittered in the lights as I turned this way and that, examining my reflection from various angles. My hair was pulled to one side; I'd spent some time at the hairdressers that afternoon and they'd tamed my unruly shoulder-length locks into a glossy chignon. For the first time in months, I was wearing full make-up. I sat down on the bed and adjusted the straps on my shoes, hoping that I'd be able to stay upright on the four-inch heels.

A knock on the door was followed by a call from Robert, "Taxi's here."

"Okay," I shouted back. I took a deep breath. I hadn't been to a gala event, or a ball, or a dinner, or pretty much any event at all since John had died. I'd not had time to buy a new outfit, so I'd dug around in my wardrobe and found this one. The last time I'd worn it had been to a wedding. One of John's colleagues, who I hadn't known well, had got married with an 'evening attire' dress code. That had been several years ago, but it still fitted well. I gave myself a final appraisal in the mirror and left the spare room.

Keith let out a wolf whistle as I emerged through the door, and I tilted my head and gave a slight curtsy in acknowledgement. Their flat was only half a mile at most from the hotel, but I'd insisted on a taxi, given the length of my dress and the height of my heels. I took Robert's arm and we left the building; two gorgeous men in dinner suits and me, heading out. Just like old times. Who needed a companion when you had these two, one on each arm?

Robert held out his arm as we left the taxi and ensured I didn't trip on the stairs. Then we hung about for a while in the bar. Pre-dinner drinks were being served and Keith rushed about from one group to another, ensuring that he greeted everyone by name, making small talk and generally schmoozing as best he could, which I had to admit was quite well. Every now and again he'd introduce me to people and I'd linger with a group, being polite, smiling, telling them that I was a widow and didn't really have an occupation. Smile, nod, smile.

I wandered over to the seating plan, where Robert came to join me.

"Tired of small talk?" he asked.

"Well, there's only so many times you can ask people the same question before you forget what you've said to who. I just asked that man over there where he lived twice in the space of about five minutes. Apparently I gave the exact same answer to his response both times, too."

We pored over the plan and found our table. Table ten. It

was to the right and about half-way up the room. We were sitting with a pair of radio producers and a couple of theatre owners. Next to my name was a seat labelled 'Sam Charlton'. I sighed and scoffed.

"I'll go and ask them to take the chair away," Robert said. "They can remove all the cutlery and move everyone round and no one else will be any the wiser."

"I'm sorry I didn't get round to telling Keith soon enough for them to change it."

"Not a problem," Robert said. He looked around him at the milling crowd, the laughter reaching a crescendo, the chatter animated and loud. "How's Collette, by the way?"

"She'll be fine." I stared into my wine. "She'll get over it. Hopefully she'll forgive me, eventually. To be frank, at least her dice with death softened the blow of Marcus having another child." I looked at him and laughed. "Silver linings and all that. Her mum came to pick up the children last night and Marcus has taken her away for the weekend, so I'm hoping she'll come back refreshed and not wanting to strangle me anymore."

"You can but hope," he said. "I'll go and get them to move that seat. Back in a mo."

I stayed where I was, studying the seating plan, seeing who else was attending. A few local celebrities, radio presenters, local television newsreaders and so on. The great and the good of the East Midlands entertainment industry. A couple wandered over to join me, finding their seats.

"Oh look, we're on the same table as Roscoe Barnes," the woman said. I had no idea who Roscoe Barnes was, but she seemed quite excited about the prospect.

After a few minutes, Robert returned. "Go and have a look," he said. "See if it's okay."

"It'll be fine, Robert. I trust you to have made it okay."

"I still think you should go and take a look. Just to be sure."

"Fine," I said, exasperated. "If it'll make you happy, I'll go and take a look." I passed my wine to him to hold while I was gone and made my way through the crowd to the double doors of the function room. I stopped in my tracks, standing still in the doorway. There, sitting in his appointed seat, leaning one elbow on the table and facing the doors was Sam Charlton.

He got to his feet when he saw me and we stood there staring at each other for what seemed like a long time.

I broke the silence first. "What are you doing here?" I asked.

He threw back his head and laughed, then started to walk towards me. "You think I'd miss this?" he said, indicating the room with his arms.

I took a couple of steps into the room, the noise of the guests outside fading away behind me, and waited for him to approach. I shook my head. "I didn't think you'd come."

He stopped a few feet away from me, sighing and looking down at his feet. He bit on his lip as if he was unsure what to say, or where to start. He looked off to the side and then back at me. I gave a brief nod, and he took the last couple of paces towards me. He slipped his hands over mine, lifting them out to the side and looked me up and down. "You scrub up nice," he said.

I pulled in my lips and tried not to smile.

He stepped back. "Look at you, Verity. You look stunning. I wouldn't have missed this for the world."

"You don't look so bad yourself," I said, moving closer to him and adjusting his bow tie.

I held onto his hands and looked into his eyes. He

leaned his face close to mine, his breath brushing my cheek as he bent forwards. We kissed, a passionate kiss, and I lost myself in his embrace, completely oblivious to what was going on around me. I cupped his face with my hands, holding him there, not wanting him to pull away, and he wrapped me in his arms, momentarily lifting me off the ground.

People had started to push past us, filling the room. The chatter getting louder as we stood there, just looking at each other, not saying a word.

A glass chinked and the room fell into silence.

"Ladies and gentlemen, please take your seats so that dinner can be served."

We pulled apart and I looked him in the eye. "I think I am ready, Sam. I think I am."

He took me by the hand and led me to towards our table. "You better introduce me to your friends, then."

## EPILOGUE

I'd been going round to feed the cat every day for over a week. I was positive that no one else was feeding her; there was never any indication of food from any other source. I'd bought a couple of bowls which I'd been taking home and washing, changing them and replenishing the food and water every day. I'd been convinced that one day I'd arrive and a relative of Jade's would have taken her away, but it never seemed to happen. And I couldn't keep going round to the house every day.

I pulled up in the car and knocked on the neighbour's door.

"Hi," I said, a little sheepishly. I hadn't seen him since he'd helped me escape the other day.

"Morning," he replied.

"I think I'm going to take the cat," I said. "It's a big ask, but, would you mind letting me in again?"

The old man shuffled backwards a couple of steps and retrieved a key from a bowl on a shelf. He changed his slippers for shoes and led me out of the door.

"You can come in with me, if you like," I offered. "I just need to find a carrier to take her home in."

"No worries," he said, opening Jade's front door.

"Hi, Peg Leg," I said, as the cat ran towards me. "Still here? How are you?"

"Meow," she said rubbing herself around my legs.

I picked her up, and she settled in my arms, purring and making little chirruping noises. "Hang on, Peggy," I said to her, putting her on the floor. "Let me see if I can find something to carry you in." I scooted round the house, looking in cupboards and behind sofas. Next, I searched upstairs, looking in the bedrooms and found what I wanted in the spare room. A cat carrier.

"Now," I said sternly when I got back downstairs. "You need to go in this." I indicated the open door of the carrier.

She threw me a look as if she thought I'd just taken leave of my senses, and sauntered off in the opposite direction, her tail forming a question mark over her back as she walked away.

I ran after her and picked her up. "There's no escape," I said and I pushed her, fighting and scratching, into the carrier. I shut the door before she had time to escape and she glared at me through the bars as if I'd just committed high treason. "Believe me, it's easier this way," I said.

I left a note on the counter with my phone number at the end and saying that the neighbour had let me in, that I had taken the cat and that I would look after her for the time being.

"She's a beautiful cat," the neighbour agreed as I carried her out of the house.

I fished into my pocket and gave the old man one of my new business cards. It had my name and phone number on it and, rather than the slogan Charlton had suggested, just the word 'investigations' underneath my name. "If you need me, or if anyone wants to know where the cat is, here's my details," I said.

When I got home, I set the carrier down on the kitchen floor and opened its door. Peggy poked her nose out, sniffing the air. She crouched down low and took a tentative step towards the door, looking around her as she went. One small step at a time, she emerged, sniffing and peering, examining her surroundings. She stood still for a while, her head swivelling, appearing to be thoroughly disorientated. Then she bolted across the kitchen, and ran straight to the living room.

I let her be, and I pottered around in the kitchen until I was ready to go out. I paused in the doorway of the living room; Peggy was on the sofa curled into a tight ball, her head tucked under her legs. She opened one eye when I appeared in the doorway, but didn't move.

"If you're happy to stay here, which you seem to be, I need to go and buy you some stuff," I said to her. "Back soon, okay?"

She winked her one open eye, then curled up a little tighter and went back to sleep. I took that as a yes.

## ALSO BY TRUDEY MARTIN

No Deadly Medicine

A Hallway of Gallows

# FROM THE AUTHOR

Thank you so much for reading Unring the Bell, I hope that you enjoyed it. If so, perhaps you'd take the time to write a review. What readers think is so important to me and, as an independent author without the big marketing budgets of traditional publishing houses, reviews are the single most important way to let other people know about my books.

Thanks again
Happy reading
Trudey

## ACKNOWLEDGMENTS

My thanks once again to Sarah Smeaton for her editing and helpful suggestions. And to Margaret Swift for proofreading. Thanks also to the friends and readers who read initial drafts and gave such constructive comments. I also need to thank the various people from the organisations and situations referred to in the book, who happily took the time to talk to me, to answer a never ending stream of questions and to give such helpful technical advice. These include Sid Sloane, Caroline Sanderson, and John Horton and a couple who wanted to remain anonymous. Thanks lastly, once again to my husband, for his constant support and love.

Printed in Great Britain
by Amazon

60449841R00203